I0614090

Althea's Awakening

by

Maggie Sims

School of Enlightenment
Book Three

This is a work of fiction. Names, characters, places, and incidents are either the product of the author's imagination or are used fictitiously, and any resemblance to actual persons living or dead, business establishments, events, or locales, is entirely coincidental.

Althea's Awakening

COPYRIGHT © 2022 by Maggie Sims

All rights reserved. No part of this book may be used or reproduced in any manner whatsoever without written permission of the author or The Wild Rose Press, Inc. except in the case of brief quotations embodied in critical articles or reviews.
Contact Information: info@thewildrosepress.com

Cover Art by *Lisa Dawn MacDonald*

The Wild Rose Press, Inc.
PO Box 708
Adams Basin, NY 14410-0708

Publishing History
First Edition, 2023
Trade Paperback ISBN 978-1-5092-4952-7
Digital ISBN 978-1-5092-4953-4

Published in the United States of America

**A widow with no knowledge of carnal desire,
a rake bored with even the most hedonistic
pleasures, and a game of truth or dare...**

Althea stepped back and took a page from her cousin's book. "My lord, fingers are fingers. I have no need of those attached to you."

Evan's brows rose. "I should love to see that. But was it as good? Did you not crave my descriptions of what I wanted to do to you? Desire the damp softness of lips against yours...either of yours? Did you not long to lie back and watch, enjoying with no need to work for it?"

Oh my. She was already wet. And panting audibly. She snapped her mouth closed and gulped a swallow.

Evan stepped into her space, raising his hand to cup her face. His thumb skimmed back and forth across her lower lip. He leaned in, whispering, "Remember, sweet. Your body does not lie."

A finger flicked across the hard point of her breast. "Unh."

Taking that bud between forefinger and thumb, he squeezed, holding her whole being still with that two-fingered touch.

"Do you need a reminder of how much better it is with two?"

PRAISE FOR

Maggie Sims

ALTHEA'S AWAKENING

"*Althea's Awakening* is an impassioned romance with a love story that is touching, smart, and wildly sexy! Althea is clever and fiercely independent but has no idea what she's in for when she negotiates an arrangement with the notoriously skilled sensualist, the Earl of Cheltenham. The earl awakens her to the pleasures of sex and intimacy, but she inspires him to desire a happiness he never allowed himself to imagine. No two people deserve each other more!"

~*Amy Sandas, USA Today Bestselling Author of the* Wright Bastards *series*
~*~

"Althea definitely wakes up in this beautifully written and entertaining story! Maggie Sims spins a fantastic tale with the perfect amount of heat and chemistry. Love it!"

~*Raisa Greywood, USA Today Bestselling Author of the* Club Apocalypse *series*

PENELOPE'S PASSION

"*Penelope's Passion* is...a wonderful story of forbidden romance from two people in very different life circumstances just trying to do the right thing for both themselves and their families...readers who like an extra spicy historical romance will not want to miss out!"

~*Golden Angel, USA Today Bestselling Author of the* Bridal Discipline *series*

Dedication

To @michelle_reads_romance,
one of my first champions

And to Becky, founder of Upturned Petticoats &
Undone Cravats and The Ton & the Tartans FB groups

This series would not be where it is without you both.

Acknowledgments

The writing community continues to amaze me with the level of support and guidance it offers. Diana Carlile, my Senior Editor, is amazing. She continually offers kind and helpful guidance and manages to make me laugh even as she teaches me a whole new language of "MM" and "WOD." My openings will get better soon, I promise, Diana!

My cover artist, Lisa Dawn MacDonald, gets me so many compliments on my covers. Lisa, those are yours, I hope I forward them enough.

Golden Angel and Amy Sandas responded to cold calls from someone they'd never heard of, begging for cover quote reviews. Raisa Greywood also agreed to write one despite multiple releases of her own, leadership responsibilities in Passionate Ink, and the holidays, because she's awesome.

Melverna McFarlane, a fellow author and critique partner, helped me strengthen Evan's second attempt at a grand gesture in this story.

My circle of author friends, Leslie Grace, Jennifer Britt, Jena Doyle, and Cecilia Rene, are always there to help with a writing sprint, plot hole, blurb review or manuscript critique.

Always, my real-life romance hero, my husband gets the biggest thanks of all.

Prologue

July 1816, London

Lady Althea Egerton fidgeted her hands in her garnet-hued skirts as she hovered near the veranda doors of the crowded ballroom. She wasn't sure what she'd expected of a demi-monde ball, but thus far, most of the activities had mimicked any Ton fête.

Her ward and third cousin, Beth Jenkins, had been vague when she begged Althea to accept the invitation to this party.

"'Tis from a sponsor of the School of Enlightenment, thus very discreet. All the attendees will be vetted, and 'tis a perfect place for me to find someone to occupy my time so I shan't be such a burden on you."

"You are never a burden." Althea shook her head at her younger cousin. But the girl did have a point. Beth had too much time on her hands and was prone to mischief. She'd only been with Althea a month when she began wreaking havoc without an outlet for her freethinking approach to life. They'd found the school to broaden her horizons and buy Althea some time, but Beth had been home for two months and already had…interactions…with the staff. Althea refused to dwell on how she'd discovered one of them.

"Downstairs will be much like any Ton ball, I

promise."

Remembering that conversation as she stared around the ballroom, Althea's lips twisted. Beth had downplayed the nature of the fête of course. The men were the same, but most were with mistresses rather than wives, and the women's gowns were quite different than Ton ladies wore. And Althea had already needed to give her cousin a quick lecture in the retiring room about touching people without permission.

Having very strict parents, followed by an equally austere husband, Althea was ready to embrace widowhood, but not to the extent some members of the Ton did at demi-monde parties like this one. And she probably should have asked Beth about the upstairs.

Beth squealed and grabbed her hand as she stepped forward.

"Oh my gosh, 'tis a reunion," she said over her shoulder to Althea as she dragged her across the room.

Two women were grinning at Beth's rapid approach, having turned from a circle of four men. One of the women was a lady, her butter-yellow dress and posture at home in any Ton ballroom, despite the fact that she might have rouged her nipples. The other, in an even paler gown, had a curtain of dark hair and honey-toned skin, making Althea wonder if she had an East Indian heritage.

Beth began breathless introductions. "May I present my cousin, Lady Althea Egerton. Althea, Miss Penelope Wood and Miss Sophia—"

The petite blonde was shaking her head. "Delighted. I am now the Countess of Peterborough, here with my husband." She gestured.

Beth blinked and nodded. "That's right.

Congratulations, my lady." She curtsied.

"Come now. We shall always be Sophia and Beth and Pen." Sophia laughed and waved a dismissive hand, and Althea understood how they'd come to be friends with Beth.

"Lady Egerton." The dark-haired Miss Wood nodded.

"Lovely to meet you both, Lady Peterborough, Miss Wood."

Sophia turned to introduce them to the gentlemen. Althea mumbled something to Lord Peterborough and Lord Slade, who seemed to be with Penelope, but her attention kept straying to the tall golden-haired man with amber eyes and a matching waistcoat. While Althea was as tall as the fourth man, a Mr. Orford, and nearly as tall as Sophia's and Penelope's escorts, this man's extra inches added to his appeal.

"…and Evan Gardner, the Earl of Cheltenham. Cheltie to most." Beth had taken over introductions at some point that Althea had missed.

Oh no. This is the Earl of Cheltenham? His rakish reputation was common knowledge. Any fascination she entertained had to stop. She could not afford to be associated with him.

"My lady. I am absolutely delighted to meet you." His voice was ardent as he bowed low over her hand, his breath a whisper of warmth against her gloved hand. She wanted to remove her other glove to run her fingers through the lustrous thatch of waves in his hair.

Oh my. That reputation is well-earned.

She curtsied, but before she could find words through her conflicted thoughts, Beth gushed over him. "Cheltie, I should have expected to see you here." She linked her arm with his and pressed her breast against his bicep in an obvious invitation.

Althea swallowed back a protest she had no identifiable reason to make.

Penelope and Sophia stepped in and gestured them away from the men to catch up with Beth, who cast a lingering look back as they found seats in a corner.

"Lady Egerton, I have heard so much about you," Penelope started, drawing Althea's attention from the beautiful earl's arse as he walked to a refreshment table to fetch them drinks.

When he delivered them, Althea lost the train of the conversation, but as the girls had all attended the School of Enlightenment together, she hadn't understood much of their gossip anyway. She'd learned what she'd needed after her husband died and left the apothecary to her, but she could see the benefits of the secret girls' school. In addition to financial and household management, and even lessons in intimacy, it offered the opportunity for lifelong friendships.

Her gaze drifted to Lord Cheltenham again. *What point is there to ogle him?* He wouldn't dance or dally with her. He'd choose a woman like Beth as his prey, whose outlook on physical intimacy matched his. Both seemed to view the goal of sex as fun between any number of willing players, which had not been Althea's experience in her marriage.

Even in the wildly remote possibility that he was interested, Althea could not afford to associate with someone of the Earl of Cheltenham's prominence and openness about shunning society's rules. Her store's success depended on maintaining a sterling character.

As the ladies rose to greet their escorts, Beth

wandered off to see if she could garner a dance with "Cheltie." Unable to watch Beth's inevitable attempts to flirt with him, Althea excused herself and strolled the ballroom. Finding herself watching yet again for Lord Cheltenham's leonine head and well-shaped arse, she firmed her lips and removed to the veranda. But a few clinched couples had her retreating to peruse the food in the refreshment room.

Finding that room safe, she dawdled, snacked on sweetmeats and biscuits, and sipped lemonade. She was thankful no one engaged her in conversation, realizing belatedly that a woman alone might be seen as looking for a benefactor, and that was the last thing she wanted. Finally, she decided to find her cousin, their carriage, and then her bed. She needed to be at the store in the morning.

After checking the open rooms on the ballroom floor, she tried the upper level. Gaining the hallway, she saw most doors were open. 'Twas a relief as she would not have wanted to knock, given the nature of the party.

Her relief was short-lived. In the first room, a man's head was visible over the back of a wingchair facing the fire. With no sign of Beth, she turned to leave the doorway.

A slurp sounded.

Frowning, she glanced back at the man.

His hand, visible on the arm of the chair until now, shifted toward his lap, and he murmured, "Hold it. Deeper."

Althea's gaze dropped to the floor, and her mouth fell open. Skirts were puddled on the rug in front of the chair. A woman was kneeling or sitting in front of him. Beth had shared enough details of past escapades that

Althea could guess what the slurp meant. But even after Beth's descriptions, the reality was shocking. She could not comprehend why a woman would do that. The point of sex, after all, was procreation, not pleasure.

Eyes wide, she clutched the doorframe. Her brain wanted to withdraw, locate Beth, and go home. But her body was held in thrall, pulse thrumming through her veins, core heating and liquefying, her breath coming faster.

Why was the door left open? Darn it, she knew she should have questioned her cousin further when she described "downstairs" rather than "the ball." Were all the rooms thus occupied?

She'd found Beth with two stable hands in an empty stall one day months ago. The guilty thrill then had kept her frozen in place. Afterward, she'd told herself it had been guilt alone. Why would she react so strongly to watching others' intimacy when she'd never responded that way to intimacy with her husband?

There was no denying her reaction though. While she did not understand these strange sensations that contradicted everything she knew about sex, she could not tear herself away. Even remorse over spying on strangers could not loosen her white-knuckled grip.

"Althea, there you are."

The spell was broken, and she turned to see her cousin stepping out of a doorway across the hall. As she took a step toward Beth, she heard a movement behind her and glanced back.

The Earl of Cheltenham lounged against the wall next to where she'd been standing, all loose-limbed grace and an easy smile. He'd been watching *her* rather than the room's occupants.

A bolt of lust shot through her. What would it be like to have him cover her like a stallion does a mare, as she'd seen in the stables? Or to be on her knees in front of him? Then chagrin washed over her. Sex was private, between two people, and she'd been caught staring.

Hot shame replacing the lust she'd felt moments ago, Althea turned away and hurried to join Beth. These illicit scenes were obviously meant to titillate partygoers of these types of affairs, but she loved her independence too much to risk it for as lackluster an activity as sex, peculiar tingles or no.

Chapter One

August 1817, Greenborough Park, Cheltenham

"Ford. I am so glad you arrived tonight before the other guests." Evan pulled Robert Orford, one of his two closest friends, into the library, barely waiting for him to hand his coat and hat to the butler. He headed straight for the buffet table with the tray of decanters. "Whisky? Brandy? Tea?"

"Whatever you want. I can see you're in a state." Robert threw himself into a damask chair by the fire, across from Evan's usual seat.

Known as "Ford" to his friends, Robert was the most easygoing of the three men, who'd met in secondary school and attended Oxford together. He was also the shortest and stockiest. Evan was tallest at a few inches over six feet, with Michael Slade, Earl of Mansfield, splitting the difference.

"In a state. Ha! Never. Lord Cheltenham"—Evan struck a dandy's pose to imitate gossip about himself—"never has a hair out of place, nary a feather ruffled. Nothing phases him, don't you know?"

"Whatever you say, old man."

Evan shot him a look. "Brandy it is then. I'm more likely to sip it and not be miserable for our guests tomorrow." He brought the drinks over to the seating area that included a low table and a settee on a silver and gold-toned rug, skirting the small desk he used when working in this room instead of his office. The dark bookcases flanking the fireplace felt as though they loomed over him as he handed one glass to the other man before flopping into the matching chair.

"Our? Your guests, you mean."

Dozens of acquaintances were due to arrive for his annual late summer rout. Men and women of all ages, some married, some actually with their spouses rather than their mistresses, and some unmarried would attend because his parties were famously beyond risqué. No one who worried about their reputation joined. Frankly, few were invited. Still, an unspoken rule was understood. Guests were not to share the specifics of these parties.

And indeed, varying the activities and pushing the envelope of scandal were why people returned each year. The Ton was all for titillation away from society's prying eyes, and Cheltenham was far enough from London to give them exactly that while being near enough for many to make the trip.

"Ford, I could use your help. I've designed the games, but I am not certain I can bring myself to play them."

"Did you suddenly find your prudish side? Religion mayhap?" His friend stared at him, glass half-raised to his mouth.

Evan shook his head, resting it against the back of the chair. How did he explain to his friend, a second son, that he was bored. Poor little rich earl, one of the wealthiest men in the country at the tender age of eight and twenty, could not muster even a modicum of interest in his own party or any of his guests.

He had hosted most of these Lords and Ladies already, had seen them naked, and fucked more than half of them. Even sex became routine after a while, and he had grown weary of searching for a new, different thrill. Many of them would continue to make overtures. Last year, he'd had not one but two titled ladies throw themselves at him only weeks after they'd pushed their daughters to snare his hand in marriage during the Season. And a few of the men had new mistresses, which in his experience meant they'd offer a threesome to show their mistress how liberal thinking they were and how close to his greatness they stood. His friends joked, but being one of the most sought-after men in society was exhausting.

"What, then?" Ford asked.

"Honestly? I am not entirely sure that I can fly the flag of interest." He waved vaguely at his lap. "It all seems tedious. Debauchery for the sake of titillation. Sex for scandal. Not because individuals attracted to one another desire to strum each other like a harpsichord for pleasure."

"You don't expect me to replace you? 'Tis you they all come to play with, man." Robert raised his brows at Evan and settled back. With his hands behind his neck and his blond hair flopping over his forehead, he was the picture of relaxation. "I'm here to watch and be inspired for new toys and apparel. Even if that crowd was interested in a substitute, it would not be me."

"I am not at all certain the herd would notice." Evan's lips flattened in annoyance at the thought of the raucous group.

"What's gotten into you, Bags?" Robert reverted to Evan's nickname since university, chosen for his investment acumen that had earned them all scads of money. "You've always reveled in all this. Hell, you started hosting these because the London scene was too tame for you."

"I'm not sure, to be honest. Mayhap 'tis Michael's betrothal. Mayhap—" Evan paused dramatically. "—I'm growing up."

They both broke down in laughter, Robert shaking his head. "'Tis definitely not that."

"Right, then. I shall make do. 'Tis a little embarrassing—the poor, wealthy earl, bored by the orgy."

"If the issue is Michael, are you looking to find a wife?" Ford's eyebrows rose. Evan's abhorrence of marriage was well-known to his friends.

"Godsakes, no. You know I'd never foist my family's health history on anyone. Besides, all any of them—men or women—want is my bank account. Why would I limit myself to a single one when I can have variety?"

"Well, then?"

"If I knew, I could solve it, Ford." Evan flipped a hand in frustration. "But like it or not, I have at least thirty visitors arriving tomorrow for a week of vice, so I shall evaluate after that."

"Tell me about some of the games, then. I want to think about what tools to have downstairs at hand and what sketches to create for custom orders."

****

Althea plucked at her skirt for the tenth time that day, glancing out the carriage window. She'd worked herself into a state on the first day of the trip, and on this final leg, she was inconsolable. "I cannot believe you talked me into this."

After the demi-monde party, Beth's behavior had remained decorous, or at least covert. When Althea lamented a few months ago that her plan to open a second shop in Bath required more capital than she had, Beth put her vast network of associates to work. She had a knack for matching people whose needs coincided, and between her experience at the School of Enlightenment and her volunteer work at a charity school in London, she'd accumulated quite a large group of connections.

A few weeks ago, Beth had skipped into Althea's office holding a note and grinning. "You need to take a fortnight away from the store, cuz. We have a house party to go to."

Althea stared at her ward with an arched brow. "I assume this is the next phase of your plan and not simply you desiring to go play in the country?"

"Can it not be both?" Beth chuckled. "I assure you 'tis the first. That is the only reason I would dare ask you to step away from the shop for a week. But there will certainly be opportunities for the second." She wiggled her eyebrows back at Althea.

"Oh, for heaven's sake. What is it, then?"

Beth bounced on her toes twice. "Cheltie is having a party. A rout, really."

"Cheltie?" Althea's heart skipped a beat, and she told herself it was alarm rather than anticipation.

"The Earl of Cheltenham."

"I know." Althea gave her a dry look.

She knew he did not take on new investments easily. He was extremely selective and generally wanted a strong stake in the business if he provided the capital. She did not want that, nor did she think he'd be interested in her venture, so it did not make sense to risk her reputation by attending such an infamous party with such low odds of getting what she needed.

She conjured up his image as easily as if the Cyprian ball had been last week rather than last year. Tall, lanky, startlingly handsome with mannerisms and expression that projected ennui with the mere mortals who surrounded him. *Another reason not to attend. I have no desire to watch him cavort with other women.*

She shook her head, even as she hated to squash her cousin's enthusiasm.

"According to Penelope— You remember her from Sarah Potter's party, and I attended her wedding to Lord Michael Slade. Michael is one of Cheltie's close friends. Apparently, Cheltie has quietly started to focus more on investing in women-owned businesses."

"Lud, I have no idea how you discover all these tidbits. That is indeed interesting. However, I know about the rest of his reputation. I am not certain I'll be— No, I am quite certain I shan't be comfortable at one of his house parties. And I understand they are quite exclusive. Invitations are near impossible to get."

Beth had smirked and waved the note. "Penelope put our names on the list. And really, Althea. You weren't comfortable taking me in or accompanying me to his London party. It seems like a silent investor, particularly when he alone might provide the full sum you need, is worth a little more discomfort?"

Althea had remained doubtful, and she preferred a female investor. However, not seeing another way, she had made the necessary arrangements.

"Please, not this again." Across from her on the

carriage seat, Beth rolled her eyes.

"He doesn't know us. I haven't needed an investor before. I fear I cannot walk up to the man, introduce myself, and ask for money."

"Althea. Stop it." Beth put her hand over her cousin's fidgeting ones. "I am certain you know how to charm people into parting with their money. I've seen you do it in the store for—pardon me, but—ridiculously priced soaps and other goods."

Althea flashed her a quick grin, smoothing the wrinkles she'd created in her gown.

Beth continued, "We will find a way."

"What if he's constantly playing..." She searched for the right word, before bursting out with, "...prurient games?"

Beth howled with laughter. "One can only hope, cuz! I can jump right in and get to know him better then spring the idea on him or pass him over to you."

Althea gasped. "No, I could not. I mean, you know I fully support whatever you want to do, but I cannot fathom it."

"I know. Sadly, your overly religious father and strait-laced husband skewed your view of men. 'Tis a shame, really. You don't know what you are missing." Beth leered at her cousin.

"Which goes to my point. I certainly did not understand my lack of freedom"—she ignored Beth's coughed *sexual pleasure*—"in my marriage. Now, keeping my newfound independence is of paramount importance. I do not want a man involved. What if people find out and only want to deal with him? It could divert attention and business. My business could become his enterprise, shunting aside the woman responsible for its success. I still hope to find a woman with enough capital."

"Please, I beg you. Stop worrying. All will be well. If you get an offer and it doesn't suit, you can refuse it. If you decline politely, no one can take offense."

"But then there will be someone out there who knows how profitable selling shampoo could be. I shall have created my own competition."

Beth bent her head and looked up at her cousin through her lashes. "Do you really think this crowd is going to exert themselves, *lower* themselves, to become merchants? Stop it."

"Ack. You are right. I am sorry."

"Now, shall we focus on the fun parts of this? You have more than ten days without having to be at the store. More, without being in London. What do you plan to do with your time?"

"Hmm. Rework some numbers for the store expansion probably."

"Oh my goodness. I said fun. What games will you play with the other guests?"

"I don't know." Althea stared out the window for a moment. "I cannot remember the last house party I attended. What games will he offer, do you think?"

"Ha. With Cheltie, one never knows. Usually there would be croquet and picnics, and dances in the evening. Mayhap cards and music. Hunting for those who want some exercise."

"How is it that you're six years younger than me, but know all this while I do not?"

Beth shrugged. "I am more fun than you?"

Althea laughed. "Right, then. Croquet. I am not sure I remember the rules, but that does sound fun if the weather improves. And I do love a game of whist. 'Tis been ages since I played."

****

"I had the servants clean your workroom this week," Evan said as he pulled chairs onto the balcony of Ford's guest suite to watch carriages arrive.

He assumed his usual deceptive lounge, leg crossed over the other and swinging as though he hadn't a care in the world as he stared out over the rolling hills of the estate he loved. He'd grown up in this manor home, running across those slopes with a hound, then in more recent years on horseback, always in search of an adventure or someone his own age.

As his parents' only child and heir, he was watched like a hawk and drilled in lessons on deportment, comportment, and all the portments, except when he could escape and roam. Now, despite his mother's presence in the dower house, he was once again alone.

Ford grinned. "Excellent, thank you. I have a new cuff configuration I think will sell well, so I started a few and will place the buckles accordingly on the lengths to order."

The rooms, done in Ford's preferred gray tones, was in the family wing on the second floor, offset from the estate entrance. None of the guests were aware of their presence, which suited Evan just fine. He needed to save his energy to be the engaging host they all expected.

Evan kept a permanent suite of rooms for his friend, a bedroom with an adjoining room that had been converted to a workroom. As a second son of an earl, Ford did not have the bevy of estates to adjourn to in the off-season, and Greenborough Park was beyond large enough for them both.

Ford had built a custom tannery business around their shared interest, sex play and bondage between willing partners, and Evan had ensured the workroom at Greenborough Park had duplicates of almost every tool Ford had in London.

"Have you had time to visit with Mama yet?" Evan asked. Ford had been like a second son to Evan's parents, often spending school holidays at the estate.

"I did this morning. She seems in good health."

"Dare I ask? Did she remember you were coming? I told her yesterday."

Ford's lips quirked in an instant of sympathy as he shook his head in the negative.

"Ah, well, I suspect the parade of carriages will entertain her, and I shall sneak away as I can to check on her." Another carriage pulled around the circular driveway, and Evan welcomed the diversion.

A tall, slim, dark-haired woman emerged, shaking out her modestly-cut forest green gown. He leaned forward, squinting. A ball of chestnut-haired energy rolled out of the carriage after her, the girl's large bosom almost making an appearance from her noticeably less modest peach dress.

He'd been waiting for this duo. Or rather, the half that was Lady Althea Egerton. After he'd met her last year, he'd asked Michael about her. There were few titled ladies whom he had not yet met—or been pursued by, for that matter. She was the widow of a merchant and ran the shop after his death, which was rare. But that fact was nowhere near as intriguing as her discomfort at the Cyprian ball. Most surprising had been her mix of guilt and fascination as she watched a man enjoying a woman's mouth on him in the upstairs hall of that party.

He'd put her from his mind as the Season wound to a close, focusing on Michael's surprise betrothal to his mistress at that very ball. But he'd barely tolerated his house party after that Season, his third annual gathering.

Robert, Michael, and he had made it a tradition after throwing the first as an Oxford graduation celebration. It had seemed the perfect way to celebrate the end of each Season with the grueling paperwork and negotiations of the House of Lords done for the year and the men looking for new challenges.

Now, Evan had mastered the nuances of Parliament, the earldom, and the bedroom, Michael was married, and Ford hated parties. Evan should have cancelled this year's but had hoped being at home would re-energize him. It hadn't.

Then he'd received a note from Penelope, Michael's countess and formerly a member of said demi-monde, asking him to invite Lady Althea and Beth. Across the bottom of the parchment, Michael had scrawled, *I'll owe you*. Not that it was necessary. If any of the three of them needed something, they had only to ask the others. That extended to spouses-to-be.

Upon reading Lady Egerton's name, his mind had immediately conjured the image of the tall lithe brunette beauty he had met a year ago. Beth had propositioned him that night, although he knew it was out of habit as much as true desire. She enjoyed sex in all shapes and forms and with as little attachment as possible, much as he did—well, used to. But Lady Althea had seemed out of place at that ball, her dark eyes wide as she turned and noted his regard, her ivory cheeks flushing red before she raced away.

So there had to be another reason these two ladies, Lady Althea in particular, were here at another demi-monde party, despite her obvious discomfort with them. He was willing to bet it wasn't simply to assuage Beth's libido. His jaded suspicion was that money was involved, which was particularly disappointing when this woman had sparked his interest more than any had in months.

Still, she might prove his only hope for enjoyment this week.

As the ladies disappeared into the house, he tilted his head. Did Althea know about Beth's education at the School of Enlightenment? He made a mental note to find out who sponsored the little hellion.

Knowledge was valuable, and Evan made it his business to know as much of the Ton's business as possible. Only then could he ensure his investment choices were sound and sometimes even one step ahead. So when a secret school for girls was being formed by several countesses and the headmistress of a charity school he already funded, Evan had sent a note to that headmistress to offer his support.

They'd determined that on the face of it, the school would best be run by women for women, although at least one other man, the Earl of Suffolk, was involved. He helped with funding and finding new teachers as needed. Evan preferred to remain a step removed, but he paid for the buildings they wanted to construct and ensured the landowner, the widow Helen Montague, received a generous stipend to stay on as headmistress.

Having a mother completely dependent on the

goodwill of her heir due to an illness she could not control had turned him into the fiercest of protectors of women. He liked the way this school helped girls learn to protect themselves quietly, as a spy behind enemy lines might.

But Lady Egerton's conservative demeanor did not lend itself to supporting a school teaching everything from money management to tipping the velvet. He tilted his head to the other side, debating. Or mayhap it did, given her shop ownership and sharing a house with Beth.

Spending a moment to wonder what those demure dresses hid, Evan's boredom slipped away and his cock twitched in interest. *Hmm. Mayhap I've found a playmate for this house party, even if she does not realize it quite yet.*

Chapter Two

Althea tried to focus on the needlework in her lap and ignore her anxiety about her cousin's whereabouts. Beth had wandered off after only a few minutes of sitting with the other ladies in the parlor. Even knowing how much Beth hated needlework, Althea would have preferred she read a book or something unlikely to offend their host, at least until she'd had a chance to present her expansion plan.

Given the size of the castle, Althea was not about to attempt to find the younger woman. She'd get lost. Having expected a manor home, brick and covered in ivy, they'd arrived to a gate with turrets of a stone tower in the distance beyond it. The fence had extended as far as the eye could see in both directions, leading Althea to wonder about just how many acres Lord Cheltenham owned.

At least their privacy was assured, given the nature of this particular party.

Althea stitched desultorily, half-listening to the gossip. She knew most of the names referenced in the conversation as clients. It never hurt to know more of the rest of their lives, to strengthen her relationships with her customers.

Finally, she could stand it no more. She poked her head out of the parlor. Her cousin stood lounging against the newel post of the grand staircase, watching servants rearrange furniture from two rooms that opened to each other, likely setting up for the evening activities.

Beth's gaze was locked on one footman's lower half with a look Althea recognized. Lust.

"Beth. I wondered if you were lost. Your needlework is here. Are you coming back?" Her comment drew Beth's reluctant gaze. She shook her head at the girl, reminding her of her promise to behave.

Beth sighed. "Cuz, I can't sit still another minute. I'm going to take a walk, rain or no rain. I'll try not to dampen our room with wet clothing from it."

"Take a servant with you."

Beth cast a hopeful glance back at the servant whose calves even Althea could appreciate and nodded.

Althea wondered what she'd find, given the number of additional structures they'd seen on the property as they made their way up the long driveway. Then she worried, given her cousin's penchant for trouble. By the time she retired to change for dinner, Althea still had not seen Beth and her worry had climbed to distress.

Then Beth rushed in as a servant finished pinning Althea's hair back. The bedraggled girl shucked her wet dress, borrowed Althea's bath for a quick splash-through, and climbed into a more suitable and drier gown.

The dining room awed both women when they first entered, and they gazed around with open mouths. Fit for a palace, it seated every last guest, despite this house party being larger than most. The table appeared to be a solid slab of mahogany, and heavy Tudor chests shared wall space with more delicate glass-fronted hutches from the last century.

Dinner was a boisterous affair, everyone chattering with excitement as they found their seats. Wine ran freely into glasses, and the energy level and resulting noise rose with each course. Althea's nerves ratcheted up with each roar of laughter and high-pitched giggle. She sat primly, her hands in her lap, wondering when she would be able to corner Lord Cheltenham for a serious conversation.

Beth kept eyeing her. Althea suspected her cousin thought she might bolt to hide in their room and was poised to stop her, which did indeed stop her. Althea barely ate, although each course put before her was more delicious than the last.

She watched their host as he laughingly deflected questions about the week's activities, declining offers of suggestions and requests for games from previous years. He seemed in his element. And why shouldn't he be? This was his home, his fête.

As the guests scraped the last of dessert from their plates, Cheltenham stood and raised his glass. "Ladies, gentlemen, and the rest of us—" He waited while the guests laughed obligingly. "—shall we?"

Beth and Althea followed the crowd to the east side of the main hall where the ballrooms sat. One was brightly lit, with some seating areas and a few musical instruments. The other was more dimly lit.

Althea tugged on their linked arms to direct her cousin to the right, toward the brighter room. As they passed, Lord Cheltenham stepped out of the darker doorway to pull in a quiet man with dark blond hair and a neatly trimmed beard who she vaguely recognized from a year ago. It appeared she was unlikely to get to speak to her host this evening then, unless she braved the darker room.

Not ready for that on the first night, she preferred to get the lay of the land.

When she slowed, Beth glanced at her. "Come, Althea. I shall stay close. There are card tables. I'm sure we can find people to play whist, and you love that game. You rarely lose."

Althea cocked her head, considering.

"Remember what I said about it being worth some discomfort? 'Twill only get harder if you wait, as one of the maids told me the evening entertainments get bawdier each night of the party."

Althea gulped.

"Come." Beth caught her hand and tugged. When Althea stepped to follow her, her cousin looked back with an encouraging smile.

Clutching the hand she held as a lifeline, Althea glanced around the crowded room. Beth was already leading them to the card tables to one side. Cigar and cigarillo smoke hung over the area in clouds, and husky feminine laughter interlaced with men crowing floated through the mist.

As they found an unoccupied table, two men approached. Introducing themselves, they requested a game.

"What are the stakes?" Althea asked.

The men looked at her, surprised by the question. They glanced around at the other tables, and both ladies' gazes followed theirs.

She gasped. The game was *strip* whist, the stakes were articles of clothing.

Her gaze darted to Beth's, and she read her cousin's silent message in her eyes.

We can do this. You are the best whist player I know. And oh! The housemaid told us to wear extra petticoats tonight and drawers—how helpful.

Althea was confident about two things despite her strict upbringing and marriage—managing her shop and her skills at this card game. Much of winning was watching people for tells, and she had mastered that by observing shoppers closely, to ensure she spent her time with buyers rather than browsers. She could do this.

She glanced around once more, then nodded to Beth and took the cards in hand. "Gentlemen, shall we draw for the first deal?"

An hour later, the gentlemen were in shirts, breeches, and hose and were debating whether the hose or the shirt would go next. Beth was, of course, offering her unsolicited opinion. "Shirts, please?"

Althea rolled her eyes as the men acquiesced, laughing and dragging their shirts off, adding them to the growing piles by their chairs.

The ladies each had a pair of shoes beside their chair, representing their one loss.

A bell rang, and when the noise had diminished somewhat, a servant announced that the card tables would need to be shifted to allow the partition between the rooms to be removed.

The men stood and bowed, thanking the women for the game.

Althea used the opportunity to slip her shoes back on and wish all three a good night.

Beth hugged her, leaning in to whisper, "Good game, cuz. Are you quite all right? You don't mind if I stay?"

While they had discussed that as a plan before dinner, Althea knew her cousin would retire with her if she asked.

"Thank you. I am not sure what I would have done if we'd lost, but I am fine. You play. I want to hear all about it tomorrow. But please, pace yourself. This is the first night of several and as you said, they'll get wilder."

"I will. I promise."

****

Evan shuffled papers on his desk, trying to find something urgent to address that would justify his lurking—ahem, presence—in his office rather than among his guests. What was left for him if he couldn't muster the courage to brave his own party? He'd never minded the women rubbing against him or even rubbing him before.

Giving up, he hoped Ford would not come looking for him. With that in mind, he rounded his desk and strode toward the hall door to close it the last inch.

Movement through the crack of space caught his eye. Franklin the footman, as Evan liked to think of him, was walking away from him toward the great hall. Evan liked having his office down a narrow side hall, off the path of guests. It afforded him the perfect opportunity to hide, er, to get work done when he needed to.

Too many guests, male and female, wanted to be in his presence all day every day. He often wondered if they hoped his money would magically appear in their pockets, his investment skills in their brains, and his charisma in their manners. He smirked. It wouldn't.

He'd have shared it with Ford if he could. Instead, he dragged Ford out of his comfort zone over and over to assist with his own constant battle against boredom.

A guest appeared at the entrance to the hallway. 'Twas Beth Jenkins. Much as he was intrigued by Lady Althea and had contemplated possibilities for her when they'd arrived the first day, he wanted to avoid this forward bit of fluff. He wasn't worried, though. Franklin had his orders. He'd redirect her.

The chit reminded him of himself. Not having the opportunities afforded Evan at Oxford, her sexual education had been ad hoc, then completed at the School of Enlightenment. In addition to sharing his carefree, take-all-comers approach to sex, she maintained a network of people of all classes, and knowledge of their needs, wants, and desires that might be even more informed and wider than his. After all, being one of the richest blokes in the land made one rather high profile and interfered with casting a subtle net for information.

He shook his head as she surreptitiously pinched her arms to her sides and pushed her stays up, then brought her hands together in front of her to tug her dress down from her waist. He had to admit she was an incredibly tasty morsel. But even from the demi-monde ball, his focus had been on her taller, dark-haired cousin.

Althea's decorum and quietude juxtaposed with her obvious love and acceptance of her wild cousin were a conundrum that sparked interest like few things did for him these days. When he'd stepped onto the upper hallway at the London party and found Althea panting against a doorframe, her eyes sheened with lust, he was beyond intrigued.

He narrowed his eyes as Beth managed to disarm his most urbane servant. *Hmm. She probably recognizes some of them from the school.*

The young man gave her a shallow bow. "My lady, this is part of the private residence. Can I help you find your way to one of the game rooms?"

"What game did you have in mind?"

His eyes dropped to her chest, more on display after her quick maneuvering. His tongue ran across his lower lip. "Whatever my lady desires."

"Excellent. I most definitely desire to see more of—" She ran her finger down his waistcoat buttons pulling back to hover in front of the placket of his breeches. "You." Her other hand rose to her décolletage, fingering the lace edging on the gown.

"That can be arranged." He gave another shallow bow.

"We'd need privacy for that, would we not?" she asked archly, glancing around the hall in this "private" section of the house. She took several steps toward Evan's office, spinning so that she faced Franklin.

The servant caught his eye, and Evan shook his head quickly, gesturing for him to get her back to the rooms designated for entertaining guests.

"Ah, yes. But—"

"Excellent. Can you find my cousin and let her know I'm going for a walk please, so that she does not come looking for me? I'll just step into one of these rooms and await you."

"Ah…" Franklin's eyes glazed as they followed her finger movements.

"In fact, let me just step in here." She grabbed the

handle of the door to Evan's office, and he jumped back.

"Not—" Franklin sounded desperate.

Scrambling several more steps away, Evan called out, "Franklin, I told you I did not want to be disturbed."

"Well, Cheltie, I'm not Franklin, and I thought your reputation was exactly that you are disturbed…in all the most fun ways," Beth said in her sultriest voice.

Damn me.

"My lord, I do apologize," Franklin said. "She slipped by me."

"I have no doubt. And no doubt how," Evan replied, giving a wry look to her heaving bosom as he turned to walk toward her.

"He is right. 'Tis not his fault. Please do not punish him for my transgression." She smirked, her head circling to take the room in. Much like the library, his office was furnished in mahogany, with wood paneling in lieu of the bookshelves. To lighten the room, he had paintings on most walls, one bookshelf behind his desk in easy reach, and sage green and gold tones in the upholstery, rugs, and drapes.

"Oh? Shall I punish you then?" Evan stopped in front of her, eyebrows raised.

"Hmm. Mayhap. What did you have in mind?" Beth asked, returning her gaze to his with a head tilt and a coy smile.

"Nice try, Miss Jenkins. And, need I remind you, not your first. Thank you anyway, though. Franklin, 'tis fine. You can leave her here."

Beth glanced over and winked, causing Franklin's woebegone expression at missing a tryst to brighten.

Evan had no doubt the chit would find an hour or two of privacy with the servant.

"Do come in," Evan said with a sarcastic twist of his lips. "Have a seat." He returned to his leather chair behind the massive desk. Lounging back, he crossed his legs and swung the top one leisurely. His gaze, however, was sharp. "How may I help you, Miss Jenkins?"

"Surely, if you're going to let me get away with calling you Cheltie, you can call me Beth." She mock pouted as she perched on a visitor chair, leaning forward to afford him the best view of her décolletage.

Evan sighed. "I think people in your life have let you get away with far too much."

She arched one brow. "Somehow, I doubt you would think that if I were a man."

"Touché." He nodded. "So…"

"I am here with my cousin, Althea—Lady Althea Egerton. She would like to discuss an investment opportunity with you."

White-hot fury flashed through him. The one woman he thought might prove interesting this week was here for money. His guess at her reason for coming had been right.

'Tis the story of my life. Why did I let myself hope for anything more?

He fought the urge to toss Beth out of his office, refraining only because of Penelope's note. The fact that Michael had added his own request made sense now. Both his friends knew his distrust of anyone asking for money; he preferred to find his own investments.

Taking a calming breath, he laid his hands on the

arms of his chair. "I am sorry, but I am not looking to invest in anything new at this time."

"Yes, Penelope said you'd say that. She also told me to tell you to listen."

Evan rolled his eyes. "God save me from forceful women. You'd better not be making this up." The note from his friend's wife had only requested an invitation.

"I beg your pardon. I absolutely would not use Penelope's name as a reference without her permission. I try to get people's consent for all things I do with…their name." She winked.

"Right, then. Let's hear it."

"Oh no. I would not be able to do it justice. Please, I am only asking that you hear Althea out. I think you will find her business plan well-organized and thought out. And word has it that you like to support women-owned businesses." She gave him innocent eyes.

How could he explain that those were different? *I seek out those women, or they come referred from trustworthy sources.* His conscience argued back. *And Penelope and Michael are among your most trusted friends.*

"What do I get out of this?" He wanted to buy himself a minute to debate more, although he knew he'd relent for Pen's sake.

"Sexual favors?"

"Ack. We've covered that." He managed not to roll his eyes, waving a hand dismissively. "And boring. Look around you. Those are freely given here, not something to negotiate with. Try again."

Beth's head snapped back at the word "boring."
If she only knew.

She cocked her head, narrowing her eyes at him.

31

He could almost see the wheels turning in her brain. After an elongated pause, she said, "A new nurse for your mother."

Evan froze, his swinging leg stilling, and stared at her without so much as a blink.

How in hell *did she find out about my mother, much less her need for a nurse?*

Ready to throw her out all over again, he leaned forward slowly and dipped his chin.

"Friend of Penelope or not, I'll thank you to keep your thoughts of my mother to yourself," he hissed out through gritted teeth.

Beth's head retracted again. "My lord, I beg your pardon. I meant no offense. Your mother is darling. I so enjoyed having a cup of tea with her when I happened on her cottage the other day. And Lucy mentioned that she needs to return home to care for her own mama now but is waiting for you to find someone."

His jaw was still clenched. Network or no, this was not acceptable. "I have no idea what inspired my staff to share confidences with you, but my mother is not to be discussed with anyone else, either here at the party or beyond, including Penelope."

"Lord Cheltenham." Beth straightened in her chair and reverted to his formal title, her voice stilted. "I would never do such a thing. When I search for servants to help friends and acquaintances, I do not use names until I have ascertained a fit. I use only general characteristics of the persons and situation. Have you ever heard word of me being a gossip?"

"No," he said slowly, running through what he knew of her in his mind. "But I have heard stories of your ability to bring people together. I just assumed…"

He grimaced.

"Ah. Well, please do not. I assure you I will be the soul of discretion. The rest of your information was correct, however. I am quite good at finding people who fit together well. And I have one or two in mind that might work for your sweet mama. I need to ask them a few questions about past service. I shall send you a note as soon as I have done that upon our return to London. The rest will be up to you. Do we have a deal?"

Evan glared at her.

She seemed impervious, returning his gaze calmly.

You just finished admiring her people skills when she was in the hall. Likening her to yourself, even. Do you not want the best network available to match a nurse to your mother's needs?

He relaxed a fraction, then nodded once to himself. He'd be a fool not to take advantage of this opportunity. A few minutes of his time for a well-suited nurse in a fraction of the time it would take him?

He stood. "Yes."

"Thank you, Cheltie. You shan't be sorry." Beth practically skipped to the door. "When shall I send Althea?"

"Tonight. Bring her to this room an hour before the dinner bell."

Hell's bells, he hoped it was an innocuous request, one he could easily accept or deny with impunity.

Beth's reference to his mother had stolen his focus, but after she left, he had a new thought.

I'll have a chance to start peeling back the layers of Lady Egerton in a few hours.

Chapter Three

Evan had watched Althea as often as his duties as host allowed since she had arrived at Greenborough Park.

The first night's dinner had been tedious, trying to catch her words from the length of the massive table and beneath the guise of listening to the guests seated closest to him as they fawned over him. Social etiquette precluded him from seating her closer, given her title and status as new to this party.

After dinner, Evan had prowled the edges of the two ballrooms. Engrossed in their own groups and games, guests did not notice. When Althea had followed Beth into the card room, Evan had perked up, wondering which game they would play or if they'd only mingle.

Given their choice, he'd anticipated seeing more of Althea's lovely alabaster skin. But game after game, the gentlemen at the table discarded clothing while the ladies remained cool and composed. Beth clearly deferred to her cousin in the betting, and Althea barely blinked. She'd known the game was a sure thing, and Evan's interest turned to disappointment at her lack of adventurousness.

Tonight, he had a bargaining chip of his own to wield.

He did his best to tamp down his annoyance at

Beth's request. Much as he loved Penelope—platonically, of course—he did not appreciate the interference in his finances. Oh, he had no doubt that Michael trusted Pen, and he deferred to Michael's choices. But for himself? With so much at stake? No, thank you.

He had hoped that Althea would be different. Why, he wasn't sure. He had no plans for anything more than a brief dalliance. But when he'd learned she was looking for money, his bitterness returned. Of course she was. Wasn't everyone who requested an audience?

Unsure if the vexation was directed at himself or her, he decided it did not matter. He'd hear her out, evaluate the opportunity as he would any other, and invest or not. He should decide that quickly though. It was never a good idea to mix business and pleasure, and he still planned to pursue her while she was here. She could not be *too* reserved if she lived with Beth, after all, and he was sure he'd seen more arousal than shock when she lingered in that upstairs hallway in London.

He paced, strangely nervous to meet her. What if her plan was not worthwhile?

I cannot upset Penelope, or Michael will take me to task. But he could not deny that this was the most excited he had been all week. Possibly all month…all year.

Stopping at the mirror next to the door, he shot his cuffs and fiddled with his cravat. He turned again to tread the length of the room, a lion in an elegant cage.

A knock turned him back toward his desk as a servant opened the door and announced Althea. At Evan's nod, the door closed behind the footman's departure.

Sable curls longer than the current fashion highlighted her porcelain skin, her dark brows and rose-colored lips the only swaths of color against that ivory. Dark eyes glowed with a fierce, intelligent light and took in everything and everyone around her. No shy retiring miss, this.

Whereas Beth's bosom was soft, bouncy, and round, like the rest of her, Althea's was shocking. Oversized for her lithe frame, her breasts were difficult to ignore. If her gaze had been any less commanding, he might not have fought very hard.

Unlike her cousin's, however, Althea's dress had a rather modest neckline, and she tended to keep her lips pressed closed, relying on Beth's natural friendly and outgoing nature to lead for both of them. "Lord Cheltenham, thank you for seeing me."

He harrumphed.

Godsakes, I sound like an old man. But 'tis not like Beth gave me much choice.

"I am happy to do so. 'Tis lovely to see you again, Lady Althea. Come, sit, and tell me more about what you're looking to do."

He gestured to the desk area.

She glanced over at the fireplace seating area but followed him, settling into a guest chair, her plum-colored skirts settling around her.

The deeper hues flatter her and stand out among the pastels the debs wear.

Bah, someone save me from myself. He was waxing poetic about a woman's color choices.

"Call me Althea, please. I am not certain what Beth told you..."

"All right, Althea. And I am Evan. Now, assume I know nothing." *Because I do.* "I'd prefer to hear about your business from you, anyway."

"Ah. Well, you may or may not be aware that my husband left me his apothecary when he passed a few years ago. I have been managing it since then. Successfully, as I can show you." She gestured to papers in her lap that Evan had not noticed until now.

"May I ask the location?" He knew it, as he knew most things about his guests. But he wanted to see how she handled the barrage of questions any investor would ask.

She named a street just south of Tyburn Road in a central shopping area walking distance from Mayfair.

"That is well-placed." He nodded once. "I may even have been in there myself."

"We have the usual offerings. Salves and tonics, beauty products, paper and ink."

"So how do you differentiate yourself?"

"I have a unique soap no one else stocks currently. 'Tis specifically for hair, to protect it and nourish it. It is called shampoo, brought over from India, and I stock it in the same fragrances as body soap. It's been one of my top sellers, so much so that I am barely able to keep up with demand."

"How will the supplier increase production?"

"The stylist who introduced it to me has asked her family to help, and they've even hired two assistants now."

Evan's eyebrows lifted. "How much do you sell a year?"

Althea named a figure.

"And what percentage of your total sales is that?"

"Ten."

He blinked twice before controlling his surprise. "Do you have any other single product that is ten percent of gross?"

She shook her head.

"I see."

He crossed one leg over the other and shifted to stare at the fire, a habit he had when pondering something.

Looking back at her, he asked, "Why do you need an investor? What are you looking to do?"

"I should like to capitalize on this while I can, before others start making similar products. My hope— plan," she corrected hastily, "—is to open a store in Bath. The Ton makes up the majority of my clients, and many visit Bath each year. A number of older people stay there year-round to take the waters. I believe the philosophy of taking care of one's self can be leveraged for my products. Shampoo in particular."

Evan rested his elbows on the chair arms, steepling his fingertips in front of his chest, and nodded.

Long before he inherited his title, before even Oxford, Evan had been able to size up opportunities— for investment, for mischief, whatever lay before him— and evaluate the risks and rewards with a few questions and some strategic thinking. A niche product in an upscale market was a perfect chance for jumping in for a short period and ramping sales and production before it became a commodity, which would mean a lower profit margin.

His thoughts whirled. His pulse raced. While the earldom, existing business ventures, and even the wildest sex had all begun to bore him, a new idea could still energize him.

Finally. Entertainment. More, a challenge. When even an orgy did not interest him, he'd worried he would never find excitement again. He weighed the pros and cons of the various ways to structure a deal.

There were a few options. A loan with payments tied to revenue, a set interest rate loan, or his preferred method, an equity stake in the shop. He favored owning a piece of the business. He could help ensure its success and afford the risk. So he chose to reap fully in the rewards rather than get a fixed payback from a loan. But first, he needed to understand what was required for the expansion and how much would come from investors.

Turning back to his visitor, he held his hand out. "If I may?"

"Oh. Of course." Althea passed him the financial summaries and projections in her lap.

Evan flicked through them, then looked up. "I shall require some time with these. If you'd prefer to rejoin the revelry, I am happy to meet again later."

He was nonplussed when she shook her head in the negative. "No, thank you. I'd prefer to wait here and answer questions as needed."

He raised an eyebrow. *Mayhap she is not as open-minded as I hoped a cousin of Beth's would be.* "Are you not enjoying the party, Lady Egerton?"

Althea winced as if recalling she was addressing the party's host. "Oh yes, thank you. And we appreciated your gracious invitation. Although—" She gave a quick twitch of her mouth in a half smile. "—I suspect it was coerced, knowing my cousin. But this is more important."

"Hmm." Outwardly noncommittal, Evan seethed internally. *Just as I thought. The request to attend was less to do with Beth's quest for entertainment and more to do with money. How annoyingly predictable.*

"Right, then. Please, make yourself comfortable. Would you prefer the settee?"

She shook her head.

"No? A drink? My apologies. I should have offered that sooner."

"Nothing, thank you."

"You're quite sure? Tea? Or I have sherry, port, brandy, and scotch." He gestured to a shallow cabinet with decanters sitting on top. "I could do with a scotch, myself." He rose, keeping her eye as he rounded the desk.

"Thank you, but I prefer to keep a clear head."

****

Althea knew she sounded prim. She couldn't help it. She was anxious. Sitting across from him for this interview was nerve wracking; she would not want to play him in whist. His face gave nothing away. While she was sure that helped his financial success, it was annoying in negotiations. But her husband had taught her not to show nerves or fear in these situations. And this felt like one of the most important negotiations of her life.

Who am I fooling? I am here begging more than negotiating. He doesn't need me. I need him.

Evan arched a brow at her as he poured himself a generous glass of whisky, his hair glinting burnished gold in the light from the nearby fire and accented by his rust-colored jacket and breeches.

Yep. Prim. She needed to work harder at not

offending her potential investor and host, however silly she found this party.

Half-raising it in a careless toast, he sipped and returned to sit. "Right, then. What do we have here?" He sorted the documents into three piles.

She watched to understand his approach. The piles seemed to be marketing materials and product descriptions, historical financial reports, and her stab at projections for the new store.

"Hmm."

Stifling a jerk at his wordless sound, she clenched her hands to combat the tremors of her rampant desire to fidget.

He spent only a few minutes flipping through the product information before perusing the financials. He set the London store data side by side with the analysis for the Bath store. As he read through the tables, he circled a few things on each. Occasionally, he threw a question at her without even glancing up, scribbling her answers down on a separate sheet of foolscap he'd produced. Unlike most men, he did not wear shirts with ruffled cuffs, and she could see why. A man of business needed wrists clear to manage paperwork.

"How long has the London store been open?"

"How many months did it take to get to this revenue stream?"

"Sales have improved steadily over the past two years." She declined to add that the timeline coincided with her husband's death and her management.

"When did you introduce shampoo?"

"Eight months ago. You can see it in the upturn of that chart." She nodded at the paper he held in his left hand, as he'd been looking at the list of figures in his right.

"How did you estimate rent for the space in Bath?"

"Will your supply still come from London and be transported to Bath? For all your products?"

He scribbled some other information in his notes, then put the pen down and sat back, looking at her. "Have you considered a different entry point into the market?"

"Do you mean a different location? I considered them briefly, but Brighton is even more expensive than Bath for space and farther from London. Distance is important if I keep the inventory management centralized through London as a sort of headquarters."

"I agree. But no, I meant mayhap not starting with a full storefront."

"Oh. No. I suppose I don't really know what that option would entail."

"I have helped a few others take that path, admittedly with products that are quite different. But the principle's the same. I could assist you as well."

Althea straightened. This was what she'd been afraid of in asking a man to invest. They wanted to step in and *help*. They assumed that was what a woman would want. "Lord Cheltenham, I very much appreciate your time. And I recognize that you have had some success with investments." *Prim!*

His condescending half grin made her aware of how vast that understatement was.

She tried to gentle her tone. "That is why I approached you. I am happy to have you direct me to possible paths, but I will take it from there. I am only looking for an investor at this time. Not a long-term adviser or partner."

She bit her lip, hoping she had not offended him. But these past two years of managing the store had been the happiest she had ever been, more so than her marriage. She had loved her husband, but in a passive, quiet way. Her father had arranged the union specifically because her husband was a placid, reserved man. So while she would not have wished him dead and missed him in some ways, she reveled in her freedom now. She loved being a merchant, despite the aristocracy's condemnation of engaging in trade. The last thing she wanted was a man stepping in and trying to take over.

Lord Cheltenham was frowning. *Oh no.*

"Lady Althea, from the looks of these reports, your London store is turning a narrow margin of profit for you. However, it does not appear to be ceding enough that you'd have anywhere near the funds needed for a location in Bath. Which means we're talking about a considerable sum. How many investors are you pursuing at this time?"

She lowered her gaze to her lap as she admitted, "You're the first."

He exhaled audibly. "I suspected as much. Allow me to clarify your situation. Whether you find one investor or ten, they'll want a portion of the proceeds. Opening a store in an entirely new location where you don't have an established reputation is risky. There are already any number of apothecaries there, a quantity you should identify, along with their locations. Even with an interest rate you'd find usurious, investors prefer not to limit their return on such a venture to a fixed amount."

Her voice was flat. "You're referring to a partial

ownership."

"Yes."

"No."

****

Evan leaned back in his chair, lifting his brows. "You haven't even heard the terms."

Resentment of the request aside, he loved this part. It was like foreplay—finding what worked for both sides, what brought the most pleasure without tipping into unwanted pain. Keeping a poker face, his hands relaxed on the chair arms while mentally he rubbed his palms together and tried to figure out what would hit the right buttons.

His cock stirred. He nearly shouted in glee.

Damn me, am I twelve?

Some men preferred a certain hair color or height or body type. Evan loved all women, along with the occasional man. And had been happy to show them, at least until the last few months. He stared at Althea.

What is different about this woman?

He had helped a fair number of women finance their futures, but rarely were they business owners who already ran profitable stores. A shop cleaning business, a laundress, almost—he smiled as he thought of Michael's wife, Penelope—a baker trying to buy a shop. And after one disastrous episode, he preferred to initiate investment inquiries, rather than field requests. But this woman's intelligence in her delectable form beckoned him.

In fact, he could only think of one woman with more business acumen than Althea. The Dowager Countess of Peterborough's skill with investing matched his, although he'd never admit it to her. They enjoyed a friendly competition, after all, but he'd never found her sexy. In part, that was because until his passing last year, she'd been happily married to the previous earl. Besides, once he'd found that she, not the earl, had purchased leather cuffs from Robert, Evan knew they would not be sexually compatible for the long-term.

This woman's body had attracted him. Her brain was rousing him further. He shifted as his cock pulsed against his breeches, then gave himself a mental eye roll and refocused.

"I am not willing to hand over that much control." Althea shook her head.

Ah. Here it is. "It could be structured a number of ways. A partnership for the one location, or an overall share of both locations."

Her jaw set. "My husband managed the store while he kept me—" She broke off and restarted. "While I managed the household. When he died, I had to learn it all at once. I am not ready to hand it over to another man." When Evan started to speak, she held a hand up. "Even if said man was willing to be a silent partner or near-silent adviser, others would inevitably turn to him for decisions. That, I could not abide."

The skin around his eyes tightened as he tried to hide his frustration. It sounded as though she wanted money with no accountability. The story of his life. He sighed. "There are ways to create the partnership so that it would not be seen by outsiders."

"That does not account for a man thinking he can take over," she retorted.

At some point, he should probably coach her on not giving away her stance on an issue quite so readily.

It put her at a disadvantage in negotiations. But not now. "Why don't you consider things, and if you're interested in hearing some possible ownership structures and figures, come visit me again before the end of the week? Or even back in London?"

She stood, her hands fisted by her side. He could see she wanted to refuse again. Or send him to hell. But she stayed silent as she reclaimed the paperwork he held out.

His annoyance at yet another supplicant looking to milk him for money and at the object of his first arousal in months being snatched away caused him to lash out. "A woman your age should know by now that nothing is free."

She halted halfway to the door but did not turn.

"You'll need to decide how badly you want this," he continued. "In the meantime, I hope I shall see you playing games again this evening."

Her back straightened and her shoulders tensed. Still facing the door, she nodded once and left.

Evan dropped into his desk chair and palmed his flagging cock. "Maybe later," he murmured. He wasn't ready to give up on Lady Althea Egerton yet.

Chapter Four

As dinner concluded, Althea's nerves ramped higher. She hoped a table in the card room would again be available and she could win a few rounds then retire without fanfare.

Her host's parting words rang in her ears, sounding more like a dare than a polite dismissal.

With Beth giving her courage at her side, she loitered in the hall to evaluate her options.

There were no card tables in either room. She wanted to roll her eyes and stomp her feet. *Variety is overrated.* In fact, variety was terrifying at this particular party. She also wanted to run back to her room and hide under the covers with a book and a candle.

"Ohh, 'tis different tonight. What are the games?" Beth bounced on her toes.

Althea gasped as Beth let go of her arm and pranced over to a footman, a gleam in her eye. Althea watched her cousin closely. She knew Beth's signs of interest in someone, and she was relatively sure that was the same footman Beth had been eyeing in lieu of needlework. She was pointing to the rooms and asking questions.

Althea shrank back against the wall, hoping one room would hold a musicale or other mundane house party choice.

She felt him before she saw him. Her host loomed by her side. She considered it looming when he was close enough that she expected to feel his breath. He may have been simply leaning in to be heard as guests crowded toward one room or another, all rustling skirts and chatter.

"Lady Althea. May I interest you in dancing?" He gestured to the right, then swept his hand to the left. "Or blindman's bluff mayhap?"

"Where's the whist?" she blurted, her hands fisted with nerves.

"Whist is so yesterday, don't you think?" he drawled. "Besides, it did not seem to challenge you much."

She cut her gaze to his sharply. She hadn't realized he'd seen them playing.

The small orchestra started, and a cry of joy rose from the occupants of the dancing room.

"Come, let us watch for a few moments. The game will not start until the quartet sets up in that room. Then the doors shall be closed so the music does not clash."

He led her to the doorway of the right ballroom.

Althea gasped. Men and women were paired, men and men were paired, and women and women were paired. But in lieu of the formal arm frame of a waltz or other ballroom dance, a man's hand was not on his partner's side. Instead, it rested low on his companion's spine, with the couple's legs intertwined, hips a scant inch apart.

She had the odd thought that a decade before this would not have been possible, but women's dresses were much slimmer with less petticoats the last few years. She shook her head and tried not to focus on the heat curling through her center from watching the bodies in close contact.

Beth was paired with the footman she had been chatting with a moment before. Distracted from her guilty enjoyment of the dancers, Althea frowned, worried Beth's actions would get the poor man in trouble with his employer.

Evan must have caught her expression. Following her gaze, he chuckled. "My servants know they're allowed to participate if invited, and they've been specially trained to meet *all* my guests' needs—at their own discretion, of course."

Althea shot him a look. Was he really saying that the guests were invited to sleep with the servants and vice versa? Oh lud, Beth would have a field day. Or…mayhap she knew and 'twas one of the reasons she was so set on this being the path for Althea to meet Evan. She frowned at her cousin again.

"Shall it be dancing then?"

She jolted, imagining the press of his body against hers. Why, her breasts would be touching his waistcoat in that close clinch. Another bolt of heat shot through her, and her nipples peaked embarrassingly. *Oh, my.*

The earl's gaze was heavy-lidded as he awaited her answer.

She licked her lips, considering. Someone pushed by behind her in the doorway, and she roused from her fog. No. She would not be lured or provoked into playing dirty games. She still did not understand her cousin's interest in sex, no matter how much Beth described it or encouraged her to experiment. Her marriage had been a good one but did not include high passion in any form. The idea of sex with a stranger left her cold. She had simply had a momentary lapse due to her strange excitement at watching the intimate dance.

Except… No. "No, thank you, my lord. I shall sit this out."

"Right, then. Onward. We shall play the game." He grasped her elbow and turned them, stepping them into the other room as the doors shut.

"What? No. Thank you, I think I shall retire."

"Madame, 'tis barely sundown. Come now, have some fun. Surely you played this as a child?"

"Yes, but…"

"This is simply a grown-up version of the game. The rules are slightly different, but 'tisn't difficult, I assure you. And 'tis loads of fun." When she started to argue, he added, "You're here, at a house party, having come all this way. You've done what you came to do. Now relax and enjoy. If you don't, I shan't be able to, and 'tis my party." He mock-pouted.

"Does that actually work with some women?" She pressed her lips together in exasperation. He'd already challenged her. She was not going to feel guilty from his teasing. She was made of sterner stuff than the Ton ladies he seduced.

"Yes." He gave a half-smile as though he knew his own charm. "I shall have to accompany you and coax you to walk with me. Or if you decline, I shall worry all evening about the guests above-stairs in"—his voice dropped—"a nightrail and in bed all alone."

She shivered, unable to stop herself. Despite her exasperation, she needed to stop his flirting. "Fine. I shall stay."

"No spectators allowed, mind you. You must participate."

The female servant he had appointed to organize this game clapped her hands, the quartet played a long note, and the room's attention shifted to the woman. Althea turned toward the speaker so Evan stood behind her. She noted the furniture lined along the walls, creating a large open area in the center of the room.

"Here are the rules. Blind man—or lady—picks the body part. Everyone must be standing. Clothing layers may be removed at each player's choosing. There are a few boxes over in the corner. Gloves will be worn—for propriety's sake of course."

The whole room laughed.

Althea blinked twice, lost.

Her host's voice rasped over her shoulder. "You'll see."

"Who wants to be blindman first?"

The guests murmured, looking around. One spied Evan. "Cheltie!"

The whole group began to chant. "Cheltie, Cheltie, Cheltie."

He turned to Althea, offering a shallow bow. "My audience awaits. I look forward to, er, feeling you, my lady."

Turning on a heel, he pushed toward the front of the room.

Althea watched in confusion as Evan strode to his assistant and exchanged a few quiet words. He turned, and she tied a cloth over his eyes. She handed him a pair of white gloves, which he pulled on with dramatic flair, causing trills of laughter among the eager guests.

A lady leaned toward Althea. "He wins this every time. So the past few parties, we have made him go first and set the bar."

Oh, no. What had she gotten herself into?

****

Evan knew that if he left the choice up to his guests, the ones who had played in prior years would choose something over-the-top. As it was, the game itself might be too much for Althea, and he didn't want to scare her away too early in the evening...or in the week, for that matter.

"Arse, it is!" His assistant called out his choice with a clap.

He could only imagine what Althea was seeing as men and women ran around the room to create a circle, facing outward. Clothes rustled, and he heard the boxes being dragged.

Finally, the servant clapped again, and the quartet started the music. She then led Evan into the center and turned him around several times before walking him toward one guest's posterior.

Taking a breath, hoping this would not discourage his new favorite houseguest, he reached forward, found the arse in front of him, and palmed it.

"Right. Next, please!" He stepped to the right and touched the person's back, ran his glove down, and palmed that very feminine arse. He squeezed it, eliciting a giggle. "Ah ha! Next!"

And round he went. He had noted there were fourteen in the room, himself included, and after nine bottoms, he reached Althea. He knew everyone's scent, but this was more. An invisible chord between them pulled him to her. When he reached for her, he knew exactly the right height to aim for and held her arse tenderly for a long moment. He could feel her nearly vibrating with tension, wanting to retreat, forcing herself to hold still. Caressing the mounds in his palms, he tried to soothe her.

He leaned in and beneath the music, almost under his breath, he whispered, "Easy, my lady. 'Tis but a silly game."

With a pat, he moved on.

When he returned to his starting point, he stood while everyone turned in toward him and starting reciting names. Still blindfolded, he pointed, named the person, waited for confirmation, and then stepped forward to identify the next.

Before he was halfway around the circle, the room exploded in curses.

One man stomped his foot like a child. "Damn you, Cheltie. How d'ya do it? Every time."

"Come now, Witherspoon, I cannot give away my secrets. What chance will I ever have to feel you up then, man?"

The room laughed as the man turned red, even as he threw his hands in the air and joined them.

"Lady Althea, I believe." He gave a shallow bow in Althea's direction.

"Er, yes."

"May I say that you have a lovely bottom, my dear?" He raised a brow, causing his blindfold to slide against his face.

"No. You may not."

"Ah, but I believe I already did." He called the next name, determined to get the last word in.

"Right." He whipped the blindfold off. "Anyone?" He held it out with a twist of his wrist, palm up, cravat dripping from his fingers. "Arses?"

People grumbled and shook their heads.

"Well, then, 'tis winner's choice."

"Go again, Cheltie!"

"Chests and breasts."

"Lips, please. With yours, preferably."

Catcalls and other lewd suggestions rang out.

Evan laughed and played along, even as he rolled his eyes mentally. There was only one pair of breasts he wanted to touch, only one pair of rose-colored lips in a pale face he wanted to kiss.

The door opened, admitting more people coming over from the dancing to investigate the games, and that pair of lips was lost as Althea slipped out of the room.

Beth bounced in, and Evan looked around quickly, spotting Robert in a corner. In desperation to catch Althea, he threw the blindfold at Robert, despite knowing he hated being the center of attention.

"What? No." His friend scowled.

"Come, please, for me. They're warmed up. They will play along nicely. And look at the curves on that one." Beth was Robert's exact type, nicely rounded and petite.

As he hoped, his friend snatched the cravat, saying, "You owe me, Bags."

But Evan barely heard him as he rushed out the door, taking the stairs two at a time to catch Althea before she gained her room.

****

He knows all his guests by name…and by arse?

Fascination and intimidation swirled through Althea while her conscience attempted to throw disgust into the mix. As always, her very strict upbringing battled with her desire to be less judgmental and more accepting of others.

How might someone recognize another's arse? She wasn't sure she could have found her husband in the mix when he was alive. Although, she'd likely know Beth's. She giggled then gasped as Evan suddenly appeared next to her on the stairs, out of breath.

"Lady Althea, please, I beg of you, allow me to apologize."

She stopped and turned to him. "For what, exactly?"

Evan stared at her, mouth slack, still gulping air.

"Mmm, right. You really do not have anything to apologize for, my lord. If nothing else, 'tis your house. Surely, 'tis your choice what games to offer and your guests' choice to participate." She paused. "Including me."

Evan smiled. "Madame, that is a lovely thing to say when you were obviously not entirely comfortable with the game. Thank you for your graciousness."

She nodded and turned to continue up the steps.

"Will you walk with me? Please?" he asked. "Given the weather, maybe the gallery?"

"Don't you have...body parts to identify?" she questioned tartly, hoping to encourage him to return to his party.

He guffawed. "I handed off the blindfold to be sporting. Please, my lady. I will tell you my secret for winning, something I haven't even shared with my dearest friend Robert."

That, she could not resist. "One turn, then, Lord Cheltenham."

"Remember? 'Tis Evan, or Cheltie if you prefer."

"Evan."

His smile at her response made her mouth twitch to

mirror it. She suppressed the urge.

Oh my, he is the most beautiful man I've ever seen.

Everything about him resembled an elegant but dangerous lion, with a bronze waistcoat and jacket a shade darker than his hair, and his dark amber eyes burning with intensity. Even the topaz and ebony cravat pin, subtly brighter than the dinner jacket, leaped out of the gold-toned cravat and white shirt.

Her heart pounded in her chest, in attraction and nerves. Outwardly, she refused to react to his flirting skills, which seemed to rival Beth's.

Once they were on the main level again and away from the revelry, she tilted her head at him as they walked. "Right, then. How do you know everyone's arse so well?"

He laughed, then kept laughing.

She stared. His laughter was at her expense, but his *joie de vivre* precluded resentment. The leonine mane, not quite blonde, not quite brown, inched closer to her curious fingers as he put a hand to his stomach and bent forward. A delicious shiver ran through her at the idea of being mauled by this particular king of the cats.

"Ah, that would be quite the story, would it not?" He stopped walking to control his laughter, dragging her to a halt with him. Between snickers, he said, "I don't, actually. I know their habits and their scents."

Huh. She supposed that made sense. *But really, all of them?* "All of them?"

"Enough to narrow it down. 'Tis why I make a full pass. I know some perfumes, who smokes, who blacks their boots daily, who drinks what. I also have a very good memory, so clothing can give it away—height, coat length, fabric of a gown."

She considered it, and another question occurred. "How did you know me? I don't wear a strong scent or smoke, and my gown is nothing special."

"Aaahhh." His smile seemed smug. "I could say process of elimination, but 'tisn't true. I am afraid that is one secret I am unwilling to share, my lady." He started their stroll again, ignoring the portraits hung along the gallery. "'Tis your turn. Tell me why you did not like the game. Too risqué?"

"I don't know how well you know my cousin, but one cannot live with Beth and not be open to activities rather beyond the pale by society's standards. I suppose I was more taken aback at the bawdiness in such a large group, but never mind. While I do not see the appeal, I do not condemn others for enjoying themselves. Beth insists I am missing out, but it must be different for everyone."

Evan gestured to a bench and sat next to her after she'd arranged her skirts. "What do you mean?"

"Oh, all that touching. And..." She blushed. Why did she make that comment about missing out? Only at such a wild party could it even come up in conversation.

"You do not see the appeal of touching someone's bum? Or even of being touched?"

"My lord—Evan. This conversation is hardly proper." She ignored the spurt of heat low in her belly at the thought of touching Evan's tight buttocks. Trying to recall if she'd ever seen or felt her husband's bottom, she frowned.

He laughed again. "Nor was the game, but here we are. At my house party, which has never been called proper." He peered at her. "Now, answer the question, please."

"You know I am a widow, do you not?"

"Yes."

"I don't feel as though I am missing any knowledge then, contrary to my cousin's comments." *Except maybe the feel of a man's arse?*

"Hmm. Tell me about your husband."

"Thomas was a dear man. He took good care of me."

Evan's eyebrows rose. "You've heard the term damning with faint praise?"

She frowned. "I loved my husband, sir."

"I don't doubt it. But was it a grand passion?"

"That is hardly your concern." Would it belie her answer if she asked him to define a grand passion? Did she want to know?

If it included her gaze being irresistibly drawn to his visage, warmth trickling through her like hot tea when he touched her, and sparks of fire at the idea of running her hands through his hair, then she'd experienced a grand passion. However, it had not been directed at her husband. Instead, 'twas much more recent and included the past few minutes. She needed to remember that she could not afford rumors, and where the Earl of Cheltenham went, rumors followed.

"Ah, but we've established I'm not proper, nor is this party. Come now, it can be our secret."

"I stand by my earlier statement." Although, mayhap behind closed doors, some improper behavior from him could prove stimulating.

"So, no, then." His gaze flicked to her lips.

She licked them, wondering how his would feel. Heat seared through her at the thought. She had never yearned for her husband's kiss, but she was hungry for Evan's.

"No wonder Beth says you are missing out." His mouth turned up on one side in a half-smile. "You've come to the right place. I shall have to consider games for tomorrow." He wiggled his brows.

"Please, do not bother yourself on my behalf." She caught herself before she leaned toward him and contradicted her words. *Lud, he is fascinating as well as exquisite. While I am curious about tomorrow's games, I cannot afford the risk to my reputation or my business.*

"No, no. 'Tis for my own pleasure of introducing you to new experiences."

"I believe I shall retire now. Thank you for the walk." Althea stood and shook out her skirts. Before Evan could rise to offer an arm, she strode away toward the stairs and her room, eager to remove herself from temptation and oversharing. She wasn't sure what had gotten into her.

Vowing to keep closer counsel the rest of the visit, she climbed into bed. Unable to sleep, she stared at the ceiling for hours, trying to picture her husband's buttocks. Her mind kept superimposing Evan's taller, broader, golden form over the fuzzy memory of her spouse. Her pulse sped up, her fingers rubbed against her palms envisioning his skin, his hair. Each time, she chastised herself and tried to blank her mind, only to go through the cycle again and again before sleep claimed her.

****

Evan lay in bed envisioning the game, remembering the feel of Althea's arse in his hands. In

59

his imagination, he stepped forward to rub his aching cock along its seam. Even through clothing, he thought it might only take a few strokes to come messily all over her lower back.

He was torn between elation at his cock stiffening after being disinterested in everything for so long and frustration that the object of its desire had to be the one woman uninterested in the more ribald party games…and yet another person who wanted his money more than they wanted him.

No matter, his imagination would suffice. He took his cock in hand, grabbed his handkerchief from the bottom of the bed where he'd thrown it, and lay back against the pillows. He pictured her in the gallery light, creamy pert breasts showcased by the scooped neckline of deep aubergine. Remembering the shoes by her chair in the card room the night before, he imagined her peeling a stocking down, then the other, then standing for him. He circled her in his mind, his hand sliding over the mounds of her bottom again, pausing to squeeze, then around her side and up to scoop a breast out of her décolletage.

His fist accelerated, and his other hand cupped his bollocks. Squeezing the purple head, he panted, wanting to draw out the fantasy.

His lips pursed, imagining the silky skin and pebbled tip of her exposed breast. Her scent lingered in his nose, and he imagined pressing against her hip as he gathered her skirts up to reach—

He grunted and shuddered as tendrils of fire curled around the base of his spine. His bollocks drew up, his pulse drumming in the iron rod under his fist, and he could not stay his orgasm a second longer. He grabbed his handkerchief. His other fist tightened and twisted, yanking brutally on his cock as it spurted ropes of scorching liquid into a fistful of silk.

His hands flopped to the bed beside him, all his muscles slackening. But his thoughts continued to circle.

Mayhap now I can focus on the best choice of amusements for the morrow.

He ran through the games he had planned in his mind, rejecting one after another. Too many different people touching. Too much skin for his most conservative guest.

Contemplating prior years' sport, he encountered the same frustration. The only matches she'd likely find acceptable were first night entertainment, too tame for his other guests at this point in the party.

How do I get myself into these situations? Damn me, I'm only eight and twenty. Then, with the edge of his frustration dulled, clarity returned. *Why am I trying so hard to please another person in the long line angling for a handout?*

He fell asleep plotting how to get Althea involved in the games. And more, to give her her first orgasm, mayhap ever.

Chapter Five

The next afternoon, Althea meandered from room to room. She sewed in the parlor, listened to music in the music room, and told herself she was bored, not surreptitiously searching for her host.

Finally, she ever so casually wandered the hall leading to his office and realized her slipper had a pebble just as she neared that door. Leaning against the wall, she slid the shoe off and bent to look at it, listening closely for his voice.

When the door opened, she jerked in shock and fell forward, catching herself with her hands, her knees coming down hard on the floor.

"Lady Althea?" Evan's bemused voice asked. "Are you quite all right? I assure you, you needn't beg for help on your knees."

"Mmmphh." She spit hair from her mouth and nearly groaned aloud, as much at being caught as the pain in her knees. She'd chosen to leave her hair loose down her back for the daytime, and it had fallen out of the ribbon holding it back from her face.

"If I may?" he asked, sobering. His hand closed around her upper arm, and he pulled her to stand. He was in buff today, which only added to her view of him as lionlike.

One knee hurt when she put her weight on it, and at her wince, he quickly guided her into his office.

Leading her to the settee, he directed her down with the gentle pressure of his hand on her arm.

She plopped down and shoved her curls back, only to gasp as one leg, then the other, was lifted and placed on the low table in front of her.

Evan stepped to the bar, distracting her from her injury with his broad shoulders and the drape of his jacket over his narrower hips. His thick mane, amber with bronze highlights, fascinated her every time they were in a room together.

He returned with two Scotches and pressed one into her hand then walked away. She heard the door shut before he reappeared, one of the forest green slippers that matched her gown in his hand. Her jaw dropped, and she glanced down. One of her feet—on the table, eep!—was slippered, and one was stockinged. Mortified, she dropped her head forward, allowing her hair to slip back along her face to hide her embarrassment.

"Have a sip, Althea. To calm your nerves after the fall."

She sipped, feeling fire burn its way from her throat to her stomach. Coughing once, she sighed and sipped again. How could she explain this?

When he sat on the table next to her foot and laid his hand on her left ankle, she jerked in surprise.

"I simply want to see if your knee is injured." His voice sounded strained, but his hand was gentle, and Althea was shaken enough by the discovery and the fall that she dropped back against the settee cushion, allowing the liberty without contest.

Up, up, dragging her dress with it, his hand skimmed her flesh. A tiny shiver skimmed her skin, but she was not chilled. Rather, a ribbon of heat trailed behind his touch.

Her head lifted, her eyes searching his, when his hand passed her knee.

He watched her with a heavy-lidded gaze and a half-smile. "I need to roll your stocking down to have a look."

One-handed, he flicked her garter open and spread his thumb and forefinger around her leg, sliding them down and taking her stocking with them.

Her lips parted. *Oh, my, he is good at that. I wonder if this will be another evening's game—undress someone one-handed.* A flash of jealousy at the thought of him doing this with another woman took her by surprise. *'Tis not like I want to play such games in a room full of people.*

He cradled her knee with both hands, his thumbs prodding gently with a hoarse murmur. "Tell me if anything hurts."

At one prod, she flinched.

"Ah. No dancing for you tonight. I shall have to ensure we have entertainment that does not require standing."

"You needn't style the evening around me, Evan, but thank you. Whist or my room are fine with me."

"Hmm. We'll see."

Leaving that leg, he made quick work of the other garter and stocking and did the same. But that knee was fine, the left one having borne more of her weight as it hit first.

His hands paused high on her outer calves, framing her knees. Nervous, she had trouble meeting his gaze and took another gulp of Scotch.

His voice still a rumble, he asked, "Were you looking for me, then?"

"What? Oh, no. I mean, yes."

He turned his head to look at her from the corner of his eye, not quite hiding his grin. "What for?"

"Uh." Smaller sip of Scotch.

"Mayhap you thought more about having an investment partner in your Bath store?"

"No." Alarm sharpened her response. Then she searched for a different reason. "Why do you agree with Beth that I am missing out?"

Oh my, did I really say that out loud? Beth had told her that repeatedly, and she'd ignored her cousin. Evan had said it once, and she could not get it out of her head. She'd snuck down this hall looking to be discovered, hoping for an opening to introduce this subject again. But so baldly?

He must think I'm wanton. She snorted. *Right. With most of the other party-goers throwing themselves at him, a mere question is wanton? I think not.*

"Althea, if you had experienced even a fraction of the pleasure I have from sex, you and Beth would never have had that conversation." His thumbs stroked over her kneecaps. Heat twisted low in her abdomen. He seemed not to realize he had done it. "And you would have had different answers to my questions about your marriage."

His thumb movement was forgotten as her defenses rose. This was the second time he was poking at her marriage. Neither Thomas nor she deserved that. Her marriage had been no better or worse than anyone else's. Anything she'd wished for was outside of the norm, but it was not Thomas's fault he was traditional.

"I loved my husband."

"And I love my friends. I'm talking about orgasms, not feelings." His voice was gentle, making her realize he had not intended harm.

"Ugh." Calmer, she could respond with a lighter tone. "You and Beth with the orgasms. She even told me how to do it, but she said herself that women's bodies are all different. Mine simply does not have the same capability."

"Shall we wager on that?"

"No!" Then her inner devil took over. "How would we judge the wager anyway?" *Lud, I've been living with Beth too long.*

"Hmm." He narrowed his eyes. "My first thought was to direct you. However, I think I need full control in order to protect my interests."

She flattened her lips. "Of course you do, Lord Cheltenham. As does every man."

"I shall ignore you likening me to other men for the moment." He stared at the fire for a minute, appearing lost in thought. "That's it. Giving control."

"No, thank you."

"Let me explain. You give me control for this. If I cannot bring you to orgasm, I offer advice on your business and an interest-free loan, with no profit-sharing. But if I can change your mind about having missed something, you must give me a stake—silent partner only with as much or as little advice as you want."

Could she live with a man as a silent partner? Would he even know if she orgasmed if she stayed still and quiet? She did not know enough about it, despite her very frank cousin.

"Oh, and let me warn you. Your body does not lie. There are involuntary muscle movements during an orgasm that cannot be faked."

Oh my, he's a mind-reader as well as an arse-reader. "Why are you offering this after I refused earlier? Do you not have a line of people waiting for your time and blunt?"

He smiled. "As you well know, I do not need the money. But I do need to see every woman I know enjoy her body and her sexuality. To hear that you disbelieve you can hurts me deeply. Why do you think I have these parties? Everyone should enjoy life, and especially sex. 'Tis the same reason I pushed Michael to ask Penelope for her hand, regardless of the differences in their backgrounds."

****

Evan hoped using mutual friends as an example would help. He thought about also referencing his servants, given their brief conversation about Beth and Franklin.

Instead, he held his breath. Silence was most often a stronger position.

His inner voice argued with him. *Why offer such a one-sided wager given the circumstances? I am so tired of people wanting my money or my body, but not my brain or my heart.*

Wait.

Heart?

Where did that come from?

Althea was quiet for long enough that when she opened her mouth to speak, he knew she'd refuse.

"No. Thank you for a very kind offer, my lord." She gave him a wry look. "But I don't believe there are any circumstances in which I'd be comfortable with a man as a partner, silent or otherwise."

She is that leery of a man taking over? Her first marriage must have chafed. Wait, if she sees no circumstances, that includes a second marriage. How could men make so little effort and keep women so uneducated that sex would not even be a factor in a woman's desire to remarry?

His inner devil laughed at him. He had been bored by sex until Althea arrived, and he never wanted to marry, albeit his reasons were different.

"You have no plans to remarry then?" He tested his theory.

"No."

The more he learned, the more intrigued he became, despite his wariness. If she had no plans to remarry, perhaps he could seduce her into a no-strings dalliance, as well as gain an investment opportunity. 'Twas all about the negotiations. After all, were negotiations not games and games a form of bargaining? He revised his plan for the evening entertainment yet again.

He needed more details. "May I ask why?"

She slid him a look, as though she considered not answering, but then said, "My parents—my father, really—was very strict with me. He is a religious man and believes piety and serenity are the most important traits in a household. When I violated those traits, he decided it was time for me to marry, and rather than go to his peers he chose from his church in our country seat."

"*His* church?" Evan interrupted.

"I have no issue with God, or the Goddess, or

Yahweh, or what anyone wants as their religion. But I found his church equated serenity with the man ruling the house and the women and children being near-silent."

"Ah. My apologies, please go on."

"I married Thomas. He was more open to discussion, but ultimately, the decisions were his. For everything. I had the utmost respect for him, and we grew to love one another. However, I shan't subject myself to a man's rule again by choice, not after the freedom I have now. 'Twas easier going from my father's household to his."

"I understand more now. Thank you."

I understand more why she dislikes the idea of a business partnership, but that doesn't negate that she's here for money like the rest of them.

After learning her reasons, he knew they were unlikely to reach a business agreement. But she had piqued his interest from the moment of her arrival, and the more she stated her lack of interest in sex, the more he was driven to prove her wrong. He had not misinterpreted her look in that upstairs hall last year. There had been arousal mixed with guilt in that flush on her cheeks, and while she might not have realized it, the points of her breasts poking through her gown had removed any doubt.

Looking back, he questioned how he had put thoughts of her aside after that. Regardless, they had all come rushing back when she'd stepped out of the carriage two days ago, and discovering her lack of interest in marriage fanned those flames. He could have her, awaken her to all the pleasure to be had without her expecting hearts and flowers…or marriage.

His blood surged and desire pooled in his mouth. He swallowed and ran through game ideas to find one suitable for the evening. Not only to keep her off her feet, but to continue to coax her out of her shell.

How positively droll. A man who insists he can cure a woman's disinterest. But of all men, he had been pursuing pleasure his whole life, knowing it would be shorter than many, given that his mother's condition was hereditary. His ability to learn quickly and find the right investments to fund his lifestyle had left him with more free time than many aristocrats, even with his responsibilities as earl. He had turned that considerable intelligence to the pursuit of happiness—mostly sexual happiness.

For a while, creativity and wildness had satisfied him. How ironic that just as he'd fallen into boredom, Althea being in the very same state of mind pulled him out of it.

"Right, then. Why don't I help you to your room, and you can put your leg up for a while. I'll send a bath up before dinner and come help you down. You needn't participate in the games if you choose not to, but I'd very much like to spend more time with you. Besides, I cannot have a guest retire to her room directly from dinner." He placed a dramatic hand on his chest, touching it with only the fingertips in mock outrage. "My reputation for house parties would be ruined. We could come in here after dinner and let the others fend for themselves?"

"Such a kind invitation, my lord. I shall consider it." She struggled off the sofa and tested her weight on her leg.

****

Evan sipped his soup and tried not to roll his eyes. He switched the seating at dinner each night so that his guests could socialize with a variety of people. And yes, so that more guests could claim the honor of having been seated next to the host, as he knew his parties and his attention were coveted.

Yet it remained the same. Someone was bragging about their exploits of the night before, the week before, or the year before. Usually, the tales were based on a prior year's Greenborough Park house party. Or else they were talking up their investments in a pitiful attempt to compete. Or waxing poetic about an investment they were considering to get his advice.

No one asked him whether he was enjoying himself, what he did the night before, how his family was. He supposed he should be thankful that he had banned political discussions from the dinner table.

Commiserating with Althea's earlier wishes, he yearned to take dinner in his room.

He watched his guests, feeling detached. They seemed to be enjoying the week, at least. If only he could prick this bubble of ennui around him. But the only time he really felt alive was with Robert, who was as comfortable as an old shoe, and with Althea, who was more like a candle in a sconce, and he was batting against it like a bug drawn to...

That was a terrible analogy, old chap. You might as well liken her to a viper.

Tempted to roll his eyes at himself as well as the guests after that thought, he pushed his second course plate away untouched. Sipping wine and sneaking glances at Robert, Beth, and Althea, he gave desultory answers to the overeager earl on his right.

He had deliberately placed Robert and Beth across from each other. He'd asked Robert to keep an eye on the wild child, and his friend had reluctantly agreed. He hoped Althea would be more available without worrying about her cousin. Althea sat next to Robert, and as she and Beth chattered across the table, Robert appeared to be very focused on Beth's posture.

Turning to Beth, Evan ran his eyes over her form, trying to find the cause for Robert's stare. Seeing nothing out of the ordinary, he continued to watch. Beth sat ramrod straight. Usually, she was quite animated in her conversation, using gestures, turning her head or even her shoulders to enhance her descriptions. Tonight, her gestures were smaller. Every once in a while, she'd wiggle a little on her chair, as though trying to find a more comfortable spot, but her back remained locked, shoulders back.

Evan smiled. The little minx was wearing one of Robert's creations. He bet if he sat near her, he'd hear a creak of leather now and then. She was likely sitting still to minimize that…or, depending on the creation, she might also be wearing an attachment that jostled when she wiggled.

He laughed, and the earl to his right looked at him in confusion before chuckling amiably and saying, "Ha, yes, I do tend to go on. What are we playing this evening, Cheltie?"

Robert had turned at his laugh, and Evan caught his eye and shook his head once with a grin of admiration before turning to his guest to answer.

In the end, he had left the game choices he'd scheduled, as he wanted to play with Althea privately.

As dessert was cleared, he stood. His assistant

announced the evening's entertainment for each of the two ballrooms, and Evan excused himself from his dinner companions and made his way to Althea.

"My lady?" He bowed over her hand then offered his arm.

She glanced up at him through her lashes, and he held his breath.

"Thank you, Evan." She placed her hand on the proffered limb and nodded.

A sigh of relief gusted out. His sidelong glance did not find any reaction if she heard it.

The guests jostled through the wide doorway of the dining room. Some sped toward their room of choice while others hung back, waiting to see who would go where. Knowing others' eyes were upon them, Evan steered Althea backward to the corner of the room, as though to have a word with her, even as the servants swarmed in to clean the table.

Evan made a subtle gesture, and a servant closed the double doors, blocking the view of the last of the trailing watchers. Turning to Althea, he murmured, "My lady. Shall we?"

They escaped out the side door the servants used and into a hallway with branches to the kitchen and to the family wing of the house where his office was located. Evan held his breath every step, waiting for her to protest and request that he return her to her room.

****

Althea had struggled to make conversation through dinner. At least half her brain was still weighing the pros and cons of playing a private, and therefore improper, game with her host after dinner.

Improper. It piqued her curiosity. Especially in

light of the past two evenings' pastimes.

She was still undecided when Evan pulled her aside to outwait the lingering diners, took her arm, and led her to his office.

His words from earlier repeated in her head...*if you had experienced even a fraction of the pleasure I have from sex... You give me control for this... I need to see every woman I know enjoy her body and her sexuality... Everyone should enjoy life, and especially sex.*

Those few minutes of seeing Beth in the stables showed Althea that enjoyment, even ecstasy was indeed possible. What if it wasn't her body, but her lack of knowledge, even after Beth's coaching? Then this sophisticated earl with a reputation as an expert in the subject, who was beyond beautiful, had echoed Beth's sentiments and lured her toward capitulation.

Her concerns about her reputation were somewhat assuaged by both Beth's and Evan's assurances of the secrecy of this party. Although she thought her fears might have been silenced more from her desire for this gorgeous, intelligent man who seemed so relaxed on the surface but held his cards close to his chest. And who better to teach her than a master of the subject?

Ha. You're making excuses for yourself now.

She debated silently as he led her to the settee he'd directed her to earlier, then scooped her ankle and lifted her leg to the low table again.

When he offered her a drink, she started, realizing she had inadvertently—or subconsciously?—accepted his invitation. She gave a mental shrug and succumbed to temptation. Her shoulders relaxed, but her breath came faster with anticipation. Her fingertips tingled.

"Sherry, please."

He brought a sherry and whisky over and settled in a chair at a right angle to her perch on the settee.

"Right, then," he said. "Have you ever played Truth or Dare?"

Well, hell. Life with Beth had sometimes felt like one long truth or dare, not that she'd change it. She loved her cousin dearly, even when said cousin was trying her patience and her personal boundaries. Those experiences meant she had an idea of what an adult version of that game might entail, given that her host's reputation rivaled that of her cousin's.

It is simply more acceptable because he is a man— a titled one at that.

"Yes." She angled her head at him, her competitive streak emerging. "I must stipulate that you have had the afternoon to think up creative options, so I am at a disadvantage."

"Fair enough. How could we adjust for that?"

They both thought for a moment.

"I may reject a truth or dare each round," Althea proposed, "and you must then offer a less outrageous option."

"I don't know if I can do that." Evan brightened. "What if every dare I give you, I must also take?" When she shot him a dubious look, he added, "Come now. That is remarkably fair. Indeed, what could be more so?"

"Fine. I am willing to try it."

"Excellent. Please, ladies first." Evan threw a hand out, palm up in invitation.

"Right. Ah, truth or dare?"

"Let us begin with something benign. Truth."

"Oh. Er…" She quickly rifled through questions.

Where is the most outrageous place you've had sex? *No, no sex, especially as he'd likely get to that soon enough.* How quickly do you think you could make me orgasm? *No, darn it!* Self-conscious about the amount of time she'd spent dithering, she blurted out, "What was your first successful investment?"

Evan smiled. "That would depend on your definition of success. To me, it was the summer I was ten. I found a girl not much older than me selling strawberries in the market when my housekeeper let me tag along. I begged the housekeeper for the fruit for a tart or pie, but she informed me it wasn't in the budget. I negotiated all our purchases that day and had enough left for strawberries for a tart. In fact, I accompanied the housekeeper for the rest of the summer break until I had to return to boarding school. It was an excellent tradeoff of my time for pie. None of my money was even involved. Of course, it did not hurt that the girl seemed to find me cute, and I managed my first kiss before summer's end."

Apparently, he could even bring a finance question around to kissing. She had to think this through. Realizing she was halfway through her sherry, her nerves having caused her to take frequent sips, she put it down on the table. She needed all her wits about her for this.

"Right, then. My turn." Evan squinted at her. "Truth or dare?"

"Truth, please." *Eh, I sound prim again.*

"Tell me what you liked least about your husband."

Darn it. If he had asked about marriage, she could have generalized. Or said "sex" as they'd already discussed her lackluster sex life. But he asked about her husband. She would not malign the dead, especially someone she had loved.

"Dare, please."

Evan's brows rose. "*Really*?" He sounded gleeful.

She frowned but was prepared to handle whatever he threw at her. Her husband did not deserve disparagement.

"Remove your shoes and stockings, please."

"I beg your pardon?"

"You heard me." Definitely gleeful, mayhap even gloating, the dreadful man.

She huffed. "You'll need to turn around, my lord."

"Hmm. I think not. Remove your shoes and stockings in front of me."

Gritting her teeth, she weighed her options. He'd already seen her legs earlier. She toed off her slippers, ran her hands under her skirts, and managed to roll down her stockings without baring her knees. *Take that, my lord*.

Evan grinned, slipping his own off and wiggling his toes.

How could a man's feet be provocative? But his were long and slender with a bit of golden hair on his big toes. She stared at them, fascinated.

"Thank you. Your turn. Truth, please." His words brought her attention back to his face.

Oh. Darn. Asking about his second investment was weak. His net worth—too crass. Family. "Tell me about your family."

He sobered. Pondered.

Ooohh. He seemed to be considering a dare, she needed to think quickly. She wasn't quite ready to invite him to shed clothing. Nor did she enjoy overimbibing, so a drink was out. One piece of advice on her store expansion. Yes.

"My parents were a love match. My father died while I was on my Grand Tour after university, and I returned home to take over the earldom. I am an only child, although I have a cousin close to my age on my father's side. My mother lives in the dower house here and is the only family I like to think about. That cousin grew up to be odious."

The recitation of facts was not what she had been looking for, but it did answer her question.

She was still filing that information away when he asked again, "Truth or dare?"

"Truth, please."

His smile looked far too self-satisfied for her peace of mind. "Say something sexual to me."

"I beg your pardon?" Was she going to answer that to every one of his requests? Or would she eventually become immune to shock?

He smiled. "Here, I'll help. I'll show you how it's done."

He leaned forward, a hand right next to her thigh on the settee. "Close your eyes and picture what I say."

She'd glanced down at his hand, but at that, her gaze flew to his. Was he referencing her shameful viewing of the activities in that room at the London party? Her brow furrowed. *How dare the host of such a party cast judgment.* Her spurt of anger died when he smiled gently at her with an encouraging nod.

Her eyes drifted shut, heightening her other senses. Her breasts sat heavier in her stays, the spot between her legs heated, and the waft of his breath over her face and neck made her shiver in pleasure.

"I remember the feel of your legs." His voice had an added rasp. "I keep imagining circling your ankles with my hands and smoothing them slowly up, up, over your knees where I linger—" He leaned in further. "My thumbs circle that sensitive area, dipping into that hollow just behind each knee, before they venture farther. That soft, creamy skin. Your thighs fall open, the muslin of your petticoat scratching without the silk stockings to protect you."

A spurt of warmth travelled through her middle, and her thighs shifted apart a few inches. When her leg encountered his hand, she started and opened her eyes. His gaze rose from her legs to hers, a wide grin on his face. Again. Darned Earl of Debauchery, he was.

At his expectant look, she realized it was her turn. Licking her lips, she thought hard. She was woefully inept, having never learned the vocabulary or even the thoughts to voice for a seduction scene. She tried tossing it back to him with a query. "And—and does that excite you, my lord?"

He leaned back, still smiling. "Ah, ah, no questions. You try it now, statements only."

Her hands fisted in her skirt, the delicious sensations from moments ago forgotten. A nervous flush crept up her neck and face. "You have an attractive form, my lor-Evan," she corrected at his head shake. "You appear to keep yourself in quite good physical condition. And-and"—the rest of her words spewed out in a rush—"I should like to touch your hair."

He was obviously fighting snickers behind his hand by the time she finished.

Her shoulders sank in embarrassed defeat. "Please,

that is the best I can do."

The sniggers stopped, and he smiled gently. "I know. 'Tis because you've been missing out. You've proven my point."

"Fine. Then I take the dare." She crossed her arms, grinding her teeth. How dare he laugh at her. She was playing his lewd game as best she could. She refused to acknowledge her hope of what dare he'd issue, given his response to her truth.

His eyes flared with satisfaction. "You didn't even wait for the option. I like it. Quite, ahem, daring of you. I dare you to invite me to show you what you've been missing."

Flames flared again low in her belly, her body heating as though it was an oil lamp turned up high. Her breasts swelled against her décolletage with her indrawn breath, and her thighs inched apart in anticipation. This was exactly why she had come in here, despite all her waffling. Somewhere deep down, she'd wanted him to push her, mayhap even to show her, without her business venture being at risk.

Chapter Six

Evan watched Althea's reaction to his dare. Fear, surprise, confusion all chased each other across her face before resolution settled in. That creamy skin surrounded by sable waves showed every expression. He dared a glance downward to her oversized bosom in the demure gown, seeing it rise and fall with nervous breaths.

She had outnegotiated him, getting her win from his proposed wager without risking even a truth. The cynical half of him wondered if it had all been an elaborate setup. No, she hadn't known what game he'd choose, and if she was going to invest time and effort in wresting something out of him, it would have been money, like most before her. Either way, he wasn't sure he cared. This was a liaison, a brief interlude in the country away from reality.

His blood heated at her determined expression. He had not been outnegotiated. He was about to get exactly what he wanted.

She sucked in a breath, and then sighed her exhale. "Evan, please show me what I've been missing."

She clamped her mouth shut and stared at him with wide eyes. The fear was back.

"Good girl," he purred. "Finish your sherry." He certainly needed to finish his whisky so he wouldn't ruin this opportunity with eagerness. "Now sit back and relax."

He rounded the table and knelt in front of her, nudging it back. "I am going to do what I talked about earlier." Moving slowly, he sat on his heels and lowered his hands to her bare ankles. They were so slender his fingers and thumb overlapped, but he kept them loose, gentle. His hands slid upward an inch at a time, catching her dress and petticoats on his wrists. When he reached her knees, he grabbed the clothing and flipped it up out of his way, the white of her undergarments stark against the dark green of her gown.

She gasped, her hands clenched by her sides on the cushions.

His blood pounded in his chest, his temples, his cock.

I haven't even kissed her yet. 'Tis like I am an untried youth, not knowing how to please a girl, much less seduce a woman. My reputation would be in shreds. Chastising himself, he laid his hands on her stockinged knees and urged them outward. He was rewarded with her thighs falling open a few degrees.

He leaned in, letting her see his intent. Tilting his head, he brushed his mouth over hers in the lightest of kisses. Feathering her lips with his breath, his lips, then his breath again, he wooed her. Her mouth opened, and his tongue dipped inside, stroking hers before retreating. He gave her time to assimilate each new sensation before adding a new caress.

Trailing kisses toward her ear, he whisper-rasped, "You may put your hands on me if you'd like. Anywhere." *Please.*

Ah, how his usual set would laugh to know he was

begging, even silently.

She raised her arms slowly to his shoulders, then inched her hands into his hair, running her fingers through the silken strands before fisting handfuls.

He shivered once. But this was for her pleasure, not his. He refocused.

Setting his teeth to her earlobe without a real bite, he swept his thumbs around her knees once, knowing her attention would again center on the motion. His hands slid upward, inch by inch.

She tugged on the chunks of hair she clutched.

And then, success!

Her spine curled, her hips shifting upward as though reaching for his hands. He grinned and let go of her ear to kiss her greedily again, grasping her hips and pulling them toward the edge of the divan. Still clutching him, she allowed her legs to fall farther open around him and arched into his kiss, seemingly oblivious to her dress up around her arse, his hands inside touching bare skin.

Exultant with his victory thus far, he needed to keep that smart mind occupied so she did not consider the impropriety.

His lips slid down her neck. Having noticed how much she enjoyed his smutty talk during the game, he tried it again. "I need to see your nipples. Are they the same rose as your lips? Oh, but your lips are quite red now from my kisses."

He released her bottom to cup her breast in the empire-waisted dress with one hand. The other, he slid upward to tug her sleeve off her shoulder.

Scooping inside the loosened neckline, he ignored the protection of her chemise and proceeded directly to skin, pulling her breast over the edge of fabric. His fingers trembled with eagerness. "Ahh, lovely. All this peaches and cream. Let me see if I can ripen this fruit to match your lips."

Glancing up to ensure she was still with him, he found her head thrown back and her eyes closed. He closed his lips on a tip, swiping his tongue across it within the wet heat of his mouth, watching for her response.

"Evan!" Her hands clenched in his hair but neither pushed nor pulled. Her head lifted, and her eyes flew open to stare at him in astonishment.

He pulled back a fraction. "Yes. Watch me."

She looked almost fearful, as she had when he had told her to close her eyes and imagine the acts he described. He was betting that she had not yet embraced how powerful sight could be in foreplay, despite her experience at the demi-monde party and here. Suspecting it might be the key to engaging her in a brief affair, he'd inserted the demand into their repartee deliberately.

Holding her gaze, he flicked the beaded point with his tongue before covering it again and taking deep pulls.

She gaped at him, breathing hard, but her stare was focused on his mouth and her nipple and she seemed unaware of his regard. Her tongue darted out to wet her lips, and her fingers clenched and unclenched against his scalp, as though fighting the urge to tug him closer.

Her innocence sent a bolt of lightning down his spine to his shaft. Even the most accomplished lovers had not caused such urgency, such need.

Yanking her dress and chemise farther down, he

shifted his attention to her other breast and gave it the same treatment. Her rhythmic grasping of his hair prompted words inviting her to direct him. But if she hadn't experienced a sexual pinnacle, she could not know what would get her there.

Next time. He barely refrained from snapping his teeth on the tip between them as his cock pulsed at that possibility.

Raising his head, he squeezed her breasts, circling the peaks with his thumbs, just as he had on her inner thighs.

Her hands fell from his hair to her sides, lax on the settee.

"I want to feel how wet you are for me, to slide my fingers through that deliciousness to your pleasure button that is even more sensitive than these," he narrated, hoping it would fan her excitement into flames. "I want to taste your nectar on my tongue and ravage you as I did your breasts while my finger thrusts into your tight hot channel in a poor imitation of my cock."

Her eyelids fluttered, as though she was unable to focus. She licked her lips, and her legs fell one more degree open.

Excellent. He took that as an invitation.

"Keep your eyes on me," he said, his voice gritty. He lowered himself back to his heels and gazed at her center. Pearly moisture coated her folds, dark curls framing swollen lips even redder than those he'd already kissed.

His fingers traced her opening, becoming soaked in her arousal as he held her leg open with his other arm. Every woman liked a different touch, so he started feather-light, brushing a damp finger around the swollen bud protruding above her womanly passage.

She flinched. In pleasure, he hoped. He stroked more firmly.

She gasped, her hands rising as though to grab him but falling away. He pinched gently.

She reared up, eyes wide. "Oh my, what are you doing? What are you touching?"

So my lady Althea enjoys a bit of squeezing everywhere. His cock pulsed, reminding him it could do with a nice squeeze as well. But teaching tonight would garner him more gratification in the coming days if he could remain focused on her satisfaction.

"You, my dear. I am simply petting you. The way you should be caressed. The way you deserve to be touched. Have you not tried this yourself?"

"Yes, but 'twas never so sensitive."

"This is what you've been missing. The key is to take it in small steps—a gentle touch first, then more firm." He grinned, a surge of lust spearing through his bollocks. He could hardly wait to see her orgasm. "Now, watch the next step."

****

Heat swirled through Althea at Evan's direction. Spots of embarrassment warmed her cheeks as pleasure ignited low in her belly, but she watched as his head lowered to her most private flesh. She stared at him, enthralled.

Lud, what will a firmer touch do?

Contrary to his words, he leaned in and blew on her sensitive flesh, and as her hips jerked her response, he licked her nub into his mouth and sucked gently. One finger prodded her weeping center and slid inside.

She nearly bucked him off her. He'd told her what he was going to do before each new touch, yet each caress shocked her with the sensations it provoked.

If his finger can do that, I have to wonder how his cock would feel.

She reached out to him again. Threading her fingers through the golden mane that continually beckoned her touch, she hesitated, still uncertain what she needed.

He paused in sucking and licking to look up at her.

Her gaze slid away from his as she watched his finger, slick with her wetness, slide in and out of her in a rhythm. No touch, external or internal had provoked such sensations, such ecstasy. Her skin was hot all over, and her hips twitched with every stroke. Where would this lead?

She keened, her nails scratching his scalp.

He grunted and sped up his thrusts, seeming to understand her silent request.

Her breath caught, her teeth clenching, and she shoved her wet flesh against him, holding his head there. She could hardly believe her aggressiveness, but he did not appear to mind.

Instead, his tongue firmed against her, and he did something with his finger inside her channel that raised goosebumps of pleasure all over her body.

She gasped, her back arching further. She wondered if she might explode. Her curled hand rose from his hair to her mouth, her teeth biting a knuckle, the edge of pain grounding her.

He flicked tongue and finger in tandem.

She imploded and flew simultaneously. Streaks of fire shot toward where he touched her and outward from that point all at once. Every part of her shuddered and contracted and quivered, an explosion unlike any she'd imagined, much less felt. A small shriek escaped from behind her knuckle as she bit down harder, her other hand still clutching his hair. Her walls squeezed his finger, her flesh pulsing against and around him, and her eyelids shuttered her unseeing gaze as her head lolled against the settee.

As the pulses slowed, Evan stilled his finger and his tongue, holding her in his mouth as her hips lowered to the settee and her hands fell beside her. She flinched in pleasure as his finger slid free of her body.

Her eyes fluttered open, awareness returning in slow degrees. Focusing on Evan, she found his digit in his mouth, his eyes hot with lust. His hair was tufted out from his head where she'd clutched it. Despite that or mayhap because of it, his glowing golden eyes and hair resembled an elegant, dangerous, beautiful lion more than ever.

With the next blink, she took in her inelegant sprawl at the edge of the divan, stocking-clad legs wide, skirts up, breasts out.

Gads, what have I done?

Unable to form words or even further coherent thought, she shoved back to sit upright and jerked her hands up then down. She couldn't decide which to cover first.

Finally shoving her skirts down as far as they would go with him still between her legs, her hands were blocked by his as he gently pulled the top of her dress and chemise up, then her sleeves.

Leaning in, he kissed her, his taste suddenly salty with…*her*?

"Well, Althea? Do you feel as though you've been missing out?" he murmured against her lips, his curving into a smile.

Evading the question, she pushed him back, closed her legs, and sat up. *Ack, and I return to prim and proper*. She needed time to think, to assimilate.

He rose and sauntered to the sideboard to refill their drinks.

She shoved her feet into her slippers and stood, stockings balled in one hand. She cleared her throat. "You have my gratitude, Evan. That was…one of the most intense experiences I've ever had."

"Intensely pleasurable, I hope?"

She shot him a glare. "You know it was. But I am done with games. I appreciate your time listening to my proposal. And…entertaining me. 'Tis late. I am for bed. Good night." With a quick curtsy, she turned and fled the room before he could even put the glasses down.

Althea did not look for her cousin. She wasn't sure she could bear finding Beth in someone's arms enjoying the sensations that had just overwhelmed and excited and frightened her.

She knew her fear had been obvious in her abrupt departure, but she didn't have it in her to care.

She was too busy evaluating the physical reaction Evan had coaxed from her body. Beth had tried to tell her how to strum that sensitive bundle of nerves. If she could ever manage to share the experience without dying of mortification, she'd gladly let her cousin say, "I told you so."

But there was no way to describe the way his words, lips, tongue, and fingers had overtaken her and built such an explosion of pleasure.

If every orgasm is like that, 'tis a wonder Beth does not get into more trouble.

The difference between her experience with Evan and that with Thomas was like the difference between the finest of silks and the roughest of wools, the richness of cake and a stale crust of bread.

And Evan didn't even remove his cravat.

The man really was an expert. The fact didn't bother her. This was not about marriage, but it was about propriety. Her body's desire to learn more, more, more, and Evan's skill at enticing her into that education could cost her customers. With sparks still flickering along her nerves from the intensity of her conflagration, she wasn't sure she cared. That bothered her most of all.

Lying in bed, she promised herself she'd worry about the store and expansion plan in the morning.

Instead, she lay in the darkness, her nightdress shifting against still-sensitive skin, and replayed each word and caress Evan had used to build a fire in her core. She recalled Beth's directions and her hands trembled over her form.

One skimmed over her breast, feeling an arrow of heat shoot from her nipple to her womanhood. The other dragged her nightrail up to hover on the mound where her thighs met at a curl-covered juncture. Slipping a finger in, she found the nub Evan had put in his mouth—his mouth! It was swollen and tender to her touch, and she rubbed delicately.

As she did, other scenes came to mind unbidden. Promising herself she would not watch others in the future, she nonetheless replayed the scenes she had witnessed. They too had built this type of fire, albeit nothing like what Evan ignited.

Beth, in a stable stall, being covered like a mare by a stable hand.

The woman on her knees, her mouth on the man in the chair at last year's London party. Her on her knees for Evan, pulses of heat running through her, stronger than she had when she'd watched from the door of that bedroom. While she couldn't imagine orgasming from doing that to him, saliva pooled in her mouth at the idea of returning the caresses he'd given her earlier.

Her finger strummed her flesh faster, her hand on her breast squeezing. But when she reached the peak, it was like a candle being snuffed out, nowhere near as bone-liquefying as the fire Evan had brought forth.

Well, I suppose that answers my question. Not all orgasms are alike. 'Twas her last thought before exhaustion claimed her.

She awoke after only a few hours, as dawn broke outside the window. With the clarity of sleep and the light of day, she found it easier to focus on her business rather than pleasure. Her independence once again was her highest priority, achievable through the success of her stores, without a man stealing a portion of it.

She had nothing more to accomplish at this outrageous party.

Except mayhap another orgasm or three.

Ignoring the internal voice that sounded suspiciously like Beth, she decided she'd simply avoid Lord Cheltenham for the rest of her life, so she needn't face him while remembering being sprawled out after coming apart under his mouth and hands.

Althea wondered where her cousin had spent the night, as she'd never returned to their room. Desperate to leave as soon as possible, she asked her assigned maidservant to quietly locate her young relative as she began packing for both of them.

Beth arrived nearly an hour later, flushed and tousled. In her agitation, Althea did not stop to ask where she'd been. "I need to leave here."

Her cousin gaped at her. "But there is another two nights of entertainment, and I've heard they get increasingly interesting. Wait, where did you go last night? Did you not play any of the games?"

"Oh, I played a game. And lost. Evan—Lord Cheltenham and I could not agree on terms. I shall need to look for other options."

Beth's eyebrows had raised at her use of their host's given name. "Right, then. We shall go home and regroup."

"Thank you." Althea had been worried her cousin would fight her for more time at this beyond-risqué gathering.

"Can we please visit the dower house quickly, though? I met Lady Cheltenham—Cheltie's mother— and she's lovely. And I promised her I'd come back."

"I suppose, if 'tis quick."

"Thank you, cuz. Come on, then."

"You don't want to change clothes?" Her cousin was still wearing her party frock.

Beth shrugged it off. "To sit in a carriage much of the day? I'll have a bath at the inn we stay at on the way home."

A woman in an apron answered their knock at the cottage. "Ah, Miss Jenkins. So nice of you to visit again. Oh, and you've brought—" She broke off, concern in her voice.

"Hullo, Lucy." She gestured to Althea. "My cousin, Lady Althea Egerton. Althea, this is Lady Cheltenham's nurse. Sadly, we must leave, so I wanted to say goodbye to Lady Cheltenham. But this also means I shall be able to interview a few candidates for this position that much quicker."

Lucy smiled. "And Lord Cheltenham agreed?"

Beth nodded and slipped past the nurse to venture down the hall to the conservatory and the older lady's chair. "Hello. How are you today, Lady Cheltenham?"

Lady Cheltenham turned toward her curiously, then narrowed her eyes. "Do I know you?"

"You do indeed. I met you the other day. But 'tis no matter. I am Beth." She gestured Althea forward. "And this is my cousin, Althea. We've been visiting with your darling son, Evan. He has been ever so gracious a host."

"Evan and his parties." The woman rolled her eyes.

Beth had given Althea a vague warning about the woman's memory. Given her new perspective, Althea wondered how much his mother knew of his house parties.

"He was always the center of activity. At school, London. I am surprised he stays here during the summer months as much as he does. But then he brings the party to him, of course."

"'Tis a shame his Lordship is hosting guests," Lucy whispered to Althea, "as today is a more lucid one. He so values those."

Althea sighed at the new twist. The light-hearted party host was a caring son. She still wasn't going to give him control over her business, but it was nice to know he was a good man, particularly after she'd allowed such liberties.

A cup of tea later, they departed. As Althea began to climb into the carriage after her cousin, she spied a tall figure walking toward them on the path from the house.

Evan!

Not ready to face him, she scrambled up.

"Althea! Wait."

Ignoring her host's call, she turned to her driver as he placed the step inside and closed the door. "Please, John, let us be off. We have a long day of travel ahead. Do not wait for his lordship."

Beth gasped next to her, and the coachman looked uncomfortable but climbed to his seat.

But before he could pick up the reins, Evan was at the carriage door, opening it.

He isn't even out of breath, the fit bastard.

She sighed.

Beth stayed silent.

Althea ground her teeth. *Of all the times for my loquacious cousin to have nothing to say.*

"Althea. I understand from my staff that you are leaving? And Beth." He nodded to each woman as he addressed them.

"Yes. Thank you for a lovely party, but we must get back. I have a business to run, as you know." Althea plucked at her skirt and avoided his eyes.

"Ah, but given our"—he paused, glancing at Beth—"conversation last night, I planned to help you, as we agreed."

Althea could feel Beth's questioning gaze on her.

Ignoring her cousin for the moment, she finally met Evan's eyes. "That is very gracious of you, my lord, but

I fear I must decline."

His mouth quirked down. "I am disappointed in you, Althea. A good businesswoman would never turn down free advice. Very well, then. Enjoy your trip, and 'twas lovely to have you here. I shall be back in London in a fortnight, should you change your mind."

Beth finally found her voice. "I shall send word of the ladies I have in mind to relieve Lucy. And Cheltie, do thank Robert for his hospitality." She winked.

Althea sighed again.

****

Damnation. Apparently, he had not been gentle enough in his introduction, and he'd scared the lovely business owner away. He'd been ready to play private games the remainder of the week if it provided the opportunity to see her achieve that sexual pinnacle again. Although he guessed she'd have run no matter how slowly he'd progressed. He just wished he knew why. A dalliance would have been brilliant between them, with no illusions of marriage to mar it.

Ignoring his guests, Evan knocked on the dower house door, wanting a few moments to visit with his mother before returning to the party.

"Mama? Lucy? How are you ladies today?" As was his custom, he opened the door to the dower house without waiting for his knock to be answered.

"We are back here in the conservatory, Lord Cheltenham."

"Ah, excellent. Such a shame the weather has been so terrible this year." He walked through the double doors from the parlor into the greenhouse-like conservatory.

"Lady Rose doesn't mind the chill or the gray. You

know she likes to watch the goings on up at the manor." Lucy gestured toward the view of the house out the large windows.

Evan's gaze shifted from the nurse to his mother, who sat in a comfortable wing chair, facing out. Knitting lay across her lap, her hands loose on the needles.

"Hello, Mama. How are you?" He leaned in slowly to kiss her cheek, never sure if she'd recognize him or be frightened.

She accepted the kiss, and he squatted in front of her to grasp her hands.

"What are you making?" While most ladies of the Ton did needlework, creating what he considered useless and ugly wall hangings, his mother had learned to knit from a nurse early on in her illness and had kept at it. He had found it soothed her and made it a requirement of all nurses after that.

She glanced at her lap and shrugged. "I don't remember."

"'Tis a pretty color, anyway. I hope it might be a scarf for you to wear on your walks." He kept his tone light, despite the wild hope that she was present and aware of her surroundings and her son today.

His mother's nurse stood and gestured that she'd make tea, and he nodded.

His mother reached out, touching his face. "You're not Henry…"

He reached up to hold her palm to his face. "No, Mama. I'm Evan. But I look like him, don't I?" He turned his head to kiss her hand, glad she remembered her beloved husband, his father.

"Yes, you do. Right, Evan. I haven't seen you in

ages."

"I visited just…"

Lucy appeared in the kitchen doorway and shook her head, reminding him not to argue with his mother.

"Right, then. What have you been doing these past few days?"

His mother tilted her head. "There is quite a lot of carriages. Are you having another party? Where is Henry?"

Evan blinked back tears. He hated having to re-explain that his father had died suddenly four years ago. She'd been lucid less frequently these past months, after a year of occasional memory loss and confusion. Her father had experienced the same illness. He could not imagine putting a wife or child through this agony of losing a loved one before their eyes. He vowed again never to marry.

Unfortunately, he was an only child, and the next in line for the earldom was a spendthrift cousin who would run through the whole inheritance in less time than Evan had taken to amass it. Evan's correspondence with his barrister was fast and furious, trying to find an alternate solution.

He tried to look on the bright side. Mayhap it was best she didn't have full knowledge. She would never approve the type of gathering he hosted.

"So is this your favorite color this week?" Trying to change the subject, he fingered the yarn in her lap. "You seem to change your preference every time you find a new skein that interests you."

"Isn't it lovely? I thought the turquoise would remind me of a sunny sky in the cold dark days of winter."

He chuckled and settled into a chair cornered with hers to sip tea and visit, chatting about London gossip that entertained her even when she did not recognize the names of those involved.

Chapter Seven

Beth quizzed Althea about Evan's "free advice." Althea in turn gave staccato answers and turned the questions to Beth's adventures with Robert, at which Beth clammed up. After that, the carriage was abnormally quiet.

Once in London, Althea dove back into the business, catching up on the books and orders for the days she'd been gone.

Beth busied herself with the charity school and interviewing nurses she thought might be a good fit for life in the country with the Dowager Countess of Cheltenham.

The days flew by with Althea being no closer to finding an investor for her expansion. Until one day, she looked up from wrapping an order for a customer to find a familiar pair of broad shoulders browsing the shelves.

"Lord Cheltenham. Lovely to see you here. Can I help you find anything?"

He smiled. "What do you recommend?"

"Is this for you or a lady?"

"A lady."

"Oh." Her tone was flat. "Can you tell me a little about her? Does she like flowers or spice, sweet or citrus?" Althea firmed her lips, determined not to let the thought perturb her. She could not stop from asking,

"Did she enjoy your party, or is she mayhap more, ahem, modest?"

Gads, she sounded jealous and prim.

He barked out a laugh. "A gentleman never tells. What is your favorite?"

She snorted at the word gentleman. "I like a variety. Sometimes 'tis about the season, sometimes about my mood."

"Ah, the entice-the-customer-to-buy-a-selection answer. Quite good."

Her lips twisted. "You are quite the cynic, my lord."

He grinned.

Wandering farther in, he peered at labels. "Where is this shampoo you told me about?"

She pointed at the very back of the store, past displays of goods grouped by fragrance encouraging customers to supplement their purchase of a soap with a shampoo or oil in their favored scent.

He followed her toward it. "Why would you put your best seller at the very back of the store?"

"There is a display in the window, but we get a good many referrals by word of mouth, as well as repeat customers. This way, they must walk by all the other products to get to what they came in for."

"Excellent. I like it."

She passed him a few of the best-selling scents— vanilla, lavender, and rose. He sniffed the first bottle. "If I said it was for me, what scent would you recommend?"

"These." She gestured to a few more plainly labeled products. They were still mostly bought by women but for their husbands, fathers, brothers. Or, she supposed, their lovers.

"Right, then. One of each, please."

"Ah, do you want to smell them?"

"Are you talking a customer out of buying more?"

"I want customers to trust my recommendations and keep returning, as well as send their friends to me. It does me no good to oversell and then have them not return because they have buyer's remorse."

"You have an answer for almost everything. Fine." He sniffed some more. "These two."

"My favorites as well."

His eyes gleamed, and he leaned in. "I shall be sure to use it before I arrive tomorrow afternoon. Beth has invited me for tea to meet the ladies she found for my mother's care. I dare you to be there."

****

Evan closed his eyes as the carriage brought him closer to Althea's house. He should be considering questions for the nurses he was due to meet, but instead, he dwelled on his visit to Althea's apothecary and whether she'd take his dare.

Walking into the store, he'd smelled her. Oh, there had been dozens of scents lingering in the air. But Althea's own personal scent, that crisp floral with a touch of pepper or spice, was layered over that amalgamation.

Still annoyed at her for running from Greenborough Park—from *him*—he'd come to London and waited a week for her to accept his offer before losing patience. Though a fortnight had passed since he'd seen her, his need to touch her, to kiss her, had not dissipated. 'Twas an uncomfortable feeling. He was not used to having to woo a lady.

Godsakes, I'm not used to being interested in ladies. More like fallen doves and Sarah's girls, who understand the game and its rules.

After his first years of society events as the new earl, he'd established a reputation as a rake. He'd flirted and danced, fetched drinks and dropped handkerchiefs, but no one received a second dance or a social call. He had been committed to not committing. No wife or son would have to endure the heartbreak of watching him lose his mind in the next two decades. Despite his indifference, Ton ladies continued to throw their daughters at him, hoping to snare his wealth and title. He'd learned to avoid them and, in fact, spent more time at the demi-monde parties than the Ton fêtes unless he needed to politick.

How is this any different? She is not some deb looking for marriage.

He didn't know. She wanted money from him with no strings. She didn't even want sex. On the surface, it appeared easier to manage or even ignore.

Or mayhap his ego was hurt for that very reason.

Damn me, my pride is injured because she doesn't want my very valuable advice, even freely given.

Despite that, he'd provoked her to attend tea.

It must *work. I desire her. I want this investment. And I wish to find life interesting again, in between planning for my rather short future.*

Evan shook off the thought, sandalwood and ginger wafting around him as he did. The scent of one of the shampoos he'd purchased made him think of her, and his cock lengthened, pushing against his trousers.

When the carriage stopped at Althea's home, he jumped down without waiting for the coachman to set the step. He strode to the front door and gave it two firm knocks.

The door opened, and behind the butler who answered, Beth giggled with a footman. She turned with a lingering smile to the servant and beckoned Evan further into the house past the front parlor.

He held his breath. Where was Althea?

Beth rapped her knuckles on the barely open door and shoved inside. "Cuz, Cheltie has arrived."

His breath whooshed out, leaving him lightheaded for a moment.

Regaining his trademark cocky smirk and swagger, he swung through the door. "Lady Althea, what a lovely *surprise*."

His gaze shot to her, consuming her tall, slender form in royal blue, somewhere between bold and navy, a perfect foil for her dark hair and eyes. Taking her hand, he bowed over it and rubbed his fingers against the pulse in the underside of her wrist.

Beth had turned toward a chair and did not notice Althea yank her arm back and hide it in her skirts.

"My lord. Thank you for coming." Her voice was wooden.

He forced himself to stop staring at Althea and took in the room at a glance. Warm purples and wine tones dominated, with gold accents in the curtains and throw pillows on the settees. The rug in the seating area was all jewel tones. It suited her.

Beth turned back with a bounce from the seating area. "Right. I've asked tea to be served thrice so the ladies will not feel like they are second choice. There are three coming, a half hour apart. If you aren't finished with your conversation with one, I shall entertain the next one in the front parlor until you do. Would you prefer here or at Althea's desk?"

Althea's gaze snapped to her cousin with a frown.

He was tempted to usurp her chair to niggle at her, but no, there was a better way. "Althea's desk, if I may. My lady? Mayhap you could join the conversation, or at least watch—" He smirked when her eyes narrowed on him. "—and the candidate and I shall use the visitor's chairs?"

Her eyes widened. She nodded, but then asked, "Mightn't the ladies not feel more relaxed if we are all in conversation on equal terms?" She gestured to where Beth still stood.

"I suppose." There'd be time enough later to ensure the chosen nurse understood the employee-employer relationship he expected. Althea and Evan chose chairs while Beth perched on the settee where the prospective nurse would join her. He crossed his legs, and his boot brushed the folds of her skirt when he swung it.

She shot him a glance but did not adjust her position.

Two hours later, his back teeth were floating, and he wasn't sure he'd ever want tea again. But he had to admit, Beth had found outstanding choices for him and his mother. Any one of them would work.

"I should like to consider this and send a note around with my decision tomorrow if 'tis all right?" he asked as they all stood.

"Of course," Beth answered.

Althea gritted her teeth, and he had the random worry they'd be smooth stumps if she kept that up.

"Beth, might you excuse your cousin and I for a few minutes?"

"Yes, of course." Beth winked as she brushed by him, the door clicking shut in defiance of propriety.

"Now, Althea," he said, "about our bet."

Her spine grew rigid. "I declined your bet, Lord Cheltenham."

"Mmm." He strolled around her in a slow circle. "I would beg to argue that point, my lady. You came looking for more than answers to questions that night. But never mind. I am going to give you one piece of advice, for a very small price."

"No—"

"Now, now," he tsked. "You haven't even heard the price. Do not be closed-minded."

She gasped and turned to face him. "How dare you? I tell you about my past, and you throw it in my face?"

Evan blinked. Oh damn, he'd put his foot in it now. She thought he was referring to her father's or husband's attitude wearing off on her.

He reached for her hand, but she evaded his grasp. "Althea, you have my most humble apologies. I was trying to provoke you, yes. But I did not mean it that way. I was saying anything I could think of to get a kiss. That was the price I wanted. I've missed you. Your eyes and lips and skin and scent. But more, your fire and intelligence. I never meant to hurt you, just to dare you."

"Oh." She bowed her head for a moment. "I suppose I might have a touch of sensitivity about that topic. You're certainly forgiven, Lord—"

"Evan."

"Evan."

"So?"

"So…what?" She lifted her eyes more than her face, chin still tucked down.

He did not bother with words. Instead, stepping closer, he slid an arm around her waist, his other hand tilting her chin up.

As she sucked in a surprised breath, he capitalized on her parted lips. His mouth met hers on a slant, tongue sweeping to tease along her lower lip, not quite entering, yet not retreating.

Her tongue crept out to meet his.

Lust surging hot through his veins at her initiative, he pressed into her, deepening the kiss. He swallowed her gasp as he nearly moaned from ecstasy.

From a kiss. What had his world come to?

Finally, he raised his head.

"You-you're wearing my shampoo." Her voice was faint.

"Yes. I have not yet had a chance to try the other one." He was fascinated that even dazzled by a kiss, she identified the scent as one he'd purchased from her store.

Having taken the moment to regain his senses, he recalled what he'd wanted to tell her. Declining to release her, he kept his arm banded around her, his other cupping her shoulder. He liked her in his space.

"There are at least three apothecaries in the center of Bath," he murmured in a lover's voice, "and a few more outside the city center. I know of one location not far from the Grand Parade that might be for rent. An excellent location."

"Ohh." Her response was everything he'd want if he were stroking her nipple.

Speaking of…but no. He had his strategy; he must

stay with it.

Stepping back, he released her. "I shall be in London for at least a sennight if you wish to discuss anything further. But for each consult, there will be a price. And they won't all be simple kisses." He winked and stepped out of her arms. "Good day, Lady Althea."

****

Evan glanced around the ballroom in the London home of an acquaintance. He only knew the gentleman from Sarah's club, but they moved in the same circles. Tonight's gathering was a sort of half demi-monde, half Ton acceptable ball. No masks were required because on the surface, it was simply a ball. Easier to do in the off-Season but still risky.

Hence why he used Greenborough Park for the house party. But given the time of year and borderline acceptability of this fête, there would be few if any debutantes he'd need to avoid.

Discretion is the better part of valor. Evan shook his head mentally. He must be really far gone to be paraphrasing the Bard.

He'd managed to drag Ford with him, despite the man's complaints about filling orders from Evan's party. Conversing with Ford allowed him to avoid all but the most aggressive would-be dance partners. And Michael and his new bride were there, which was a pleasant surprise. Of course, Penelope had started in the world of the demi-monde, but Michael's family desired strict adherence to society's rules.

'Twill be like university, only Michael is the first to get his girl rather than me. Happy for his friend, Evan bore no ill will about being outbid for Penelope when she'd auctioned herself off. It had all worked out for the

best for both Michael and the little baker.

Evan spied Althea and Beth sidling along the ballroom wall from the entrance. Althea wore another deep hue, this one a deep emerald, with a square neckline. Beth was in her preferred pastel peach.

He grinned. *What a nice surprise. I should have expected Beth to attend and bring her cousin. No wonder Ford gave in.* He suspected Beth was entertaining a dalliance with Robert. Mayhap she'd bring him out of his shell a bit.

Her presence and the nature of the ball provided a perfect opportunity for him to woo Althea into a casual affair that would suit both their appetites. Nudging Ford, he angled his head toward the duo.

His friend harrumphed, shrugging with a straight face.

Evan shook his head with an indulgent smile. "Shall we?"

Michael and Penelope were in their path around the edge of the dance floor, and the ladies reached the couple at the same time.

Evan bowed over each lady's hand, saving Althea's for last so he could end up next to her. "Fancy meeting you here, Lady Althea."

He could not have asked for a better opportunity to woo her into an affair than this particular fête, given its nature.

She slid him a sidelong glance.

Beth bounced. "Tell us how this works, if you will, please, Cheltie."

"'Tis my understanding that downstairs is for the tame—ahem, I mean, Ton." The group obliged him with chuckles. He watched Althea's face closely as he described the rest.

The setup was quite similar to the demi-monde party where they'd first met a year ago, but given the end of the Season, even more of the so-called reputable members of the Ton attended. They simply ignored the other half of the gathering.

"Upstairs is for the more adventurous," he continued. "All the doors in our host's home have peepholes. Anyone is welcome to make use of a room for whatever activity they choose, but anyone else may watch. If the door is open, then either the room is unoccupied or the couple welcomes people to step in to get a closer look."

Althea's eyes widened and her jaw dropped. "What about for other times? Couldn't the servants use them?"

He shrugged, having no answer. He didn't much care and didn't think his host did either, or the man wouldn't have created the holes. He probably had them on the servants' doors as well so he could in turn watch them.

Evan's mind raced. He was sure Althea liked to watch, despite her prudish upbringing. How might he coax her out of her shyness to watch a tableau?

The pretty shop owner is competitive.

"I dare you." His voice was a thread of sound next to her ear as he leaned toward her.

She turned to him so quickly she nearly banged her nose on his jaw. He inched back but remained close, grinning.

"To what, exactly?"

His brows lifted, and his lips curled into a pleased smile. That wasn't a no.

Chapter Eight

Lud, what was he daring her to do? She'd given her curiosity a very strict lecture to avoid the party's more salacious entertainments, even if Beth attempted to coax her upstairs. Why hadn't she anticipated Evan's presence? This was the lion's den, never mind his kingdom.

Her pulse, elevated from the moment she'd walked in, started a lap around a racetrack when she'd spied Evan's hair. She'd been lost at "peepholes," her guilty pleasure. She had no idea why someone would put those in his own house, but a sudden flash of Evan's face between her legs negated any attempt to care.

The guilt remained. Sex was private and for married couples. But she knew she'd ignore her conscience no matter what the dare was.

Beth doesn't agree. Nor does Evan. Clearly, this homeowner does not, either. Who am I to argue?

"I'd dearly like to know what you're thinking about, Lady Althea."

Althea suspected Evan mocked her prudish ways with the use of her title, but refused to acknowledge the taunt.

"But for now, I'll answer your question. I dare you to venture upstairs. Either side of the door will suffice." He waited, brows still raised in query.

Thanks to the man before her, Althea now

understood her body's reaction to viewing intimate acts.

Was it the performers? Their pure enjoyment and obliviousness to their surroundings? The novelty? Darn her cousin. 'Twas Beth's fault she was in this position. Her cousin's overactive appetite for fun in all its forms had led her to Evan, who had encouraged these prurient activities. Althea knew she was blaming everyone but herself, a grown woman, but she was not ready to face her desires.

Her reputation was at risk again by attending. Being seen upstairs would surely affect her sales. But she could not resist. Would watching titillate her again? Did she want it to?

If she were honest with herself... Yes. She wanted the rush of pleasure it brought her to watch and what it would lead to. She wasn't stupid. Evan's attempts to seduce her with her own desires were obvious. But her competitive nature and the memory of that explosive, amazing orgasm were compelling.

The idea of another lesson in ecstasy made her breath catch. Her chin dipped an inch, then angled up so she met his gaze.

His brows quirked. "*Really?*" He drew out the word as he rubbed his hands in glee. "Right, then. Shall we find some champagne? Then mayhap a dance?"

She angled her head toward him. "What? I thought—"

"Trust me, please, Althea?" He gestured for a servant with a tray of glasses. "The wine will relax you, and the dance... I hope the dance will heighten the mood, the anticipation."

"Ah. Then by all means, lead on." She touched his arm. "But please, is there a back stair? I don't want to be seen."

"Just to see others, eh?" He chuckled and covered her hand with his.

Her lips twisted at his perceptive comment, but she couldn't argue.

They danced closer than during a Ton-approved Season ball but not hip to hip as the dancers at Greenborough Park had.

Every turn teased her with the promise of his thigh sliding between hers. Every pull of his lead offered the chance to lean in and press her breasts to his muscled chest. But his thigh did not slide and she did not arch. Instead, her body heated. Her breasts swelled and became sensitive, as did the private folds between her legs. She panted with arousal, hoping no one would notice or they'd assume it was from dancing.

Afterward, he placed her hand on his arm again, and led her to a hallway and a rear staircase. "Tell me if you desire to return below-stairs at any time or wish to leave altogether."

She nodded, biting her lip.

'Tis Cheltie. Purveyor of all things sexual. He shan't judge you.

Her conscience chimed in. *But you need him for business. And you've already been more intimate with him than you can afford, given that very reputation of his.*

'Tis just walking the hall, seeing what there is to be seen. No intimacy.

But you want that intimacy with Evan, don't you?

She rolled her eyes at herself. If she was going to do this, she needed to stop the internal debate so she could learn whether 'twas something she enjoyed.

On the upper level, an only slightly smaller crowd mingled as though window shopping in Mayfair. Couples strolled arm-in-arm, ladies put their heads together to titter, and men did that thing where they lounged standing upright.

Althea turned her face into Evan's shoulder.

He patted her hand. "No one is watching us, I promise. The activities behind those doors are far more interesting to most." He stopped at the first door and peeked through the viewing hole. Shaking his head, he said, "Not the right place to start."

Curious, she glanced back as he stepped toward the second door, but she deferred to the expert. He viewed that room, shook his head, then proceeded again.

Althea was growing impatient and afraid her nerves would get the better of her. She tugged on his arm to slow him. "What am I missing, Lord Cheltenham?"

"A woman on her knees before a standing man. Have you seen or experienced that act, my dear?"

Althea needed a beat to process. "Uh, no."

She hadn't seen the act itself at his London party, only guessed from what Beth had described and from the positions of the man and woman in the room. Her heart pounded once at the thought of seeing exactly what the woman had been doing kneeling in front of that chair. Would Evan teach her that as well? What would his cock look like? She only had the vaguest notion of Thomas's shape and size. Sex had been in a dark room under the bed covers, and he'd never invited her to explore. She licked her lips.

"As I suspected. I'd rather show you a woman receiving pleasure than one pleasing a man. At least to start." He winked.

Oh my, that means he might teach me soon. She sighed dramatically. "I suppose I'll trust your judgment then, my lord."

His breath gusted out on a quiet laugh before he peered into the third room. "Ah. Here we are."

Stepping back, he put Althea in front of him with his hands on her upper arms, protecting her from the view of others in the hall. She leaned forward to the peephole.

The woman was on her back at the edge of the bed facing away from the door, hair spread about her on the bed. Her breasts mounded over her rose gown's décolletage.

As mine were back in the library at Greenborough Park.

Cravat, waistcoat, and jacket still in place, the gentleman stood between her legs. He held her legs in a wide vee, and his member thrust into her through opened trousers. As Althea watched, his hips sped up, driving into her harder as well as faster. The woman raised a hand to play with her breasts as the man trailed one hand to where their bodies met.

Like Evan did in the library.

Althea's panting breath caught. Evan's temple nudged hers sideways so he could peek before drawing her back to the viewing aperture.

His hands drifted down her arms and around to her waist. One hand rose to cup a breast while his other played at the crease of her thigh over her skirt. Her nipple peaked, begging for his attention, and moisture seeped from her folds. Would he bare her? She should worry, given their stance in a hall half full of partygoers, but she did not. Her pulse throbbed between her legs, craving his fingers, his mouth, or his cock.

She leaned back, tilting her bottom out to search for his cock. *Ohh.* Relief was short-lived when she felt his size. Desire flamed higher. That would feel so much different, so much more, than his finger had.

His hips canted forward, and his lips brushed against her ear, breath feathering over her cheek.

"Do you remember? How it felt when I touched you?" His voice was rougher even than in the library. "Your breasts, their rosy pointed tips? Your lips...the ones where his hand is now. They were even darker than your nipples. All swollen and wet for me."

His fingers slid under the neck of her dress to play with her breast, flicking the hardened nub. His other hand flattened against her swollen folds right through her dress and petticoats. He thrust the heel of his hand against her mound in a rhythm that mimicked sex, his fingers pressing more gently, teasing her sensitive bud. Her hands rose to grip his wrists. She pulled him into her, his front to her back, loathe to leave the peephole even as her body cried for full-length contact.

Feeling his hardness pulse into her bottom, she wiggled against it, adding stimulation that shot forward to meet his fingers.

He grunted, squeezing her breast. "You do remember. I do as well."

Althea was lost to memories fueled by the couple in front of her.

I don't even know their names, but I know the shape of his cock and the color of her nipples, and they arouse me. Well, they...and Evan.

Apparently, spying on intimate acts was indeed a

shameful secret interest of hers, but the titillation was heightened by Evan behind her. The hands touching her were pleasurable by themselves, but 'twas the memory of his hands on her bare flesh as well as his skill that ratcheted her excitement ever higher.

The woman moaned and writhed on the bed. Althea undulated against the stiff rod digging into her bottom, then forward into his hand. She arched to nudge her breast more into Evan's hand.

He accommodated her movements, grinding his hand against her swollen, hot, damp center in time with her mini thrusts.

"Do you remember my mouth on you? My finger in you? Pistoning like his cock is in her?"

Althea could barely hear him over the rasp of her breath, but suddenly, they heard the couple in the room give a series of short shouts as they reached their pinnacles. The woman's last shout rose to a scream.

Althea's hips shoved back at a furious pace.

Evan pushed her fully up against the door, his fingers pinching her nipple, his teeth latching onto her earlobe. His hand searched for and found the slit in the side seam of her dress to access the pocket of her petticoat. Ignoring the pocket, he dragged the petticoat up, up, up, until his hand was on her flesh, branding her with its heat.

"Yes. Yes, I remember. Yes, please, Evan." Need tore the pleas out of her in a lust-roughened whisper. If only there was another pocket so she could help. If only she hadn't worn a petticoat. She might collapse if his fingers did not reach her core to hold her up with the sweetest and darkest of touches.

His fingers slid over her outer lips, swollen and

most likely the color he suggested, slipping on the moisture leaking from her.

She sighed, her relief countered by her body's immediate demand for more. Lud, her knees might give out even with his hand under her.

He unerringly found the perfect spot, the perfect pressure on her nub, and began to pat it.

Her back arched in pleasure, lightning jagging from his fingers on her nipple to those on her pleasure point. Her mouth dried as she gasped for air, lost to his touch.

There was no hall, no risk. There was only him surrounding her.

Unable to widen her stance, she leaned against the door, the unyielding wood a relief to her balance.

His cock was a hot poker riding between her buttocks, and his forearms were anchors she clung to.

His hips and hand had taken over her gyrations, driving into her and back, his pace so rapid fire it felt almost like smacks against her sensitive nether lips and protruding nub, teetering on the edge of pain and pleasure.

Twice more and everything tightened in her abdomen. She managed to mostly stifle her hoarse cry. Ecstasy coursed through her, and her swollen folds pulsed as one against his hand. Her own slid over her skirt to squeeze his hand harder between her legs.

He held his hand still and drove his middle finger in against the contracting flesh.

Her heartbeat pulsed in her ears as she shuddered over and over again before sagging against the door, leaving only his hands and the press of his body supporting her. His cock pressed against her bottom one last time before he carefully withdrew his body and hands, helping her regain her balance.

Regret and worry slammed through her as she regained her senses. Hearing voices around her, she opened her eyes to scan the crowd milling in the hall. *No one is staring, but what if someone recognizes me? This man makes me as wanton as Beth.*

She shook her head. No. It was unfair to blame him. She hadn't even known he was coming. 'Twas Beth who got her here, and Evan who dared her to go upstairs, but she was an adult. These were her decisions.

But she could not afford these risks, or both she and her cousin would lose the roof over their heads. 'Twas fine for this wealthy titled man to flaunt society's rules, but *her* shop would suffer for *his* reputation. This could not be.

She forced herself to turn to Evan and not to wonder what carnal affairs were there for the watching in the other rooms along the hall. "My lord. Thank you for a lovely evening, but I must leave."

Althea almost ran for the stairs without waiting for him to accompany her or even respond.

****

Evan stifled his groan, swallowed his disappointment, and had another quick conversation with his cock. *Denied again. I'll get back to you later.*

Beyond being almost painfully aroused, he felt shaken, off-kilter. He'd chased this woman down his driveway as she ran away from him and his party. Then he'd sought her out at her store. Then he'd seduced her in this hallway. All were actions he'd always dismissed, even disparaged. 'Twas simply not how he dealt with women. He didn't do relationships. He barely handled women at all. He generally allowed them to handle him.

With much more success. Gritting his teeth, he meandered to the grand staircase. Below, Althea was already rushing Beth toward a servant holding their cloaks.

Not bothering to return to the ballroom, he followed them out and walked the line of waiting vehicles to his own. Sprawling across the seat, he lifted one leg up in an effort to make room for his swollen bollocks and cock. He raised his hand to sniff at it. Althea's essence exacerbated his trouser predicament.

Finally, he reached his townhouse. Given his choice of parties, amusements, and servants, he'd never cared if his household saw him aroused, but it occurred to him that he had not actually had to worry about it. He'd never come home dissatisfied.

Nor am I now. Giving Althea pleasure, finding a bit of debauchery that she enjoys and taking her over the edge while fully clothed gives me all the satisfaction I want tonight. And confirmation the prim little widow likes to watch.

He snorted a laugh under his breath. *Beth is her perfect house mate, at least for now.*

He declined to examine exactly what his subconscious meant by "for now." There were more pressing matters. Literally.

In his suite, he had his valet assist him with his tight-fitting dress boots and then dismissed the man for the night. Stripping off his clothes, he laid back on his bed done in creams and golds. His cock pointed at the ivory canopy over the four-poster, still drooling over the memory of being nestled between Althea's bottom cheeks.

He swiped his hand around the liquid seeping from the tip and fisted himself. His other hand rolled his heavy bollocks as he remembered the feel of her pointed nipples, the rasp of her breath. He smelled her arousal mixed with his, as though she were in the room. His eyes drifted closed to picture her hips twitching against him, her arse nudging his cock. He pumped his hand faster, remembering the speed of her hip motions.

As his fingers twitched from thinking of her hot core pulsing against him, he exploded, thrusting through his hand over and over. Lava curled up from his spine, his testicles, and shot through his cock, spewing his seed across his stomach and chest and onto the sheet. His hand slowed, the other dropping to the bed by his hip.

Evan hoped he'd enticed her enough to come to him, even if only under the guise of business. But he was afraid he had not. She was proving to be far more of a challenge than any woman he'd met.

****

Four days later, Evan was still arguing with himself about patience and his rules not to chase women when there were so many available and willing, as he stood outside her shop again.

Penelope had to have a birthday soon. Or a bakery-opening gift. Mayhap something without vanilla notes, though. She had enough of those. He wondered if there were any feminine shampoo scents with cardamom in them. The little baker's treats often had hints of cardamom and ginger in them from her East Indian great-grandmother's recipes.

And now I'm hungry, too.

He stepped into the shop, all his senses reaching for Althea. He could not see or hear her, but he could feel her.

A clerk approached him. "My lord, how can we help you today?"

"I need a shampoo for a friend of mine, a baker."

"May I ask, is the baker a gentleman?"

"No."

"Right, then. Let me see."

"Lord Cheltenham?" Althea's voice sounded, and his pulse sped, his palms growing a tad damp.

He found her coming from the back room in a purple gown so dark it was almost black.

The clerk turned, saying, "This gentleman is shopping for a lady friend who is a baker. Did you want to assist him?"

Althea never missed a step, but her face froze, her smile going stiff.

"You met her." Evan noticed her reaction and hastened to explain. "Penelope. Lady Mansfield."

One brow arched. "And does your friend know you're buying gifts for his wife?"

"Ah, no. I figured I could sort that part out later." Heat flooded his cheeks.

"Come on back. Let me see what I have." She searched along the shampoo display. "One moment, please. I believe I have a new scent that might be just the thing. 'Tis in the storeroom, not even out on the shelves yet."

She disappeared through the door.

His finger tapped against his thigh, pulse racing.

He had no plan. *He had no plan.* He never did anything without a plan. Yet today, he'd come here with the sole intention of seeing her. Wooing her. Wanting her. Oh, he'd contemplated his options. She was a widow, after all. A discreet liaison would not go amiss. And she seemed to like the privacy and lack of obligation.

With that sudden thought, he looked around. The other two clerks were busy helping other customers. None were looking in this direction. Turning the knob quietly, he stepped through the door to the back room.

Chapter Nine

At the sound of the door opening, Althea straightened from the box she was opening. Assuming it was one of her clerks, she swung round as she asked, "Is there a prob— Evan? You should not be back here. I shall bring it out if I can find it."

"No one saw me, I assure you."

She'd ducked into the back room because she needed a moment to recover from seeing him. A flush had swelled up her chest and cheeks at the thought of facing him after behaving like a wanton chit in the middle of a hallway. She could not afford such mistakes, even if his powerful shoulders and height had blocked them from view.

Since Greenborough Park, she had repeatedly tried to recreate the sensations he'd culled from her body while lying in her bed at night. One hand on her breast, one hand between her legs, exactly as Beth had told her for years and she'd dismissed. But when she'd stroked the nub Evan had found for her and even experienced the zing and zap of the climb Evan had brought about, she was disappointed.

She'd tried several more times, of course. Being an intelligent woman, she should be able to improve. But every time 'twas only a faint echo of the explosion at his hands. From then on, she hadn't bothered. Then he had put his expertise to good use again four nights ago.

And here he was in the lips—er, flesh, again.

In the storeroom, dust motes from the box she'd opened floating in the light, she took in his copper jacket and buff waistcoat accenting his hair and eyes. Lud, he was handsome. All golden lion, lithe and dangerous, and on the prowl. He faked harmless well, but she knew his reputation.

And his skill.

She shushed her inner voice and tried to concentrate.

She licked her lips, not realizing she was staring until his mouth quirked in a wry grin.

"It seems you missed me, Althea." His voice was a low rumble, like thunder in the distance promising a storm.

Yes. Please bring the lightning.

No. They were at her place of business. A public space.

She swallowed and dragged her gaze from those lips. Afraid of what she'd see in his eyes, she glanced down his body, noticing the breeches tight over a swell and hands fisted at his side belying his easy smile.

Her cousin had educated her enough, along with her marriage, that she'd understood the games she and Evan played at Greenborough Park and the ball earlier in the week had been very one-sided. She had spent considerable time wondering what his cock felt like. If it had some of the same skills as his lips and fingers.

Beth would say I owe him. But I have no idea how to give pleasure. I was never taught, even by him.

This isn't about good manners. Widows may have more leeway, but you are a business woman. You do not.

The last thing she wanted was to gain a reputation as a loose woman. None of the Ton ladies would be caught dead patronizing her store again. At the moment, she had the mistresses' and the wives' business. Losing one half of those sales would be harmful even without plans to expand.

Althea stepped back and took a page from her cousin's book. "My lord, fingers are fingers. I have no need of those attached to you."

His brows rose. "I should love to see that. But was it as good? Did you not crave my descriptions of what I wanted to do to you? Desire the damp softness of lips against yours…either of yours? Did you not long to lie back and watch, enjoying with no need to work for it?"

Oh my. She was already wet. And panting audibly. She snapped her mouth closed and gulped a swallow.

Evan stepped into her space, raising his hand to cup her face. His thumb skimmed back and forth across her lower lip. He leaned in, whispering, "Remember, sweet. Your body does not lie."

A finger flicked across the hard point of her breast. "Unh."

Taking that bud between forefinger and thumb, he squeezed, holding her whole being still with that two-fingered touch.

"Do you need a reminder of how much better it is with two?" His lips slanted over hers, his knee sliding between hers.

She did not, but she did crave that level of pleasure she could not achieve alone, and she'd spent enough time wondering. Before she could rein herself in, her curiosity won out. Bracing her hips on a table behind her, she slid one hand between them, palm out, to cup the bulge in his breeches.

Oh my.

He moaned and took a half step back to toss her up on the table then stepped away to lock the door.

Oops. She'd issued an inadvertent invitation. She tried to scramble upright on the table to slide off, but he was back, the lion stalking its prey. Succumbing to her desire for another lesson in bliss, she sighed as she surveyed his tall form. At least he'd locked the door. And she wanted to see that part of him she'd only just gotten a hand on.

Her nipple still pulsed from his gentle pinch, and she craved his lips back on hers.

Before she could reach for him, he leaned over her to scoop her breasts out as he had at his estate. He paid homage to them in turn with his lips, tongue, teeth, and fingers.

She changed her mind. She did not need a kiss if he wanted to put his mouth to such good use. Her back arched to thrust her breasts into his face, his hands. She melted onto the table as her blood sang in her veins and wetness gathered between her legs. But darn, she'd wanted to touch that bulge again and she could not reach. Papers rustled under her as she writhed in pleasure and determination. She slid her leg between his, shifting to make him ride her knee, desperate to feel the cock she'd been so curious about.

"Althea. Godsakes, give me a minute or I shall lose control, you gorgeous girl. You drive me to distraction."

"No. No minutes. You've had a fortnight. Please. The girls…the shop…" She could not even form sentences, but she needed that bulge revealed and put to good use. Never before had sex felt essential, like air to breathe or water to drink.

"You are not ready for what I want."

"Yes. Please. Your—" She swallowed hard. "—your cock."

There, she could talk dirty, too.

His eyes widened. "Damn me, you're a quick study. But no, not like this, fast and furtive. Never fear, though, you shall have pleasure."

He dragged her skirts up.

Her exposed breasts blocked her view of what she wanted to see. The air against them felt decadent and erotic, and she loved it. Her desire ratcheted even higher.

Struggling up to her elbows, she found coherence and a pout. "At least let me see it."

"Damn—" One hand dropped her skirt to grip himself.

"Please?" She'd beg if she must. Heaven knew, the pleasure she'd experienced at his hands was worth begging. She could only imagine what he could accomplish with his cock. And she could admit— silently—to an intense curiosity to see a cock clearly for the first time. A dark marriage bed and peepholes did not count.

"All in due time. You first."

He pushed her back to lie flat. A moment later, her skirts were bunched above her hips, and his gaze was centered between them. Watching him, she could almost feel the touch of his gaze whisper across sensitive flesh, raising goosebumps of awareness. Bathing in his regard like a warm bath, she arched. If only she could return the favor.

Then she felt wetness trickle out of her. Abruptly self-conscious, she tried to close her legs in embarrassment, but his hips were in the way. His fingers tweaked a nipple again, his gaze still on her bare flesh between her legs that ached for his hand, his lips, his cock.

He licked his lips. "My word, you smell and look delicious. I must have a taste."

His fingers left her nipple, and he lowered, his hands shoving her thighs wide and dragging her closer to the edge of the table. He draped her legs over his shoulders.

His magical lips caressed her most sensitive flesh. She bowed upward. "Yes. Yes. Please, Evan. More."

A finger slid into her, then two. But the lips retreated. She gasped with need. How could he stop after she'd begged?

"Pinch your nipples. I want to see you give yourself pleasure."

Oh my, like the couple beyond the peephole. I should have guessed he'd have a plan. There are advantages to intimacy with an expert.

Her hands cupped her breasts, pinching with finger and thumb, somehow creating an ache and relieving one at the same time. She enjoyed her own touch, but it did not gratify her to the extent his did. Her nub ached for the wet warmth of his mouth again.

More moisture slid between her buttocks, and she could not bring herself to care. Need burned through her, and her legs tightened around his shoulders.

He chuckled once, then his lips once again surrounded her engorged bundle of nerves, and his tongue flicked in time with her pinching.

"Ah, ah. Evan." No longer coherent enough to beg, she reveled in the heat of his mouth, the wash of sensation over every inch of her, like fresh bathwater, warm from the fire, being poured over her.

She flicked her nipples faster, urging him on, and he responded. His fingers thrust at the same pace, and his tongue licked in tandem.

A deluge of hot pleasure soaked her. Even her scalp tingled, and within seconds her back curved and her hips took on the rhythm, thumping against the table.

He sucked hard, and she came apart, bottom off the table, legs locked around his head as she contracted around his fingers and under his tongue. Her hands fell from her breasts to brace herself so she would not be sucked under the waves.

She covered her mouth to muffle her scream as her whole body shook. "*Evan.*"

He softened his lips, sipping as his fingers petted her for a moment. Her legs slackened around him, her spine relaxing against the supportive tabletop. She wasn't sure she could move.

He stood and unlaced his breeches.

Suddenly energized, she rose on her elbows again to stare.

"Yes, sweetheart, you wanted to see. Now watch what you do to me."

His cock leaped out to point at her, seeping liquid from its tip.

Now I know why he said I looked delicious.

His member was dusky red, straight, and thick, its helmet looking like an impressive and mayhap slightly scary creamy delectable treat. She wanted to lick it and taste it. Her tongue swept across her lips, saliva pooling in her mouth.

He wiped his hand gently, carefully for her sensitivity, through the wetness between her legs, and brought it to his cock, adding the moisture he'd created and smoothing his hand along the stalk again and again.

Her inner walls contracted again, craving that thickness between them. But she knew Evan was determined to control this interaction.

His gaze ran over her, and she pictured what he saw. Eyes glazed with pleasure as his were, lips wet and parted, breasts plumped, with hard rosy tips begging for more pinches, and legs spread wantonly around her damp swollen folds where his face had just been.

He groaned and grabbed a handkerchief she hadn't noticed beside her. His hand slicked up and down, faster and faster until he held the handkerchief over his swollen rod and shuddered, his eyes closing, his back arching as his hips thrust into his hands.

He staggered once and brought a hand to the table as he leaned over her to kiss her.

She smelled herself on him. Strange, but not unpleasant.

The door rattled, followed by a knock. They both started.

"Althea?" One of the shopgirls needed her.

****

The next hour was a blur of fumbling answers to questions and hiding from customers in the back of the shop, until Althea gave up and went home, leaving the senior shop clerk to close. She'd made Evan leave via a back door that let out onto a foul-smelling alley. He hadn't argued about a purchase, which cemented her belief that he'd come to seduce her again.

She'd fallen right into his hands, risking her business. Despite her self-directed anger, and her concern over how she'd keep her hands off him if he continued to pursue her, she could not stop thinking about his cock. She still hadn't gotten to touch it, much less taste it. Worse, the poor man had only had a self-induced orgasm, whereas she was up to three Evan-gifted ones.

Beth was coming in from her volunteer time at the charity school and had just ordered tea to the library when Althea entered and flopped down across from her, throwing her feet on the delicate matching Hepplewhite footstool.

Beth tilted her head. "Cuz? Are you quite all right? You appear flushed."

Despite their relative marital status, Beth was her font of knowledge for this. She needed advice.

"I've just had the most explosive sexual experience of my life in the back room of my shop. 'Tis no wonder I am flushed!"

"What? Do tell!" Beth sat forward on the settee. "With whom?"

Althea gave her a withering look.

"Ah. Cheltie does get around. It seems he was able to live up to his reputation. Come now. Share with your best friend and family member."

"Only because I need advice. Please, you cannot breathe a word of this to anyone. The shop will suffer, never mind my reputation."

"I promise, I promise. Now spill."

Althea started back at the beginning, describing the bet she'd declined, the game, the dare. Then the second dare at the London party and the most recent interlude.

"But, cousin, I must also confess something. Part of the reason I sent you to the School of Enlightenment was because I stumbled across one of your, er, interludes in the stables."

"Oh, that," Beth scoffed. "I was actually hoping it would help convince you to try sex."

Althea's eyes bulged. "You saw me? Why did you never say anything?"

"Me? Why did you never say anything?" Beth laughed, arching a brow. "I glimpsed you hurrying away is all. If you recall, I was rather busy at the time. Regardless, 'tis quite all right. I don't mind. The more, the merrier, and all that. And I know why you sent me away. If I had stuck to the stable hands, you might not have, but I am very grateful for my time there."

"Oh." Althea sagged against her chairback in relief. Then another thought occurred. "Beth, there were two stable hands watching before I arrived. You say you don't care, but I still can't comprehend that." She referred to their long-running debate over the etiquette of intimacy.

Beth snorted. "Before Evan, you thought sex was for procreation, not pleasure. I see you're not trotting that tired argument out now."

Althea's cheeks warmed.

Her cousin continued. "Look at Aphrodite. She had many lovers, and she lounges around naked in most of her depictions. I'd wager her motto was the more the merrier, too."

"It just feels wrong to watch others in what is specifically referred to as intimate moments."

"What if their definition of intimacy is inviting anyone interested to participate in that, bringing people together in a different way?"

"I cannot fathom it."

"Well, then, let me ask this. If Evan had neglected to lock the door, and your employee had entered just before he took you over, would you have cared? Would you have even noticed?"

Althea looked down at her hands in her lap, suddenly back in the room behind the shop. Would she have minded her employee seeing her with her skirts up around her waist, in the throes of passion? Certainly afterward, but at that moment? She didn't know. Unable to meet Beth's eyes, she remained silent.

"Is he as well-endowed as they claim?"

She looked up to find Beth grinning at her, apparently willing to drop the inquisition. "Who is they, and—never mind. Beth, please. Now is not the time for idle gossip. What do I do, cousin?"

"Right, then. Sorry. You have nothing to lose by taking some advice, which he's already offered. However, he's come to you twice now." Beth raised a brow. "Cheltie never chases. He doesn't need to. You shall likely need to go to him."

Althea shook her head. "But now he is insisting on sexual favors in return."

Beth grinned. "'Tisn't the worst idea in the world, from the look of you. And they say he is a very generous lover."

"If by generous, you mean he has brought me over three times with not even a single opportunity for me to return the favor, then yes, he is very generous. I might even feel guilty if I didn't feel quite so…satisfied."

Beth giggled.

Althea sighed with a smile before remembering the

problem at hand. "Please stop talking about *they*! I cannot afford a scandal, however marginal I am in the Ton. My shop sales will suffer, and expanding to improve sales is the entire reason I am in this predicament."

Well, that and Beth's solution being the party at Greenborough Park. No, that's not fair. She was trying to help.

Althea stood and paced a path along the length of the low table, from the fireplace to the end of the area rug and back.

Beth sat back and sipped tea from the tray a servant had brought in, thankfully during a less prurient part of Althea's summary of her situation. "Cuz, apart from the risk of rumors, what do you want? A month ago, you'd have told me you had no interest in sex. But that is not the case now, is it?"

Althea threw herself back into the chair. "Gah! No. Blasted man. And you!"

"Me? What did I do?"

"You told me about it all. And that pushed me into making claims he felt forced to disprove. 'Tis all your fault!"

Beth snorted.

Althea snorted.

Then the two of them burst into giggles and laughed until they were crying.

Finally, wiping the tears from under her eyes, Althea straightened in her chair again, reaching for her lukewarm cup of tea. "Here, I'll give you the words I know you are slavering for. You. Were. Right." She stuck her tongue out at her younger cousin.

"Oh my, I've been rubbing off on you. Or Evan

has—literally." Beth snorted, seeming on the verge of descending into giggles again. She took a deep breath and sent Althea a level gaze. "Look, you have the upper hand at the moment. He has come round twice, so even though you must go to him, 'tis clear he wants you and will flex on the terms. Use the negotiating tactics he would. If your biggest concern is rumors, trade sex for advice. Just make sure he agrees to keeping it secret."

****

Evan arrived home from Althea's shop, shampooless, with his hands still shaking.

'Twas the first time he'd spent his seed with another person in the room in months. No wonder 'twas a bit of a shock to the system.

But it was more. He desired more than an afternoon's interlude. He'd wanted to scoop Althea up and take her home and make love to her all afternoon. Hell, he'd wanted to spear into her then and there, if only his conscience wasn't so darned interfering.

Pouring a generous whisky, he slumped in his desk chair and stared at the fireplace in his library. When he raised his glass to sip, he caught a whiff of her arousal mixed with his seed. His cock twitched in his breeches, eager to continue its path out of this dry spell.

Did I push too far, too fast? I did not accept her offer of intercourse. Surely, that will count for something. So now what?

Did he continue purchasing items in her shop, hoping for another assignation? He'd gone there twice and to her house once. Should he give up and walk away? There had to be some other woman out there who could make his cock hard again. Or if there wasn't, some other investment to pique his interest.

He sipped whisky, watching the firelight play over the tans and golds of the room's upholstery.

If Ford told him he had pursued a woman this much, he'd likely laugh and tell his friend to move on, rather than keep at it. Although, given the modicum of success he'd had today, his advice might be to continue his efforts. She had given herself to him, despite his idiotic chivalry and terrible choice of time and place.

With that, he took one more sip and put the whisky aside to go through his correspondence. On the top were two letters that overrode his indulgent memories of the afternoon.

Nancy Lincoln, the woman he'd selected as a nurse for his mother, had written to accept his offer of employment. And a note from Lucy indicated she'd been struggling more the weeks after he'd left, as his mother's memory was slipping more frequently and she became angry when she was confused.

He'd had letters like that one before, as his mother's dementia progressed to a new stage. Each time, he returned home in the hope that his presence would soothe her and because each advancement reminded him that his time with her was limited. Whether she valued it or not, he did.

He called to the butler to ask his manservant to pack for a short trip back to Cheltenham, and he scribbled a note to be delivered to the new nurse, along with a small pouch of shillings. He indicated that if she could leave in two days, she could travel in the comfort of his coach with him. Otherwise, the money pouch should cover her fare and to please apprise him of her planned arrival date.

Two days later, Nancy arrived with a small trunk

and she and the trunk were being loaded into the carriage. Evan stood on the stoop, pulling on his gloves as he waited.

A small carriage pulled up behind his, and the figure alighting caught his eye. *Althea.*

"My lord. Oh. You are leaving."

"I must. Is Beth with you perchance? I should like to thank her for finding Nancy for me. I am going to get her settled and check on my mother. I've had a letter…" His shoulders tensed.

Althea laid a gloved hand on his arm, ignoring decorum. "Of course. I understand. Beth is in the carriage." She gestured.

"Alfred, I shall be right back." Evan called to his coachman.

The man saluted.

Offering Althea his arm, he accompanied her back to the smaller carriage and handed her inside. Stepping in, he found himself crouching before them, as there was only a forward-facing seat.

He was pleased to note Althea's gaze gravitating to his thighs and calves, pronounced in this position.

"Beth, Nancy is accompanying me to Greenborough Park. You have my gratitude for finding her. She is lovely, and I think will work out very well with Mother."

"I am so glad, my lord. I suspected you might choose her. Please tell me how it goes." She nodded at him, her eyes flitting between him and her cousin.

"Althea, why did you come?" He did not have time to waste prevaricating.

"Oh. I—you had offered advice in return for—we were interrupted at the store—ah, you had invited me to discuss your advice on how to expand..." Her voice rose at the end as though uncertain.

"Ah. I would love to. Unfortunately, it shall have to wait. I try not to wait too long between visits to my mother."

"Shall I call again in a sennight? Or mayhap you could send a note 'round when you return?"

He squinted at the floor, thinking. *She came.* His brain stalled on that. *I must go, but how do I continue to reel her in?*

Finally, he conjured the beginnings of a plan. "It might make more sense for you ladies to meet me in Bath. We could evaluate things in person together. Since you travelled to Greenborough Park for the party, I assume you have someone who can cover the London shop for you?"

She nodded, her eyes straying to his taut legs again. He swallowed his grin.

"Well, then. Shall we say a fortnight and half from now?" He named the guesthouse he stayed at when visiting. "I shall procure two rooms for you."

"Thank you, Evan." Althea nodded, glancing at Beth, who sat watching them with a wide smile.

"Is there aught else I can do for you before I go?" His lips quirked in his trademark half smile, and he dropped his eyes to Althea's lap. If it had been a year ago with different women, he'd offer to give them both a quick fingering in tandem. Hell, he'd done it before, and he'd wager Beth had participated in similar fun. But he no longer had any interest in touching anyone other than Althea.

"A kiss, I think, please." Althea and he both whipped around to look at Beth at her statement. "Mine can be on the cheek, of course." At Althea's continued glare, she corrected, "uh, or the hand. Althea will need one on the lips after coming all this way."

Evan shook his head at her but palmed her hand and brought it to his lips. "Delighted, Miss Jenkins." Turning to Althea, he ignored Beth's intrusive stare and leaned in to whisper in the hope that Beth could not catch his words, "Althea. I did not wash my hand or face for a full day. I look forward to our next visit."

Althea flushed but licked her lips and left them parted.

His brushed hers, the barest of rubs. Once, twice. A touch of his tongue to her lower lip, and then he pulled back. "I dare you to think of me."

Chapter Ten

Ford was already at the estate when Evan arrived. They often traveled in tandem, so were either in their London residences and spending the evening at White's or Sarah's, or out at Greenborough Park together.

After the annual bacchanal, as Ford had named it, he was almost always inundated with orders, as well as new design ideas. Evan had expected him to hunker down in his London home to work, but he had excused himself to the estate after the demi-monde ball last week.

Given the letter that had prompted this trip, Evan deferred his curiosity about Ford's sketches and designs until he saw his mother and did his best to ensure she did not fuss at the change of nurse. Then he hoped to convince Ford to accompany him to Bath.

He quickly arranged for a room for Nancy to ease his mother into the change and asked the butler to give her a tour before he strode back outside through the cold rain to the dower house.

Lucy met him at the door and reported that Lady Rose was having a calm day, although foggy, and she thought it might be a good time to introduce Nancy, so Evan returned to the house for her.

When they walked into the cottage, he introduced the nurses and then walked through to the conservatory, the others trailing behind him.

His mother started at his appearance. "Who are you? Why are you in my house? Lucy! Help! There are strangers in the house."

Her calm day had deteriorated, as it often did toward evening. Evan's heart broke for the hundredth time. It did not matter that this happened more often these past months. It was a fresh stab of pain, worse than any rapier, every single time.

This, this is why I will not marry.

He lowered himself to a chair swiftly, to appear less threatening. "Mother, I am Evan. Your son."

"You are not my son. I do not have a son. Where's Henry?"

He leaned in, reaching for her hands, but she veered back with a gasp. Dropping his hands, he said, "Henry can't be here right now, Mama. He sent me."

Turning, he looked to Lucy for guidance.

Nancy caught his eye. She was shaking her head and took a step back into the shadows beyond the doorway of the conservatory. Evan looked to Lucy who was next to her, just inside the kitchen on the other side of the threshold. She, too, made a negative gesture.

Turning back, he tried to at least visit with his mother. "How are you today? Have you been knitting?"

"Lucy, where are you? Please, this gentleman is pestering me."

Lucy stepped in, hands gripping each other at her waist. He was sure it was a less than ideal position to be in, but he'd made it clear to her at the start that she would be Rose's advocate. If he was upsetting her more than Lucy thought acceptable, she could direct him to do whatever she thought best. He'd run through the same guidance with Nancy in the carriage this morning.

The new nurse might as well see this scenario so she knows there are no repercussions.

"Sir, I think 'tis best that you leave Lady Rose for today."

"Of course."

Evan stood. He refrained from kissing his mother's cheek in farewell, knowing it would upset her, even as the lack of affection jabbed him again.

"I hope I can visit with you tomorrow, Moth—Lady Rose."

Lucy laid a hand on his arm as he passed. "I can spend some time with Nancy out of sight of your mama, to start the transition."

He nodded, unable to speak through the lump in his throat. Lifting a hand in a desultory wave, he walked out into the rain and leaned against the stone wall next to the front door of the little house.

Evan buried his head in his hands and sobbed.

****

After changing into dry clothes, Evan searched for his friend. When he entered the guest suite's sitting room and converted workroom, he sighed, glad to have Ford so close. Relocating a half-finished piece that looked like a bustier comprised mostly of straps with metal rings holding them together, he gave it only a passing glance as he settled into the chair he'd cleared.

Robert finished punching a few more holes for stitches with the sharp stitching awl and put the bundle of leather in his lap aside. "Bags. You look tired."

Evan appreciated his friend's discretion. Tired was better than looking like he'd been crying his eyes out.

"Just worried. I brought the new nurse back with me. But mama is easily vexed by changes in routine."

He shrugged.

"Would a Scotch help?"

"It certainly would not hurt." He smiled at Robert when he got up to pour them each a drink.

As he passed Evan the drink, he asked, "Do you want to talk about it?"

"Eh. For every visit she recognizes me, there are more and more when she doesn't. 'Tis hard to see your mother standing in front of you and remember that she is not really there anymore. I miss her."

"I am sorry. Do you remember her going through this with her father? How old were you at the time?"

"I was young. So no, I don't recall it. I just know what she told me later, when she warned me about the possibility of it happening to me…and first, to her."

"And did she give you any tips to help cope?"

"No. Her focus was on ensuring I lived as full a life as possible, as I was liable to have it curtailed. And to remind me that she would always love me. But how—" He choked up again and took a fortifying sip of whisky. "—can she love me when she doesn't recognize me?"

Robert shook his head. "I don't think it works like that, Bags. Love underlies it all, for a parent. She did everything she could to prepare you for this time and to mitigate your pain when it became difficult, out of a place of love."

"Well, it did no such thing. And I cannot imagine doing that to a wife or child."

"How did you find a new nurse so quickly? You've been gone less than a month."

"Didn't I tell you? Beth had agreed to help me find Lucy's replacement. It was how she got Althea her audience with me. That and her relationship with

Penelope."

"Ah. I wondered what brought about that interest in an apothecary, beyond the attractive owner. You usually seduce the owner but decline the investment. That girl is wily. And she knows Penelope. Interesting…"

Evan agreed. "The chit knows everyone. Her network rivals mine, and Charlotte's." He referenced the Dowager Duchess of Peterborough.

"Really? Why does she need such a network?"

"She excels at bringing people together who need each other. Or someone who needs help with another who has the exact thing the other needs. 'Tis hard to explain. But just as one example, as soon as they arrived, she discovered that I needed a new nurse for my mother and offered to find one for me. In addition to matching people well, she seems to love it. She told me 'twas because she enjoys finding people's place to fit in this world. My guess is 'tis also because she has struggled to find her own."

"Hmph. Well, mayhap I should hire her. While I've managed to restock leather, I am short on buckles and other accessories. And my blacksmith is getting older and has been talking of going to live with his daughter and son-in-law to spend more time with his grandchildren."

"Just say the word. She'll likely have you three candidates in a fortnight."

Robert looked pensive, and Evan shot him a sharp glance. He should find out more of what was going on between Robert and Beth. First, he needed to ensure the transition from Lucy to Nancy progressed smoothly. Then mayhap in the carriage where Ford would be a captive audience, Evan would quiz his friend, assuming he could convince Ford to join him.

Robert played right into his hand. "How was the rest of your time in Town?"

Evan knew he was really asking how the mad chase after Althea had gone. It was out of character for Evan to pursue a woman for any reason, so his friend's curiosity was well earned. "Frustrating. Slow. But, finally, productive, I think."

He'd given Robert a quick summary of the investment and Althea's concerns before he left.

"She invited you to invest?"

"Not exactly. Care for a trip to Bath?"

****

Evan had procured rooms for the group at a small but luxurious guesthouse near the river, a short walk north of the city center. The men's rooms were on the first floor, above the public rooms, and the ladies' rooms were above them.

He always stayed there when visiting Bath because he shared ownership in the property with the manageress. He rarely visited the resort town, so he preferred this to renting or owning a house.

Althea and Beth had not yet arrived, so he and Robert strolled toward Stall Street where Evan had invested in extending the development of much-needed housing begun two decades before.

As they passed the Pump Room, Robert gestured and joked, "Mayhap taking the waters would help, old man."

"Damn me," Evan responded, "if every biddy in there wouldn't perk up at the sight of us and drag their daughters over. No, thank you. But go right ahead."

Robert shuddered and shook his head as they continued on. "Right. We've seen the two apothecaries on the main street. And the owner of the one said there are three others, two up near the Royal Crescent and one down here. Given the continued expansion down here, it feels as though the area could sustain one more if Althea is so inclined."

"Possibly." Evan had a different idea but wanted to see the southern part of the city for himself first. After they'd found the apothecary, he scanned its offerings, buying a random tonic to endear himself to the shopkeeper. Then they headed back to the guesthouse.

Discovering that the ladies had checked in, Evan continued up to the second floor while Robert stopped at his own room.

Knocking on Althea's door, his heart beat faster, and his hands grew clammy. He dragged off his gloves to gain some relief.

Hearing footsteps, he patted his hair. When was the last time he checked his hair for a woman? He rolled his eyes at himself, composing his face quickly as the door opened.

"My lor—Evan."

"Althea." He nodded, taking her hand and brushing his lips over it, noting her dark chocolate gown that blended with her hair, pinned back but left down. "I trust your travels were without incident?"

"Yes, thank you. Although now Beth has disappeared. You needn't have gotten us two rooms. We shared at Greenborough Park if you recall."

He slid his gaze to hers with a small grin. "Ah, but there I had my study for private…conversations."

She blushed.

"If we can locate Beth, I have Ford with me. I thought we could all have a quiet dinner tonight and get started looking around tomorrow?"

"Certainly," she said. "I am going to check next door in the pub. She is likely flirting with the bartender."

Evan suspected otherwise but preferred not to defame her cousin if he was wrong. "I will gather Ford. Come by my room when you are ready. If need be, we can all stroll the block and look for your cousin together."

Once she closed the door, he ran down to Robert's room and knocked. "Althea cannot locate her cousin. Any thoughts?"

His friend gritted his teeth. "No. But did you check your room?"

Evan frowned at him in puzzlement. "Why would she be in there?"

"She may have thought— Never mind. Let's check, shall we?" He gestured for Evan to cross the hall.

And there she was, backlit by the window, which showed how few undergarments she was wearing under her blush-toned gown.

"Rob— Oh, Cheltie. Lovely to see you." She gave a shallow curtsy. "I beg your pardon. I thought this was my room but just realized my mistake. I believe I stopped one floor too early. If you'll excuse me, I shall correct that immediately."

Evan bit back a snicker at her nervous babbling. At least she recognized she was in trouble, and not just with her cousin.

As she started to brush by him, Evan caught her

arm. "My dear Beth. Entering a man's bedchamber is naughty. I believe you should be punished, don't you?"

He was not sure if she knew he was aware of her schooling but given that knowledge and his familiarity with her penchant for trouble, he knew he could take liberties.

She gasped but did not appear afraid.

He suspected it was in a combination of excitement and nerves.

"Don't you?" he repeated. 'Twas only fun if both parties enjoyed it, after all.

She bit her lip, and he heard a shuffle. Glancing over, he saw Robert had turned away. Excellent. He was certain both parties would appreciate his sternness.

"Yes, my lord." She fluttered her lashes.

"Excellent. I agree. Unfortunately, I need to speak with Althea after dinner, but Ford here"—his friend whipped back around with a glare—"is quite good at correcting naughty girls' bad behavior. He may even have some toys—ahem, tools—which could help manage that behavior through dinner?" He raised his brows at his friend.

Robert narrowed his eyes and nodded thoughtfully.

Beth's eyes brightened.

"Right, then. You two work out the specifics," Evan said. "Althea is coming to this room in a few minutes, and we shall await you downstairs."

****

Althea followed Evan to the small seating area at the back of the guesthouse lobby to wait for Beth and Robert. She sat, intrigued when he pulled out a short pencil and a scrap of foolscap and sketched out the layout of the city with the curve of the River Avon curling around the east and south end of town.

She'd visited before and done the same with Brighton to determine the best opportunity for expansion. She'd also considered a second location in London, but the shops for the aristocracy were all concentrated in one area, where her existing shop already sat.

Evan marked Xs on the rough map, showing her where he'd already found apothecaries, including one that hadn't been there on her previous trip. "We'll want to visit them again, of course, so you can see their offerings. I perused them, but you'll have a better eye to who might offer the fiercest competition."

She named the two in the city center, saying, "I have already visited both of these. I did not like the quality of their wares or their proximity. I'm hoping to find a niche where there is a growing clientele or an underserved group."

He grinned, and she preened a bit. She had a good head for business, but having one of the richest men in England acknowledge that acumen was still flattering.

Once Beth and Robert joined them, they braved the drizzle for a tavern a few blocks away that Evan recommended. Conversation remained light, with Beth squirming and Robert remaining quiet, his eyes on Beth much of the time. More than ever, Althea worried about everyone having their own rooms, knowing her cousin's penchant for trouble.

But her attention kept veering to the predatory cat to her right. Flashes of that leonine mane between her thighs created a hunger that had nothing to do with the food on her plate. Thrice now, he'd taken her to heights she'd never dreamed with his mouth and hands. Would she survive his cock, or would her heart give out? And what a cock it was. Despite not having much opportunity to compare, she was certain Evan's befitted a lion.

Mayhap I should worry about myself, not Beth.

She squirmed a little, and Evan's glance flicked to her in surprise. She licked her lips, wondering if he'd want her mouth on him the way he'd put his on her.

His eyes followed the movement of her tongue, dropped to her bodice, then rose to meet her gaze. Glancing down, she realized her nipples were hard points poking through her camisole and dress. Flushing, she looked up again.

"You realize that I have paid my price for the shop storeroom," he drawled. "Tomorrow, we start anew with an exchange. Investment information for opportunities to illuminate the world of intimacy for you."

Althea panted, unable to find it in her to consider risks or repercussions. Instead, she worried about the separate rooms. She would not have the strength to turn Evan away if he knocked on her door during the night.

****

Althea slept restlessly, half hoping for a knock at the door, half fearing it. All for naught, as she had no nocturnal visitors. Nevertheless, she leaped out of bed in the morning, ready to investigate her potential competitors and mayhap even possible locations for her shop.

The four gathered for pastries and tea before going their separate ways. Robert and Beth, with a maid trailing them for propriety's sake given Beth's unmarried status, planned to stroll the city and sightsee, then visit a forge Robert hoped to partner with.

Althea and Evan began retracing the route Evan had followed the day before. After the first two shops, Evan led her away from the water, showing her the Circus, the Royal Crescent, and the surrounding area where the most affluent residents and visitors stayed. Then they walked down past the Grand Pump Room and Roman Baths to Stall Street again. He first pointed out the construction of row houses underway, then the area beyond Stall Street yet to be built before ushering her into the final apothecary of the morning.

She exclaimed and sniffed and examined the goods in each shop, from candles to tonics to soaps to inks. Back on the street, she'd take a pencil and her notebook from her reticule and scribbled a few notes about the quality and variety of offerings in each shop.

Evan led her to a bakery for a cup of tea and a pastry, which she ignored until after her thoughts on the final store were noted.

Finally, she sat back and sipped her tea. "Thank you. This area is busier than when I was here last year. I had no idea of the growth. I'm even more excited now at the prospect of a store here. I wonder if I can improve on the time to profitability."

"What do you think of the quality of items sold in these stores versus yours?"

"Two were comparable, the first was a mix. Some items seemed inferior. The inks looked watery, but I'd have to test them on paper to be sure." She had bought one for that purpose.

"What location would you choose if there was an appropriate space?"

"With the two in the center of town, I think either

up near the fancy houses or down here with the newer homes could work. But you mentioned two other locations. I'd want to know where those are before I decided. And probably see them."

"Right, then. Shall we? I obtained the location of one from the guesthouse manageress. 'Tis a bit north of our rooms but walkable, if you're willing. My guess is that the other is north and west, past the Royal Crescent, so we can ask up there."

The next shop was the fanciest, and Althea wandered around for longer than she had in any of the other stores. As she sniffed and fondled and rubbed, she listened to Evan chatting with the lady at the counter. Althea estimated she was in her forties, with dark hair pinstriped with silver pulled back in a bun and a modestly cut midnight blue dress.

Half-listening to Evan's questions, Althea gleaned that the clerk was actually the proprietress. Her sourcing was not through London. It was direct with more local businesses. And she, like Althea, mixed her own fragrances for soaps and candles. She also shared the location of the last apothecary, indeed in the part of town Evan had guessed. When asked why she did so readily, she waved a hand as Althea approached.

"You'll find they carry different items than I do." She kept her sneer from her tone, but a sniff escaped.

Althea could guess that it catered to more of a working-class crowd. Or mayhap tried for upscale but the quality was not as good. Her pulse ticked up in anticipation. She wanted to find out. Having so many similarities with this shopkeeper, Althea was anxious to see if they thought alike regarding competition. That could help her if she planned to compete as well, although she found herself strangely reluctant to interfere with another woman's business, particularly one she'd liked so much in this first meeting.

Back on the street, Althea bounced on her toes as she walked, trying to rein in her excitement.

Evan grinned at her antics.

She ignored him, flapping her hands before placing one on his proffered arm. "That shop, that owner, is the most like mine. She will be my closest competition."

"And yet you seem…happy?"

"Lud, did you see the workmanship of her pens? And those inks! I cannot get inks that thick and dark without them looking like shades of black or brown. But hers were rich in color. You should have asked where she found those specifically."

"Ah, so you were listening."

"Of course." She smiled, squeezing his bicep. "You asked excellent questions. How do you know so much about this type of shop?"

"Many businesses share similarities. For Penelope's bakery, there is still sourcing of raw materials to be done, quality of goods to be assessed, and such. Most shops will have some of the same challenges, and I've helped others before."

"What other businesses have you helped?" She tilted her head to look at him.

"Recently, I've focused on women who want financial independence. Many of those are more service businesses. Laundresses and the like."

"Why?"

"Why do they more often offer services?" he asked, glancing down with a crease between his brows.

"No. Why do you focus on them?"

"For a few reasons, but the biggest is my mother. While I would not share this with most people, you've met her. Did Beth tell you why she needs a nurse?"

"Not really," she said. "'Twas not her place to share."

"She is losing her memory. Rather like the elderly, but much earlier, and 'tis worsening."

"Oh, Evan. I am sorry. That must be terrible for you as well as her."

"I worry what would have happened to her when my father died, without me to take over the earldom and to help manage her care. Women have very few paths to financial independence and very few ways to learn the skills needed for some of those paths."

"Wouldn't other family have taken her in?"

He shook his head. "Not in my family. Without me in the picture, my second cousin would have gotten the title and the entailment and would have not only thrown my mother out on the street but likely have gone through the estate in a matter of months. He still could if I die."

"That is terrible." She shook her head, remembering him mentioning that cousin when she had first asked about his family. She assumed he'd circumvent that by marrying eventually. Hating the idea of him marrying, she returned to his previous statement. "But 'tis ever so forward-thinking of you to help women where you can."

She debated bringing up the School of Enlightenment but knew that was not allowed. Still, the school could benefit from Evan's help, and she thought he would find it a worthy investment.

Chapter Eleven

The second northern apothecary was inferior, just as Althea had suspected. They quickly returned to the guesthouse, and Althea ordered baths for her and Beth for an hour from then. She heard Evan doing the same as she ascended the stairs.

After a short rest with a cup of tea, she lowered herself into the warm water in the hip tub the staff had brought. Her maid had found her favorite shampoo and soap from the luggage. Althea turned the bar in her hand, rubbing and sniffing it to ensure the quality was everything she remembered, in light of the products she'd seen earlier.

Reassured, she washed quickly, then leaned over the tub so her maid could wash and rinse her hair.

As her maid finished securing her dress, a knock sounded. Her maid answered the door, returning with a note. As Althea unfolded it, another knock came.

The door opened before she could respond, and Beth's face appeared. "Cuz? How was your day?"

Althea shook her head at her cousin as she entered without waiting for an invitation.

"Quite productive, thank you. We walked so much." On the verge of asking Beth about her day, Althea remembered the note in her hand. She scanned it. "Oh. After the four of us dine this evening, Evan would like to discuss my expansion plans further, in order to determine what we do tomorrow. Do you mind? Would you like to join us?"

Beth threw herself on Althea's bed. "Thank you, no. I don't mind at all. I am sure I can entertain myself." She smiled.

Fighting the urge to roll her eyes, Althea frowned at her cousin's failing attempt to look innocent. "I am serious, Beth. No scandals. No employees complaining to management and getting us thrown out. Behave. 'Tis only a few days. Surely you can control yourself."

Although, the more Althea thought about it, remembering her dilemma of wanting and not wanting Evan to knock, the more she began to understand Beth's penchant for trouble. The pursuit of that level of ecstasy could indeed eclipse one's good sense.

No. Keep business and pleasure separate.

But she could not help the thrill that accompanied every thought of Evan's price for each piece of advice. She shivered, wondering how many tips he would provide and where it would lead them. She chose a burnt orange gown, ignoring the internal voice that said it reminded her of his hair. Finding a scarf, she tossed it around her neck with the ends trailing down her dress and pretended her nipples poking through her dress were from cold.

They had supper in the private dining room upstairs at the pub next door, with only one of the few wooden tables in the room set for four. Evan and Robert both wore plain black jackets and trousers, unlike their colorful ballroom attire. Beth chose a mauve gown that flattered her, as always sporting a decidedly lower neckline than Althea.

After dinner, she and Evan remained in the room

while Beth and Robert made exaggerated yawns as they left, leaving Althea to realize she really ought to have asked Beth for more details about her day out. She wondered if either she or Evan would hear noises from a neighboring room later.

Or both of us if we're in the same place. No! Focus.

She turned her attention to Evan. "My lor—Evan. What did you think of the various shops, given your knowledge of investments?"

He sat back, whisky glass perched on his leg in one hand. "Ah, we'll get right down to it, eh? I shall warn you, I have had a superb idea, and it will not come cheap. Are you prepared for a steeper price?"

Gads. He's making me agree aloud, so I cannot say I was coerced. She could not bring herself to care. In fact, she wasn't sure which she wanted more—the advice or the tariff.

Her gaze held his as she nodded. "I am."

A satisfied smile flitted across his face before he sobered again. "My thoughts mirrored yours. While I don't know the details of ink or other goods' quality, I found the overall atmosphere, pricing, and level of service at each location in line with your evaluation of the offerings."

Althea was immediately drawn back to her excitement as she left the second-to-last shop. "I need to assess who I want to compete against, but also the cost of finding shop space in the various parts of town. My preliminary plan was based on average rents from the paper when I was here last."

"Hmm."

She arched a brow at him, knowing he was

drawing out the anticipation for his *superb idea*.

"I was thinking... Two of the shops, the Stall Street location and the one near the Crescent with the proprietress, are larger than the others. But they don't seem to carry more inventory. Do you agree?"

She tilted her head, picturing the two shops. "Mayhap a bit more, but not much. Instead, they use the space to display their goods in a pleasing way. London is so cramped; I could never afford to do that."

"Right, but you sell plenty. And you group different products in the same scent to promote larger purchases, do you not?"

"Yes, I keep excess inventory in the back room, in order to set up displays for maximizing sales. But I'm not looking to help my competitors. Why do you ask about this?"

"What if you chose one as your partner?"

She threw up her hands. "Ah! There you go again. I don't want a partner. You know this."

"No, not investor, not an equity partner. More of a...sharing space type of agreement."

"Oh?" Her brow furrowed in confusion. She could not imagine it, but she could see from Evan's expression he'd deduced much of it already, and she was eager to hear his idea.

"What if you picked the north shop, the one closest to your quality and offerings, but with different scents and better inks."

She nodded, gesturing for him to continue.

"You could agree on scents that complimented each other. Even mayhap make some shampoos in *her* scents." He leaned forward, his words coming faster with his enthusiasm.

Althea leaned in as well, her chest rising and falling, mouth dropping open in excitement. *This man's brain.* Lud, how she wished she had the opportunity to learn more about him. But there be dragons.

"You get some shelf space in the store here, and she gets shelf space at your store in London. Limited product offerings, so that you do not have competing items, but I think it could be hugely profitable with much less capital needed to start up."

"Ohh…" Althea's voice trailed into breath in wonder. She stared at him, flushed with pleasure and excitement. *This is almost as good as the orgasm he gave me.* She giggled at the random thought.

Evan looked at her sharply. "What's funny?"

Her eyes widened. Lud, she'd laughed out loud. Hopefully, he was not offended, but if she admitted her thoughts, he'd realize where half her attention had been focused during the trip.

On the other hand, they were away from London, away from the Season. Slowly, she held his eyes and sat back, knowing her nipples were hard, her chest flushed, and her breathing fast. "I love the idea. I find this quite exciting. Mayhap even better than sex."

****

Evan stared at her. He'd had a hard time keeping his hands and lips off her the entire trip, envisioning her laid out on the table in the back room of her shop. In Bath, that beautiful brain of hers had spun him even higher.

He'd already been contemplating what remuneration to demand. To have her goad him after his repeated challenges was more than he could have hoped for. He knew she knew what she was offering, from her steady gaze to the deliberate arch of her back, offering her breasts with their deliciously pointed tips begging for his teeth.

He took a deep breath to steady himself and shook his head, firming his lips in mock consternation. "I thought you'd learned that sex can top just about anything." He shook his head in mock sadness. "This is why I offered my terms. It seems another lesson is in order. And look, we have another convenient table."

The pub staff had been in to clear dinner after Beth and Robert left, delivering his whisky and a sherry that Althea had not yet touched.

Now she grabbed it and took a gulp.

He appreciated the courage required to make the tacit dare and understood her nervousness. After her second sip, he stood and took the glass from her, then set both of their drinks aside to pull her to her feet.

Running his hands down her arms, thumbs skimming the sides of those pert, heaving breasts, he watched her skin pebble behind his touch.

He raised a hand, palm facing her. "One moment."

He released her and strode to lock the door. As he returned, he pulled out his cravat pin and yanked the neckcloth open.

Reaching her, he cupped the back of her head and placed his other hand at her hip to hold her tight as his lips descended on hers.

Her low moan reverberated through his mouth into his chest. He nearly shuddered in response, amazed at how aroused he could get from a dare, a kiss, and a moan. He who was so jaded and had done most of what two—or three or four—people could do together…many times.

Turning her from where she stood in front of the chair she had occupied, he gripped her waist, lifted her the few inches onto the table, and spread her legs to step between them.

Her eyes pleaded for another kiss, so he obliged.

Sherry and Althea made a heady combination. Her unique mix-of-apothecary scent encircled him, intoxicating him more than whisky ever had. Part of him contemplated reckless behavior, tearing aside her clothes and thrusting into her there and then. But as bold as she'd been, she was still remarkably innocent for a widow, and he needed to woo her. His jaded half laughed at his desire to make their first time special.

He drew back, took a deep breath to regain his equilibrium, and arched a brow, proclaiming, "You do realize that because the other lessons did not work, this one will have to be more thorough?"

She'd begged for his cock last time, and he could not bear to wait another night to give it to her, but he was determined to stretch this encounter out and make it beyond amazing for her. He desired more time with her, despite the fact that neither of them wanted forever.

Her eyes brightened and breath caught, but she placed a hand on his lapel. "Please, I do not want to get pregnant."

He admired her for speaking her concerns about a subject society considered taboo. His own family situation meant he was always prepared. He nodded. "Trust me, Althea. I will take care of you."

When she returned his nod and dropped her arm, he let out a breath he didn't know he'd been holding, relieved at obtaining permission. The trick would be drawing it out for her without torturing himself for too long.

His hands slid up from her waist to her ribs, and his thumbs brushed her nipples, back and forth through her dress.

Her eyes fluttered closed, and her head angled back.

He dragged her dress off one shoulder, taking her head tilt as an invitation to run his lips from beneath her ear to along her collarbone.

Damn me, she's delicious. Whether 'tis shampoo or perfume or her, he wanted to run his nose along every inch of her, then his lips, then his teeth.

He laid her back and tugged her dress farther down until her breast popped out. Her ample breasts on such a slender frame awed and gratified him every time. His head lowered, and he caught the tip between his teeth and flicked his tongue over it.

She squirmed beneath him, her hands clutching his jacket.

"Too...many...clothes," she panted out.

"Ah no, sweet. I am just warming you up. I need a bed for the main lesson." He gritted his teeth at the thought. His trousers were so tight it felt like all his blood was in his cock, leaving none in his limbs for even the short walk to the guesthouse.

He straightened and placed each of her feet on a chair, leaving a third seat behind him. His hands slid up the insides of her legs, gathering her skirt on his wrists before tossing it back to expose her. With the wind whipping off the River Avon at night, she wore an extra petticoat and pantaloons. He dragged the underwear down and gripped the top of her thighs. His thumbs spread her nether lips.

Her eyes closed, and she turned her head to the side, pink rising on her cheek.

"You are gorgeous, love. Don't be embarrassed. I could look at you"—he stroked a thumb down her open folds—"and pet you all night."

She opened her eyes to peek at him eagerly.

He laughed. "If you look at me like that, I might think you were faking needing a lesson."

Her lashes lowered, and she produced an extravagant yawn.

"I thought so. Right then, let's make sure you are warm for the walk back to the guesthouse, as you'll not be wearing drawers." He folded her undergarment as small as possible and stuffed them into his breast pocket, pouffing them out to look like a dandy's handkerchief and smiling in anticipation.

She watched him with a furrow of concern between her brows.

Reaching around, he picked up his whisky glass and sat on the chair he'd left between her legs.

When she started to rise to her elbows, he put a hand to her sternum and urged her back down. "No, lay still. I am going to enjoy my after-dinner drink."

She lay back, legs twitching once in discomfort from being exposed.

He dipped a finger in the amber liquid and ran it around her nub then down to her opening, then repeated the action twice more.

After a gasp, she lay still.

He grinned. Her lips were more swollen and a darker rose than when he'd first lifted her skirt. Leaning in, he licked and slurped the whisky from her. Mmm. The liquor and salty flavor of her arousal made a tasty combination. Mayhap his new favorite drink. As her hips lifted to follow his lips, he drew back and flattened her again.

"Patience." He dipped a finger, then swirled. Dipped, swirled. Needing to taste her again, he sucked the burgeoning nub, then licked again, pushing the ever-harder nub against his front teeth as he searched for every last drop of Scotch.

"Evan, please." Her hands clutched his hair, holding him close.

"Please what? Did you want to talk more about the partnership with an apothecary here?" He barely held in his chuckle.

"Wha-what?" Althea seemed to have lost the thread.

His cheeks were going to ache from incessant grinning. This was beyond fun. "I seem to recall you saying that was as good as sex."

"Ugh, no. What was I thinking? I was so wrong, so wrong. You win. Evan, *please.*" She tugged on his hair.

"The more you pull my hair, the slower this will be. We're not leaving until I finish my whisky. And you're not going over until you're in my bed." *I think.* He shifted the iron rod in his trousers to a slightly less uncomfortable angle. It was a good thing he'd arranged for a private dining room.

Her hands landed with a splat on the table, and he stifled a snort of laughter.

Dip. Swirl. Suck. Lick.

Her hands twitched.

His cock responded with a lurch.

"Ah dammit, I can't wait any longer." He threw back the Scotch and rose. "Let's go."

****

For the half block walk, Althea attempted to weigh the pros and cons. She was a widow, yes, but also a business owner. She knew she could not sully her reputation without her shop being at risk. But they were in Bath, and Evan, while being known as a libertine, was well-connected and well-liked throughout the Ton. He could help put any gossip aside.

But her self-confidence struggled. Why was he doing this? He could have any woman he wanted with a crook of his finger. Certainly his choices had to be better than a sheltered, rather uptight widow. She was going to embarrass herself.

Her body didn't care. The craving he awakened in her simply sitting across the table or walking the streets of Bath with her was beyond anything she could have imagined. His intimate touches opened a whole other world to her, and she needed to know the rest, even if he walked away after tonight.

She shied away from that thought, not liking it or her reaction to his theoretical departure. Was she coming to care for him? If he ended things, would she be hurt?

She could not settle on any one thought, and by the time they'd entered the guesthouse, she'd stopped trying. She only knew that she needed his naked body against hers and damn the consequences.

Evan had her in such a state, she'd been ready to start unlacing her gown as soon as they turned the stairs out of sight of the lobby, but she resisted, clinging to his hand as they ascended. They tried his room first, but hearing banging from the room across the hall, they continued on up the stairs.

Althea grinned when Evan's cheeks ruddied and he bit out, "Ah, Ford does leather work, mayhap he's working."

She rather thought it sounded like a bedframe against the wall and breathed a sigh of guilt-ridden relief. She should probably worry about Beth's behavior, but at least no one would be on the ladies' floor to hear her own bed knocking.

Finally, they gained her room, and she turned as he dismissed the maid and locked the door.

She stepped into him, gasping again, "Evan, please."

He threaded uncaring fingers through her updo and cradled her head as his lips slanted over hers.

As he obliged her unclear request for a kiss, she pushed at his jacket and progressed to his waistcoat buttons, fumbling in her haste.

He laid his hand over hers, and she sighed into his mouth before dropping her head in embarrassment.

"I can't imagine you've undressed a man very often. I'm happy to have you practice on me, but mayhap another time. I need you too urgently right now. If you'll allow me?" His voice was soft, reassuring.

She nodded and watched him, eyes darting to each patch of skin unveiled as his waistcoat disappeared. His throat, a strong muscled column with his Adam's apple bobbing when he spoke or swallowed. His wrists as he undid the cuffs of his shirt, covered in that same gold-colored hair that she loved. Then his chest, as the shirt came off as well.

Her fingers reached, tentative. He took her hand and brought it to his chest before dropping his arms to his sides to allow her to explore.

And explore she did, with both hands now, up his chest to his shoulders, rounded with muscles, down his arms to the light dusting of gilded hair before skimming to his nipples. When she circled them and flicked her finger over the tip, he groaned and grabbed her hips.

"Turn around, Althea."

He had her out of her clothes in record time. She smirked. *Another advantage of being with a rake.*

"On the bed, please."

She climbed on and shivered at the cool sheets against her heated flesh. It should had been chilly walking back without drawers, but she hadn't noticed at all.

"Are you warm enough?"

"Gads yes, I feel as though I might burst into flame."

"Excellent, that was my first goal."

His first—

His actions distracted her from finishing that thought. Leaving two candles burning by the bed, he stripped his remaining clothes off.

He stretched out next to her and skimmed his hand down her body. Her thighs slid open. When his finger dipped into her channel and retracted to circle her nub, just as he'd done with the whisky, her hips arched.

Withdrawing, he reclined. "D'you know, I may have been going about this wrong." Her head had turned to watch him, and he smiled. "I have been teaching by demonstrating. But there is no better way to learn than by doing something yourself." He gestured down his body. "Why don't you give it a try?"

She sat up, all her brave desire to explore and taste

him deserting her. *Give* what *a try? I have no idea what to do. I am going to disappoint him.*

Despite her marriage, she was a novice. "Uh, I think I need more teaching."

"Come now, you had your hands on me a few minutes ago, and I saw you licking your lips. You can do this. I shall help." He gestured. "Straddle me."

Oh. Yes, please. She threw one leg over and settled her weight on his upper thighs.

"I very much enjoyed your touch on my chest," he said. "What else would you like to touch? I am at your disposal."

Her gaze dropped to the swollen stalk pointing up his belly from almost between her legs. She imagined she could feel the heat from it radiating toward her core. Her fingers slid, smoothing inch by inch down his stomach, feeling his muscles twitch at her touch. Finally, her fist curled around his cock and tightened involuntarily at the heady combination of smooth and soft over hard and hot.

Evan grunted, and his hips jerked, the rod in her hand twitching.

She glanced up to check if she'd hurt him, but he smiled and nodded at her, banked amber flames flickering in his eyes as he watched her.

"Oh." She slid her hand up and down experimenting, a wan imitation of what she'd seen him do in her shop's back room.

"*Yes.* You're an excellent student." Evan's words hissed through clenched teeth as he threw his head back.

Marvelous. It seems I can affect him as he does me. What else has he done that I liked?

Remembering, she licked her lips. She didn't think she'd need whisky to enjoy this, she'd been waiting so long. Saliva pooled in her mouth, and her breasts ached for friction.

She scooted down his legs, not caring that she left a trail of moisture along his thigh where her folds brushed. She wanted to rub her nipples on his leg hair, but 'twas his turn. She was several orgasms ahead of him in their interludes to date.

Holding his cock away from his belly, she stared at it. It looked enormous up close, and she had no idea what she could fit in her mouth, but she desperately wanted to try.

Tentative, she licked from where her thumb held the base all the way up to the tip then swirled her tongue around to capture the liquid seeping from this silk-covered iron rod.

Salty, but interesting. She wanted more.

After licking around the head once again, she slid her lips over it and down until he hit her throat.

"Damn me, Althea. So good. You don't have to. Please." His head tipped down, the flames in his gaze no longer banked.

She suspected Evan wasn't sure what he wanted to say, but she ignored him anyway. 'Twas her time, her toy. He'd had his.

She sucked and pulled, pushed and licked, up and down until he grabbed her hair to hold her still. She whimpered, her mouth wet and open. Her breath stuttered, her breasts were unbearably sensitive and swollen, and a surge of heat dampened her core, saturating his leg.

"No more. I want to come inside you, sweet."

She sat up quickly, and he chuckled. But when she tried to dismount, he grabbed her thigh and held her in place.

Oh. What now? She watched him eagerly.

With his other hand, he grabbed a small finely woven sock off the bedside table. It appeared to have a tiny ribbon garter at the top.

She stared as he pulled it over his cock. Not a sock. A cock sock? She didn't care what it was called. He was protecting her as he'd promised.

At his beckoning, she rose to her knees and scooted forward. He held the base of his cock with one hand and ran a finger through her folds to spread her wetness around her opening. She held her breath, the warm bath of pleasure washing over her skin as he strummed her higher.

Then he urged her down with his hand back on her thigh, and she groaned as his tip breeched her.

"Tell me if I hurt you or 'tis uncomfortable in any way," Evan grunted out, remaining still. His hands urged her hips downward an inch before falling to her thighs to let her take him at her own pace.

She sank, slowly at first, then thrust down to impale herself on him. "My word, Evan. It never felt like this with—"

Althea bit her lip, belatedly realizing it was assuredly terribly poor etiquette to refer to past relationships of any kind.

But Evan seemed to understand. "You needed the right teacher. Now, please, Althea. Move."

She rose and fell, rose and fell. His cock felt huge inside of her, stretching her walls, dragging along sensitive nerve endings. But the ecstasy wasn't rising like it had under his hand.

Then he grabbed her bottom and angled her toward him. Her swollen bud scraped against his pubic bone.

"Oh!" *Even in this position, the expert guides and controls me. Amazing.* She stopped thinking and focused on the friction she'd been craving. Inside, outside, everything was bathed in heat and the fire burned hotter with each plunge.

He threw his head back, gritting his teeth. "Again."

She rose and fell. Her hips tilted, and she lost control. Her movements sped up, her hips circling and jerking as she raced up the mountain, her sole focus on the crest.

Evan held her hips more gently and watched her intently. She was dimly aware that his attention was also on her pleasure rather than his own, but she could not concentrate enough to worry that no one was ensuring his enjoyment.

Her downward thrusts became faster and rougher, their skin slapping together. With each plunge, Evan's stomach muscles contracted.

Oh good. That spot feels as good to him as it does to me.

Finally, on one particularly hard thrust, she keened, on the precipice.

His hand shifted to where they joined, thumb gently squeezing her already-spasming nub.

Her hips made small rocking motions against his hand, his cock hitting something equally pleasurable inside her, until everything exploded. She screamed, her eyes clenched shut, and she drove down on him to hold still as her muscles spasmed around him. Her fingers dug into his chest to cling to him through the storm.

As the pleasure waned, she drooped over him, belatedly opening her eyes to find his. He was watching her, waiting patiently but with tightened jaw. Only when she straightened a few inches did he grab her hips tightly and drive up into her once, twice, before groaning and twisting under her with his own orgasm.

Althea wilted onto him again, feeling the aftershocks of both of their orgasms. As her head hit the pillow next to his, she whispered, "I hope you have lots more advice for me, my lord."

Chapter Twelve

For three days, the four of them explored Bath, walking the neighborhoods around the two apothecaries Althea chose as her first and second choice to partner with. At breakfast, Evan helped her run numbers for various partnership scenarios, with different stores, levels of inventory, and product lines. Although *helped* might be exaggerating. He felt more like an audience than an adviser, as she seemed to have the matter well in hand. At dinner each evening, they hashed out pros and cons of partnerships. They tried to guess what any concerns or requests would be and formulated responses.

At night, he gave Althea a tally of his recommendations and informed her of his expected compensation. Sometimes, he demanded full access to her body, others he preferred that she return his attentions as he reclined and enjoyed.

For all his worldly past, he was continually shocked at how new everything felt. Each time was more explosive, more elevated than the last. Afterward they lay facing each other and talked until sleep pulled them under. They'd taken turns peeling the layers of their lives away.

The third night, he dared confide in her about his mother.

"We spoke briefly about my mother's memory.

Her condition is hereditary. Her father suffered from it also. And she likely passed it on to me. I have roughly another decade or two safely."

"I cannot imagine the difficulty of living with that knowledge." Reaching for his hand, she squeezed it, the simple connection feeling more intimate than the acts they'd engaged in for the last hour.

"Given my struggles with Mama, I cannot find it in myself to put a wife or children through that."

"I understand." She nodded against the pillow, her hair a blot of black ink against the pillow in the dark room. "But what of the earldom, given what you told me of your cousin?"

"I do not know yet. I have my solicitors looking into it, and as I said, I have a decade to solve that issue."

They were silent for a few minutes.

"On a lighter note, will you tell me about your membership to Sarah Potter's club?"

He chuckled, relieved at the change of subject.

"I like trying new things. New foods, new places, new positions. When we found that after our wild university days, it was a great way to learn new ideas from professionals. And it has certainly helped enhance my party games."

"But you've never seemed interested in spanking me…" She trailed off uncertainly.

"Is that something you'd like to try?" Evan asked, running a hand down her cheek.

"I am not sure. I guess I'll try anything once, but it does not hold a particular appeal. I assumed it did for you, given your membership."

"My membership there is more about networking

and finding new people, new interests, even new business ventures. You'd be surprised how much work gets done there. Sometimes more than White's."

"So no spanking will be required. I must say I am relieved."

"Mayhap 'tis something we should try. If you find you enjoy it, I'd be happy to oblige. Everyone has their favorite parts of sex. Mine is discovering my partner's preferences and then finding new ways to deliver those."

"You don't have particular tastes of your own?"

"You misunderstand. I get more pleasure out of delivering a new experience, but one still tailored to the tastes of the woman—or man—I'm with."

Her eyebrows ticked up. "You've been with men?" At his nod, she continued, "But as you are here with me, does that mean you prefer women?"

"Honestly, I've never cared. It was more about the individual and the fun to be had. But"—he shrugged the shoulder he wasn't lying on—"now, I find I simply prefer *you*." He leaned in and sipped on her lips until she pulled free.

"What do you think my favorite parts of sex are?"

"Are you ready to admit you like to watch?"

She ducked her head, and he knew she was blushing despite not being able to see her skin pinken in the dark. "'Tis shameful."

"Not if those you are watching prefer to be watched. Hence that last ball."

"Oh." Her breath gusted in a sigh over his throat. "Now I see what you mean about your taste. That experience was titillating on its own, but you built on it and made it even more exciting. For me, at least."

175

He heard a quiet giggle, and the bed shook. "You find it funny that I gave you three orgasms before I got any, do you?"

She laughed harder.

"'Tis quite all right. You can make it up to me now." He rolled her to her back.

She leaned up to meet his kiss, and he growled his hunger into her mouth. An idea sparked, and he pulled back, shifting his knees under him to lean over her.

"Let us test your preference about spanking."

"What?" Her eyes widened in alarm.

He smirked and sat back. "Roll over. On your hands and knees."

"Evan…"

"Trust me not to hurt you." He almost added *please*, but it rather belied the point of a spanking to beg to administer it.

Eyeing him warily, she rolled over and rose to her knees.

Smoothing his hand over her bottom, he again admired the creamy skin, so pale in the dim light from one candle and the night sky through the open curtains. Her dark hair cascaded over her upper back, a perfect contrast. His hand looked tanned and broad against her lithe form. Raising it slowly, he watched her bottom tense for impact and waited. He wanted this to be fun, not painful, and tense muscles would make it hurt more.

When she took a breath and relaxed, he aimed for the fleshiest part of her arse, scooping under to angle upward. The resulting smack was sharper than the true impact.

She jolted but did not yell.

His hand barely stung, and he held it aloft, again

checking her reaction.

After a moment, she wriggled her bottom once.

Perfect. The small bite of pain has become a burn of pleasure.

Aloud, he warned her, "Ah. The universal sign for more. I shall be happy to oblige."

His hand swooped down again, directed at her other cheek. The need for her boiled in him. He could not wait any longer for the slide of her skin against his, her now-warm bottom nestled against his groin as he brought them both satisfaction.

Before she could process her reaction to the second spank, he grabbed another sheath and covered his cock, and surged up to slide home.

"Evan." His name was a hushed gasp from her lips.

They had not yet tried this position, so he probably should have warned her. No, there was no should in sex, other than making sure one's partner was pleased by every action.

"Yes, Althea?"

"You're so deep."

His cock throbbed inside her, and his response was guttural. "Is that a good thing?"

"Lud, yes. Move, please."

"We haven't finished the lesson." He grinned at the back of her head and spanked each of her arse cheeks once more.

He was rewarded with another gasp and wriggle. "Oh my."

He withdrew slowly, then thrust fast and hard.

Althea lowered onto her elbows and grabbed a pillow. She screamed into it before shoving back against him.

He repeated his slow glide out, quick thrust in, knowing her reaction would be even more extreme given the angle she'd just created with her drop.

A long squeak erupted from the pillow.

Grabbing her hip, he abandoned his spanking lesson. Instead, he gathered most of her hair in a fist, arching her back farther, and drove his hips faster.

He listened to her sounds from the pillow, swallowing back his orgasm. Finally, unable to stand it any longer, he released her hair, planted one hand on the bed beside her, and reached the other around to tap her nub.

She convulsed, her back undulating while her arse plunged back at him in erratic strokes. Her little button hardened and quivered under his finger and her channel throbbed around him.

Grasping her to him, he plunged twice more, hot lust surging up as her inner muscles squeezed his release from him.

More sated than he could ever remember being, Evan collapsed to his side, drawing her with him so they spooned, and tamped down his concerns about losing her, about what would happen in London, or Cheltenham, or a decade.

****

How was I so bored by any and all forms of copulation, with anyone I wanted, man or woman, only a month ago?

Evan could barely look at Althea without his cock rising in his breeches for all to see. He could barely kiss her without leaking in his drawers. For all his knowledge of the most lascivious acts, it was the simple touches that undid him when she was the one touching.

The most intimate lovemaking with her body sliding against his.

But where would it lead? She still needed investment money, and he was as reluctant to mix business and pleasure as she was. Neither of them wanted to marry, albeit for very different reasons. A part of him still wondered if she was trying to incite him to gift her the money rather than asking for a stake in the business. Her business acumen stimulated his mind—and sometimes his cock—as much as her figure aroused his body. A cunning woman might have thought that was a way forward, using one of the few tools that society allowed women.

Sometimes, he was tempted to give her the funds she needed. If he squinted enough, he could argue it was like his first investment—negotiating for strawberries and a kiss or, now, shampoo and sex. He always ended up talking himself out of it, though, wary after too many requests in recent years.

A note had arrived from Greenborough Park, reminding him that his myriad investments needed monitoring. He also wanted to check on how the new nurse was doing with his mother. And he needed to show his smiling, carefree façade in London to maintain his reputation as the blithe rake with more money than sense. Constantly scared the gossips of the Ton would become too curious and look at his family, he liked to ensure he created enough gossip, whether spending money lavishly, dabbling in the demi-monde, or whatever else he could think up, to ensure the focus was squarely on him.

His time in Bath with Althea was at an end. She was meeting with Emily Anders, the owner of her first-choice shop, near The Royal Crescent. They had not talked about what was next. Nor had he asked Ford whether he'd return to Cheltenham or follow Beth to London.

Mayhap a break would give them time to consider what they wanted. Althea could check on her London shop, and he could find a solution for her investment needs. When she was near him, he had trouble focusing on anything other than the next lesson he wanted to teach her about the pleasures of the flesh.

He looked up from the hall table in the guesthouse as the door opened. Althea swept in, her expression triumphant. He knew before she said it that the local shop owner had been interested in a partnership.

She plopped down in the chair across from him. "Evan, it was amazing. She was so flattered by my interest in her inks and other products. And I had to leave three bottles of shampoo with her, so that she could try the different scents for herself and her lover."

He raised his eyebrows. "You had one of your scents for men with you?"

"Yes, but she didn't want that."

Interesting. He'd worried that a male shop owner's interest in a partnership might involve attraction to Althea, given her beauty, but he hadn't considered this scenario. No matter. In either, he'd already thought of ways they could use it to their advantage. And it was clear the shop was well-managed and the partnership had a basis in good business.

"Right, then. What's next? Did you both identify the products you want to swap, or are there other items you'll need to ship for her to test and vice versa?"

"Other than the shampoo, which she'd never heard

of, we have agreed on the products. She will send her shop's turnover figures with me tomorrow, so we can each estimate inventory we'll want. Then I will know the investment I require. I hope obtaining that funding and organizing the necessary paperwork will be quick?" She tilted her head at him in question.

Evan's lips flattened. Despite her reference to paperwork, she seemed to be asking him how quickly he would get her funds and how formal he'd want the documentation to be. His answer was brief and vague. "I will help you with organizing. I am sure it can be expedited."

"Oh good. Oh, Evan"—she grabbed his hand where it sat in a clenched fist on the table, not noticing as she petted him in excitement—"I am thrilled with this solution. I cannot thank you enough." She bit her lip. "Although, I am sure I could try, given what I've learned." Her lashes swept down, then up.

Evan's groin tightened as his fist loosened. He'd figure out the next steps tomorrow. Tonight was for celebrating.

****

Evan woke early the next day. Given the close quarters, and their distance from London, they'd given up any attempts at secrecy from their staff or Ford and Beth days ago.

He lounged in bed as Althea directed her maid to pack her trunk, waiting to see if she'd say something about their future to him. He regretted the need for maneuvering, waiting to see if she'd speak first, but not enough to bring the subject up himself. Frankly, he still didn't know what he wanted. Letting her decide seemed the best course of action.

As her maid folded clothes, Althea perched beside him where he sat propped against the pillows, covers in his lap below a naked chest. Flicking his nipple with a nail, she smirked. "Mayhap 'tis time to dress, my lord?"

He caught her hand and brought it to his lips. "I thought you preferred me without clothes?"

"I do." She sighed, lowering her head.

He braced himself mentally.

Peering up at him through her lashes, she said, "'Tis our last day here. You haven't told me where you're going."

"You have voiced concerns over rumors affecting your business."

"Yes. And those haven't changed." She looked down at their still-joined hands, then back up at him. "I was wondering…if you came to London and kept a low profile, I could give you a key to the back door of my house?"

"Ah, so I shall be your dirty little secret?" What was he saying? And why did he feel hurt at her offer? 'Twas the perfect opportunity to extend their relationship with no commitment. He mentally rolled his eyes at his mawkishness.

Her lower lip jutted out. "No. Well, yes. I guess so. I'd come to you, but 'tis so much harder for women to roam about undetected and so much higher risk if we're caught. You know this."

"I do." He rallied his emotions. "I was teasing you. We can do that for a little while and see how it goes. I must go to Greenborough Park, though, at least for a sennight."

"Oh." He could not help his thrill at the disappointment in her voice, particularly after being told he'd have to sneak around because she didn't want to be seen with him.

"And eventually, I will have to be visible in London. I have investments to maintain, and relationships, Parliamentary and otherwise, to nurture."

She frowned.

"Not sexual ones, my sweet. I assure you our exchanges take all my focus."

She mumbled under her breath and appeared worried, but the maid was finished packing and they needed to start their day.

Evan gestured and Althea stood, providing a modicum of a shield from the maid as he pulled his clothes on to return to his room and see to his own packing.

As they said their good-byes and he saw the ladies into their London-bound carriage, he reminded himself that a short casual affair could hurt Althea's business but was no skin off his nose. Why, then, was he still irked by her request for secrecy?

****

As Ford snoozed against the squabs across from him, Evan stared out the window and pondered Althea's need for money, balanced with their relationship. Despite hours of cogitations, he was no closer to a solution when they arrived at his estate.

It was late enough that he did not want to disturb his mother, so he sent a note to Nancy that he'd visit in the morning, and he and Ford settled in the library with a cold supper and whisky.

Trying to avoid rehashing his thoughts from the drive, Evan opened his mouth to heckle Robert about Beth, only to have Robert beat him to it.

"Will you see the lovely widow Egerton again?"

Evan narrowed his eyes at his friend but carefully kept his relaxed countenance, one elbow leaning on the chair arm, legs crossed with one swinging. "Will you see the bubbly Miss Jenkins again?"

"Eh." Ford shrugged one shoulder. "I wouldn't say no, but that girl has a mind of her own, so 'twill be her choice."

"Ford, we've been over this. You know you have much to give, right, old chap?"

Another hitch of the shoulder was his only reply.

"And any woman, titled or no, would be lucky to have you?"

Robert nodded but would not meeting his eyes.

"Beth seems particularly suited to you," Evan persisted, "as she cares little for the Ton's unending rules."

Ford mumbled something into his glass as he sipped whisky.

Evan raised his brows. "What was that?"

"She's rather high profile, ain't she?"

Ah. And therein lies the rub. Shakespeare aside, Evan pondered. "Why d'you think that is?"

A mumbled, "Dunno."

"Her connections are unparalleled. And you know that is high praise from me, given my own. But hers are quieter and include working class networks. I don't think that is it." The parallels between Ford's and Althea's concerns were undeniable, and Evan suspected the reasons were similar.

Ford finally met his gaze with questions in his eyes.

"I suspect that her unconventional upbringing and,

er, interest in sex make her conspicuous, don't you?" Evan asked. Althea's underlying fear was business whereas Ford had dreaded attention from his peers since his childhood, but both abhorred the idea of society's focus turning to them.

"Hadn't thought about it."

Evan raised a skeptical brow but let the comment slide. "If 'tis that, it seems as though there is a simple enough solution."

He waited.

Ford frowned as he chewed a bite of meat and cheese dabbed with mustard. He swallowed. "What's that?"

"Fulfill her sexual needs in private, and she won't be on the hunt in public."

His friend choked, despite having consumed the food already.

"Mmm. Ta, Bags. Ever so helpful." He rolled his eyes at Evan.

Evan chuckled.

But Ford's next words sobered him. "You haven't answered my question. Will you see the widow again? Are you investing in her business? It certainly seemed like you had a specific interest in it down in Bath."

It all poured out. "She daren't risk a dalliance for the scandal. Rumors could hurt her business given that her clientele are the ladies of the Ton."

"Is an affair what you want?"

Evan glared at him, bringing both feet to the ground and leaning his elbows on his knees. "What else?"

"You seem particularly well matched."

"Bah, Ford. You aren't implying that I'd consider

marrying her? You know how I feel about marriage. Or should you accompany me tomorrow to see Mother again?" He was practically spitting the words now, angry at the unfairness of it all. "I will never subject loved ones to that, nor shall I risk a loveless marriage with the threat of dementia in my future. Besides, she doesn't want to marry again either. Which doesn't leave me with much choice in the matter."

"Oh, please. You have talked more women—and a few men—out of their knickers when you've put your mind to it. You've wooed the toughest opponents in Parliament to your views. And you've negotiated the best financial terms I've ever heard on any number of investments. If 'twas simply her wishes, we would not be having this discussion."

Evan nodded. "You're right. 'Tis my reservations more than anything." He hoped that would end the conversation, but Ford wasn't done.

"Have you heard from your solicitor or the investigator?"

"No, but that reminds me. I haven't even looked at the post since we arrived." Evan stood and crossed to his desk to shuffle through the pile of correspondence there. Finding a missive from his barrister, he dropped the rest and returned to the small table with their repast.

Breaking the seal, he scanned the note. He took a fortifying gulp of whisky and read it again more slowly. It held terrible news, made worse by Ford's prodding. He'd hoped there was another heir or another way. How did every other Peer of the Realm have family coming out of the woodwork looking for an inheritance, and he had only one cousin? One who was avaricious at best.

"What is it, man?"

"They could not find anyone else. No relations other than my profligate cousin. No children who might come of age before I turn fifty and likely lose my mind. Nothing. No one. Not even a female relative I could try to direct it to with court paperwork."

"So even if he doesn't spend through the fortune you'll leave, it all dies with him anyway, unless he has a child in the future?"

Evan nodded, slumping in his chair, dropping his forehead into his hand.

Ford shrugged and gave his words back to him. "It seems there is a simple enough solution. You marry and beget an heir."

****

Evan visited the dower house the next day. Cautiously hopeful when he found his mother lucid, he regaled her with stories from his trip to Bath, expounding on Althea's expansion plans.

Halfway through, she roused. "Who is Althea? Is she the little brown-haired girl who visited me?"

Excited at her memory of recent events, Evan leaned forward. "No, that was Beth. Althea was the tall dark-haired cousin."

"Oh." His mother frowned in confusion.

Knowing how fragile her hold on the present was, he veered the conversation toward what she remembered. "Beth and Robert seem interested in one another. I am hopeful they will end up together."

Rose nodded. "But Evan, dear, what about you? I want to see you married and settled happily. None of us are getting any younger."

Evan hung his head. He couldn't say that he didn't want to end up in her chair, with his child sitting across from him hoping to be recognized.

His mother patted his hand. "Tell me more about Althea."

And so he did, promising to bring her some shampoo. His mother dozed off as he talked, not unusual these past few months, and he sighed in pleasure that she'd been truly with him this visit.

Despite his mother's inattention, he liked talking about Althea. There was so much to admire, mayhap to lov— No. That would be dangerous. She'd come to him for money, and he did not mix business and pleasure. For one moment, he contemplated winning her over and having her forever before he shook his head to clear it of the impossible vision. Ford should mind his own affairs. Besides, Althea had made it very clear she had no interest in losing her independence to marriage.

Leaving Rose to nod, he stopped in the kitchen where Nancy was helping the house servant prepare a simple supper.

"Sounded like a good visit, my lord?"

"Yes. How has she been, and how are you faring?"

"'Tis grand here. So beautiful. Your mother is a love. There've been a few tantrums, and I know her struggles will increase. But I appreciate the work, and 'tis nothing I haven't done before. Please do not worry yourself, Lord Cheltenham. She is in good hands."

"Thank you, Miss Lincoln. I shall return tomorrow."

His mother did not recognize him the rest of the week, one day reacting in fear to a stranger in her home, other days thinking he was his father or a family friend and wondering where her little boy was.

Evan was wrung out by the end of it and in awe at

the nurse's sustained equilibrium. He tried to emulate it, telling himself his mother was mostly lost to him, and he simply needed to provide the best care for her physical shell. But that made him unendingly sad.

London felt like an escape as he sat back in the carriage with a sigh, Ford in his usual position facing him. His trickle of relief at departing brought on guilt, despite conversations with his mother early in the disease's onset where she'd encouraged him to live his life and rest happy that she had loved hers.

As the house grew smaller in the distance behind them, he remembered the quandaries that had plagued him on his last carriage ride. None had been resolved, and in fact, his choices were more limited than before given the results of the investigation. More than ever, he knew he ought to marry. However, even on his most optimistic days, he hated the idea of his wife or child left dealing with his body when his brain was lost. After this most recent visit, the day was not one of his more hopeful.

Not ready to tackle that problem, even as he recognized that he was procrastinating, Evan turned his thoughts to Althea. *Do I give her the funds outright?*

An image of her walking away from him, money in hand, and spurning his attentions rose in his mind. He refused to be taken advantage of, even for such a paltry sum. The investment and their relationship must stay separate, but he'd promised to speed the process along.

Who else will invest the capital she needs without an equity stake, so I can keep her in my bed?

She had not yet committed to accepting any male investor. He needed a plan and his very best negotiating skills.

Chapter Thirteen

Althea bounced on her toes in excitement. Evan had sent a note around saying he had arrived in Town and would call on her late that night. She should leave the back door open.

Waiting for him to give guidance on paperwork had been agony. She'd visited her solicitor as soon as she'd arrived and wanted Evan's opinion on the drafted documents for the partnership she'd received. Waiting for further lessons in ecstasy had been just as torturous.

Checking that there was time before dinner, Althea ordered a bath and went to find Beth. When the younger woman was not in the house, she frowned, concerned that Beth had decided not to wait for Robert's return and returned to the stable boys she favored when in London without other options. But a peek out there had her sighing in relief.

The butler reminded her that it was Tuesday, one of Beth's scheduled days to volunteer at the charity school. She rolled her eyes at herself. If she was not so addled with thoughts of Evan, she'd have realized that. Tuesday was the only day she was home from the shop and Beth was not. Sunday, when the shop was closed, Beth was home. They had chosen this schedule so she could review finances and orders for the shop in peace, and Beth would have other time in the house to herself, giving each of them some space.

Beth arrived an hour later as Althea stepped out of her bath. Taking advantage of its presence, Beth stripped and lowered herself into the water freshened with a few buckets heating on the hearth.

Althea told her the news of the men's arrival.

"You're sure Robert is in Town also?"

"Yes. The note said so."

"But the note was from Cheltie?"

"Yes."

"Stubborn man." Beth grumbled at her bath water as she scrubbed herself.

"What shall you do?" Althea had enough to juggle with the business expansion and keeping her relationship with Evan quiet, but she hated seeing her cousin despondent. Then again, with Evan coming to her house, privacy suddenly felt important.

Beth grinned. "What you don't know can't get me in trouble, cuz."

Althea rolled her eyes. "I am in too good a mood to worry about it. Just be careful, please."

"Yes, mother." Beth stuck her tongue out at her, flicking water toward where Althea sat, still in a wrapper. "What are you planning on wearing this evening?"

"I do not know. He's coming here, so I shan't dress to go out."

"Right. You should absolutely dress to stay in, cuz."

Althea raised questioning brows.

"Do you remember the corset I talked you into that you thought was scandalous, but was perfect for under that one ballgown?"

"Yes. But if I'm not going out—"

"Take one of my chemises. They are shorter than yours. And likely a little lower cut on average. Wear it under that corset. No knickers under the chemise. And your wrapper. Have a bit of wine or sherry and *lounge*."

"I don't normally lounge in a corset. Especially without a dress over it."

"That does not matter. You are dressing for a man. The idea is suspension of disbelief. He shan't focus on the improbability. He'll see your breasts on display, your waist sucked in, all under the thin veil of your wrapper. Lounge in your room, of course. I shall leave my door closed, you leave yours ajar, and send the servants to bed early."

The store and partnership papers were forgotten as Althea focused on seducing—to the best of her ability—the most sexually knowledgeable earl in Britain. Her body hummed in anticipated pleasure. The folds of flesh between her legs, so recently cleaned and dried, grew swollen and damp again.

She struggled into the corset and threw on her day dress to go ask the kitchen to send a supper tray, Scotch, and wine to her room for the evening. The staff was well-trained enough not to ask about her sudden taste for whisky. After her meal had been delivered and she'd dismissed the servants for the night, she ignored Beth's closed door and pretended to believe the girl was inside as she crept down to unlock the back door. She'd give Evan a key when he arrived.

In her room, she removed the dress, leaving on a chemise and the daring cream satin and bone corset that Beth had helped her don. Drawing her simple white wrapper on, she caught her reflection in the mirror before she tied it around her. The satin was a shade warmer than her skin, the wrap a shade paler. With the fireplace behind her, she could see the silhouette of her cinched-in form through the muslin. She ran her hands down her body as she watched, sucking in a breath as she imagined they were Evan's hands. Her nipples poked through the thin chemise, the corset framing each breast but not covering it.

Hurry, Evan.

She sat, sipped wine. Stood, then paced. Sat again and sipped. Seeing a drop of red wine caught on the rim of the cup, she swiped her thumb across it and brought it to her mouth to suck at the wine.

The door swung open farther, and there he stood, his gaze heating when he discovered her state of undress. He, too, was less formal than usual, having forgone a cravat and waistcoat and wearing a dark jacket and trousers.

He stared at her thumb, still resting on her lower lip. On instinct, she pushed the length of it into her mouth, hollowing her cheeks as her throat worked to suck it. She nearly groaned at her own eroticism and wished it was his cock.

"Althea. Damn me, I missed you."

She pulled her hand away. "Show me." Her voice surprised them both with its huskiness.

He closed and locked the door, strode to pull her up, and jerked her to him.

Althea gasped at the heat of his body against hers, feeling it more intensely with fewer layers than usual between them. She shoved at his jacket but lost focus and clung to him when his lips found hers, plundering and sucking at her mouth. They needed to be skin-to-skin, that very moment, or she might expire from need.

Her chemise chafed the hard tips of her breasts, and her hips flexed forward against his.

His hands were at her waist, then her wrapper was gone. His jacket hit the floor. His teeth clamped gently on her lower lip, and he licked it once before releasing it to mutter, "You want me to show you?"

"Yes. Oh please, Evan." She dared to palm his cock through his pants, and a rush of heat filtered through her. *That. I want that inside me. I'm not sure I care where.*

"Oh, you want to see that? Right, then. You shall see it up close." He pushed her back down in the chair, tore off his shirt, and unbuttoned the fall of the trousers.

"Yes. This." Her hands were there before he'd peeled the edges back, drawing him out carefully. Her tongue swept out to lick her lips in hunger. "Delicious."

"You'd best check."

She glanced up at him through her lashes. "I'll be glad to."

Her tongue swiped across the weeping head before her lips swallowed him, coming to rest in the fur at the root of his cock.

"Ahh, Althea. Never mind. I want to fuck you. I can't stand it after so many days apart." He tugged at her hair.

She shook her head and did not release him. She knew he would not pull her hair too hard, so she was in control. Just to be sure, she latched on to his muscled buttocks, holding him against her.

She swallowed, and he jerked in her mouth. Sliding back, she sucked in a breath and engulfed him again, keeping her rhythm smooth and leisurely, as though they had all the time in the world and were not both straining to come together.

"Please, please, love. Either faster or let me get inside you."

She drew back. "You are inside me."

Ohh, she liked Evan begging. Usually, she was the one pleading for him to hurry.

"Gah, you know what I me—" He lost his words as her lips hit his cock again.

She sped up, one hand rising to roll his bollocks. His spine arched. "Althea, let me get a handkerchief."

She shook her head slightly and kept impaling her mouth on him.

"Ahh, ahh." His hands gripped her hair, blunt nails scraping against her scalp as he clutched her to him, his spine arching his hips toward her farther as he held her still.

Nearly choking on him, she trusted him not to hurt her. His cock thrashed in her mouth, heat spurting down her throat as she swallowed against him. She felt more contractions and heard more grunts at her gulp, so she did it again.

Finally, his hands gentled, and he straightened. "Right. Your turn."

She licked him clean as she leaned back slowly.

He picked her up and threw her on the bed, flipping her and untying the corset faster than any maid ever had.

She smiled into the pillow. Such an expert.

Rolling her over, he shoved the chemise up. He dipped his mouth to a pebbled peak, and his fingers slid through her wet swollen folds.

Her hips rose to meet him. An embarrassing three strokes later, she was spasming against his hand, clutching his head to her breast.

As he gentled his movements and she released his hair, he looked up at her. "It seems you missed me as much as I missed you, love."

She blushed. And found her heart twisting at his chosen endearment. If only…

"Yes, my lord. Now what shall we do? Cards?"

He laughed. "Oh no. I have many more plans for tonight." He rose over her, and she saw that he indeed appeared to be fully recovered and full of plans.

****

Having sated the worst of their hunger for each other, the next night, they managed to have a conversation before tearing each other's clothes off and falling onto the bed.

Althea's review of the partnership papers was animated. She showed him the figures she'd modeled as to the investment needed.

Despite his relaxed posture lounging in his chair with his leg swinging, Evan held himself stiffly as they reviewed the entirety of it. Unsure whether he was uncomfortable with her estimates or the subject as a whole, Althea hurried to put the documents aside.

He shot her an inscrutable look. "Given this much smaller figure than you originally needed, how are you feeling about an equity investment versus a loan?"

She sat back, crossing her arms. *Well hell. We're back to this.* "My answer remains the same, my lord. I thought you understood my reason."

"I do. I am not trying to provoke you. I simply wanted to reaffirm. If I am to help you, I need to know the options. Your preference will limit the level of interest, given the level of risk in a small business. And

I'll need to consider what rate of return will justify the investment."

Althea was confused. What interest was he talking about? That last night in Bath, he'd said he'd help her, and that it would be faster and simpler that way. She still wanted all the formal documents in place, but surely, he had this smaller amount to invest and would not need to go to others.

However, his stiffness precluded her asking. She did not want to seem presumptuous, and he knew the details of the world of investing better than she did. She nodded.

Evan's gaze roamed over her simple day dress and loosely pinned hair. He asked suddenly, "What happens when I need to be seen about London again?"

Why had he changed the subject? She pushed a stray curl away from her face with a frustrated motion. "I have not considered that. I thought we had a bit of time. I have been focused on the business developments."

"We do have time. I was simply curious if you'd reached a decision."

She frowned. Hadn't they already resolved this?

"A few of my investment circle are having a soirée in a sennight for their business partners and co-investors, as well as a few business owners looking for investment." His leg still swung. "If you are not willing to attend on my arm, I could certainly invite you as a prospective business partner. It could prove quite lucrative."

"Oh yes, I should love to talk about my shop to more of the Ton." She heaved a sigh of affection and relief. Even if she wouldn't go with him, he was willing to introduce her as his associate. 'Twas very supportive and enlightened of him.

He nodded. "And which shall it be? Alone or with me?"

"Er." *Why is he pushing me? He knows I am not willing to risk my reputation, even if he says his friends are open-minded. Will he be angry if I decline?* "I'd prefer to come alone, Evan." She held her breath waiting for his reaction.

His lips twisted. "Right, then. If I am to be your dirty secret, then we should get back to the dirty part of the evening."

He gave her a lopsided grin and kept his tone light, but she feared she saw a wryness to the twist of his lips.

Never mind. She'd pleasure the hurt right out of him, with all he'd taught her.

****

Evan strolled back to his townhouse. The darkest hours of the night were not entirely safe, even in Mayfair, but his clothes and height—and his attitude—stopped anyone from accosting him.

He almost wished they would. He could use a good fight right now to get some of his frustrations out.

Damned infernal independent woman. He had hoped after Bath she'd trust that he had her best interests at heart. It seemed his wariness was warranted about investing with someone he was in a rela—

Fucking. The word is fucking.

But Ford's words had taken root in his mind, as much as he hated the idea of marriage. If he needed to marry, he could not envision anyone other than Althea. She constantly challenged him and made him raise his game. He'd never been so engaged mind, body, and soul with a woman. Even his youthful infatuations with sexually aggressive ladies who taught him some of his best tricks had been one dimensional. This was all-consuming. And while he didn't know if it was love, Ford's plan was the most straightforward path to ensuring the preservation of his earldom and fortune.

If Althea had been willing to bend even a little, he might have been able to convince himself she wasn't pursuing him for quick and easy funds and clandestine lessons in lust. But she had failed to clear even the first hurdle. She was still set against giving up even a small piece of ownership, which meant he had no foundation for trust.

He didn't want her to pursue him for his money, but he wanted her to be open to…pursuing him. He sighed. *Ford would laugh at me for going 'round and 'round like this.*

Mayhap if his family legacy did not include mental health issues, he could see past a lack of trust to marry for heirs. But similar to his nightmares about torturing someone who loved him by not recognizing them, he could easily picture someone who didn't love him abandoning him to an asylum. In fact, he was sure that was what his cousin would do, so why would he marry if not to avoid that?

No, he needed to find someone else to fund her expansion, so he could relax and enjoy a free sexual relationship with the beautiful and willing widow, until such time as they went their separate ways.

It seemed his best path was to avoid caring too much for any woman, even Althea. He hoped it was not too late to choose that direction.

Over the next two days, Evan wrote notes to fellow

investors, particularly those who liked to support women's ventures, mentioning the upcoming soirée. Lady Charlotte was unavailable, which surprised him as she'd only just rejoined society after mourning her husband's passing. He requested a private audience with her for Althea the day after the party.

The following week, Evan dressed and ascended into a dark and lonely carriage, resenting not being able to show Althea off to his associates. He hoped one of the investors attending would decide quickly to support her, leaving plenty of the night for his preferred prurient activities, with no obsessing about nuptials.

Normally, he would also want to scout new investment opportunities at such an event. He found it helpful to look a businessperson in the eye to judge sincerity, fire, and intelligence. All three were needed to succeed in London in the era of Prinny's whims. But tonight, his goals were to find the right fit for Althea, then get her naked and enjoy the safe part of their arrangement.

With two dozen attendees, the party flowed between the dining room and a connected parlor of the host's home, dozens of candelabras keeping it bright and warm. Evan mingled and lounged, keeping a close eye on the door.

Finally, Althea swept in, once again in a dress of a deep jewel tone, this time amethyst, striking with her dark hair and creamy skin.

Her fingers fiddled with her reticule as her gaze flitted around the room, searching for him.

She found him as he stepped forward from a small cluster of sycophants, and her shoulders dropped away from her ears.

He bowed over her hand as he had other business people he'd invited, giving it a surreptitious squeeze to reassure her. Tucking her arm in his, he strolled the rooms, stopping to introduce her to the various business owners and investors. He offered a comment about their role, then allowed each to share their passion with her and her with them.

There were a few he knew better than others and had co-invested with them in several enterprises. To offer proof of her business acumen, he told one friend about Althea's shampoo and jokingly offered his hair to touch.

Althea shocked him when she opened her reticule and pulled out a few small bottles, likely repurposed from perfume. "No need. I have a few scents here for you to choose from. I brought samples for those most interested."

She removed the stoppers and offered them to be sniffed.

"How enterprising. Cheltie said you were intelligent beyond your years. I should have known his instincts were spot on, as usual."

Evan bristled at the flattery, then recognized his reaction as jealousy. He'd never been jealous. He didn't like the sensation.

Attempting to put his emotions aside and focus on Althea's success, he promenaded with her toward the next investor. Patting her hand on his arm, he said, "'Twas a nice touch, bringing the samples. Not something I would have thought of."

She smiled.

"Let us solicit a few others. Mayhap we can get some competing bids and bring your interest rate down."

Althea stopped. "Evan, I confess, I am confused. How many investors do you think I'll need? How much do these people usually offer?"

"Most here would fund your venture individually unless they thought it held a very high risk." He started them strolling. "If that was the case and a few were interested, they would meet and see if it made sense to each take a smaller piece. But yours is not what we would consider high risk. 'Tis why I think we'll have more interest."

Althea stopped again and turned to him. She took a breath as though to speak, then closed her mouth, looking pained.

"What is it?"

She raised her gaze to his. "I thought you said you'd be my investor."

"What?" He frowned, his voice raised. Seeing a few heads turn, he realized they were making a scene. He took her elbow and guided her out of the room and toward the back of the wide entry hall. "Why would you think that?"

"In Bath. You told me you would help. And thus it could be expedited."

He gritted his teeth. And here they were, back to his never-ending situation. Another person who wanted money from him. He'd been right not to trust her. His jaw clenched, he ground out, "This is me helping."

"But—"

"But nothing. You said yourself, you don't mix business and pleasure. This was my solution. Why on earth would you think otherwise?" He threw his hands up in agitation.

"I just thought…"

As it had in Greenborough Park when she declined his reasonable offers of investment, anger overtook him. "I know what you thought. After all, my friends call me Bags because I always had a bag of money to bail them out." His mouth twisted as he continued, his voice pitched high to mimic her. "No, I don't want anyone to have a stake. I just want money and sex with no strings attached. Oh, and it has to be on the sly." He lowered his voice back to his natural range, shaking his head. "That is not how it works."

"I beg your pardon, Evan." She was frowning at him, her mouth a taut line in her face. "'Twas a simple misunderstanding, hence why I asked you about it now. You needn't be rude. I do know how *it* works. Life works quite differently for you titled gentlemen than it does for any lady, Ton or no. And you said all along you understood that. As for the rest, I fought hard for my independence, and I intend to keep it. Again, I thought you understood and supported that. It is clear you did not."

He spun on his heel toward the front door, ignoring the tears coursing down Althea's face. He needed a drink and solitude. "Good night, Lady Edgerton," he flung over his shoulder. "Best of luck with your expansion endeavors."

Chapter Fourteen

Althea stood in the shadows at the back of the hall with her hands fisted at her sides. She was both furious and hurt at Evan's unjustified outburst. He'd said he would help her and referred to her as a potential business partner. Surely, he could understand her assumption. Instead, he had yelled at her and mocked her.

Her mind swirled with everything he'd thrown at her, but the soirée was not the place for it. They both could not disappear without gossip starting. Turning, she made her way to the retiring room and bathed her face in lavender water until her eyes were less red. When Evan's accusations started replaying in her mind, she shoved them back down to be dealt with later.

After all, he thinks I am a good businesswoman, and 'tis good business to put this opportunity first. Even her inner voice sounded bitter and angry.

In the parlor, she circled the room, quietly wishing the people she had met a good night and accepting offers to visit with those interested in hearing more about her venture. Evan had already arranged a meeting with the Dowager Countess of Peterborough for the morrow. She loved the idea of a woman investor investing in a partnership of two women's businesses. She'd follow up with the others as needed after seeing how her meeting with Lady Peterborough went.

Two of Evan's cronies were joking about besting Cheltie as she approached them to say her farewells. One looked around the room and frowned, then turned to her. "Speak of the devil, where is he?"

"Er, I am not certain. I believe he may have left."

"Left? He is always the life of the party, the last to leave."

She didn't doubt it. Her mouth twisted in a sneer as she walked out to her carriage.

How dare he? No matter how he meant it, if he's going to refer to me as a business partner, he should give me the respect of hearing me out.

Her mood vacillated between anger and angst for the carriage ride.

At home, she threw her gloves on the bed and yanked her dress off without waiting for her maid. She tugged pins from her hair with no thought to pain in her scalp.

She stomped in circles for a moment before grabbing her wrapper and stomping across the hall to Beth's room. Barely stopping herself from pounding on it, she tapped. Leaning her head close to the door, she heard a rustle and turned the door handle to peer in.

"Beth?" she whispered. Then thought to ask, "Are you alone?"

A snort and a muffled response came from the bed in shadows. "Yes. Come in."

Fumbling ensued before a candle was lit, then another.

Beth sat up, curls in disarray around her, covers at her waist. Uncaring of her nudity, she hopped out and put a wrapper on. "Brr. Stoke the fire a bit, would you, Althea? You look like you need wine." She wandered over to a decanter and two glasses on a tray, poured them each one, and brought them to the armchairs angled toward the fireplace.

"Sorry to wake you. I can go." Althea hovered uncertainly.

"I am up now. And you know I don't mind. After all, 'tis usually me waking you. Or someone reporting my troublemaking." Beth curled into one of the chairs, tucking her feet under her, and gestured for Althea to take the other.

It was Althea's turn to snort. "True. Oh, Beth."

"What is it, cuz? Did the investment soirée not go well?"

"Why could you not have left me in blissful ignorance?"

"What? What did I do?"

Althea shook her head, knowing she wasn't being fair. "Nothing. I was trying to joke and failing miserably at yet another communication." She stared into her wine.

"A bit of help here, please? I am lost."

"Evan introduced me to a number of investors, several of whom were interested."

"Do you need multiple investors? I thought he was handling it."

Althea explained the misunderstanding and repeated the vitriol Evan had spewed at her.

"Huh. Not well done of him, at all." Beth gave a half-smile at the wry look she received for that understatement. She took a gulp of wine and waited for Althea to do the same. "Cuz…"

Althea cocked her head.

"I will support you in everything you do. You

know that. And I am forever grateful you took me in." She sucked in a deep breath, and her next statement rushed out on the exhale. "I sort of see his concern."

Althea bolted upright. "What?"

"Hear me out." Beth held her free hand out, palm facing Althea in supplication. "Look at him. Think about being him. You have a sick mother you are trying to protect. You have absolute scads of money. And you've a reputation for being the most accomplished sexual maestro available for both ladies and lords."

"But—but—*he* pursued *me!*"

"He did. And none of what I'm saying makes what he did right or less rude. But you know the Ton and their games. Evan has lived in that environment for years, after inheriting his earldom very early. For many of them, there are ulterior motives behind their ulterior motives. I can understand how he might be somewhat jaded. And might wonder if you'd set the whole thing up, making him pursue you."

"Bah. He should have been able to distinguish that the first night in his library at Greenborough Park."

"Agreed, and I don't doubt he will return to that when he's over his upset. But if I had not offered him help with his mother's nurse and known Penelope besides, he likely would not have even heard your request. He is that discerning."

Althea gaped. "You did that? I did not realize you helped him with the nurse in order to buy me time."

"Eh, I would have done it anyway, you know that. 'Tis all in the presentation." Beth grinned and winked.

Althea managed a small chuckle for the first time that night. "I did say I wanted to keep our relationship secret. He'd said he understood the risk to my reputation. But, tonight, he seemed hurt by that, as though he thought I was embarrassed by him."

"He's accustomed to all sorts of people falling all over themselves to attract his attention. I'll bet poor Cheltie's ego was a bit bruised." Beth seemed to take satisfaction in that idea.

Althea certainly did. "So now what?"

"Now, we sleep. Tomorrow, we plot—I mean, plan." Beth winked again.

****

Althea woke refreshed, surprised at how well she had slept. Rolling over, she considered her petite cousin. Beth might be wild, mayhap even a bit crazy, but she was the best friend Althea had never had, and she loved that girl. She just hoped they would not end up two spinsters together forever. Or worse, knowing her cousin, two spinsters with a baby or two, fathers unknown, and young virile male servants for Beth's entertainment.

Her lips quirked. That scenario might be better than simply two spinsters, now she thought about it. If she got nothing else out of her—relationship? education?— with Evan, she had a new appreciation for the pleasures of the flesh. And mayhap a friendship with the Dowager Countess of Peterborough.

Lady Peterborough! Althea shot upright. She was supposed to visit her today. She wondered if, even now, the widow was calling for a bath to try the shampoo sample Althea had sent over with a summary of her business proposition.

Althea smiled. She'd bring Beth. From what Evan had told her, she suspected the women would do well together, even if one held herself in tight control and the other was a free spirit.

I should learn from Beth. Of course, she still needed to be circumspect in bed partners for her shop's reputation. But in other things, she needed to relax and enjoy more and worry less. Damn Evan to hell, anyway. Even if he was justified in his concerns, that was no way to treat her, especially in the middle of a stranger's home.

I don't need him. With Charlotte's help, I hope not to need any man. I was perfectly happy without him, and I shall be so again.

Althea ignored her inner voice that wanted to argue she had not been happy. She'd been getting by. Any happiness she'd had was because she was blissfully ignorant, but she could not return to that state.

She rang for a servant, requesting tea and toast for both her and her cousin, and crossed the hall to wake Beth and request her company to call on Lady Peterborough.

On their way, they had the coachman stop by the apothecary so Althea could run in and gather a small basket of gifts. A larger bottle of shampoo, a matching soap, scented oil for her bath, and a pretty pen and ink she had brought back from the Bath store to show the quality of product she was gaining through this partnership.

Standing in front of Lady Peterborough's townhome, she realized it was barely midday, quite on the early side to call on acquaintances. Before she could debate returning at a later hour, a butler swung the door open.

"Oh! Hullo. Lady Althea Egerton and Miss Jenkins to see Lady Peterborough, please."

"Ah, ladies. She is expecting you." His eyes flicked to Beth and back, but he refrained from commenting whether Lady Peterborough was expecting one person or two.

"Thank you." Althea followed Beth inside where the butler gestured them to wait while he announced them.

He reappeared with Charlotte right behind him. "Lady Althea! And who have we here?" She advanced, smiling, with her hands held out to them.

Althea met her hands and returned her finger press. She grinned back as she introduced Beth.

"Come in, come in. Austin, have someone bring tea and scones please."

Beth bounced in happiness, and Althea slid her a sideways look.

"Try not to eat them all," she muttered.

Checking that Charlotte was still facing away as they entered her parlor, Beth stuck her tongue out.

Althea rolled her eyes but could not stop smiling. She was determined that this day was going to be a good one, happy as well as productive. Evan be damned.

They sat, and Althea began, "Lady Peterborough, I—"

"Charlotte, please."

She nodded. "Charlotte. And 'tis Althea and Beth. I am ever so grateful for your time. Please accept this as a token of my thanks. 'Tis a few products from my store that will appear in Bath to complement the shampoo scent you selected, and a pen and ink set that is the highest quality I've ever seen. Those are from Emily Anders, and I've asked for inventory to stock in

London, as I feel sure they will sell well here."

"Oh. The Bath shop is also owned by a woman, eh? I love that so much."

"I thought you might." Althea could not stop smiling.

"Right, let me see your projections then."

Althea handed over her marketing packet, and Charlotte perused the documents for a few moments. Althea was impressed by the speed at which she flicked through them.

After an agonizing few minutes, Charlotte sat back, dropping the papers to her lap. Her face was inscrutable.

Althea braced for questions or, worse, a rejection.

"My word, I am quite certain we can take care of this whole thing, almost without a man in sight. Sadly, I have not yet found a woman solicitor. But never mind, that too shall come." Charlotte's grin was ear to ear.

Beth clapped once but subsided at a quelling look from Althea.

"Right, then." Althea permitted herself a small smile to answer that of her hostess. Then she squared her shoulders and accepted a cup of tea. "Here are the terms I would like…"

****

Evan had been in high dudgeon leaving the soirée. He'd gone to Ford's townhouse, where his friend watched and poured whisky as Evan paced and railed. After two drinks, Ford had talked Evan down to where he could at least see how his words in Bath could have been misconstrued.

Once calmer, Evan could see that. But he could still envision a scenario in which Althea had staged the entire thing or one in which she took advantage once he had opened the door. Or one in which she became complacent in their arrangement and believed he would gift the money rather than invest it with the expectation of a return.

After only three days, he was making himself crazy with his imaginings interspersed with his craving for Althea. He invited Ford to accompany him home to catch up on correspondence and visit his mother.

At Greenborough Park, he was faced with the letter from his solicitor he'd received last visit. He'd left it out on his desk to remind himself that this too was a problem he needed to address. Upon seeing it, he was thrown back into frustration at Althea's presumptions.

To think I'd considered marrying her.

Franklin, the ever-amenable footman, made himself conspicuous with errands into Evan's study, bending for things he'd dropped, clearly having had his uniform tailored to be more form-fitting than it had been designed. Evan suspected the young man thought he could help Evan fuck the bad mood right out.

Despite the man's tight buttocks, broad shoulders, and extraordinary calves, Evan could not even coax a pulse out of his cock at the thought of sex with Franklin. No, the form his cock wanted was taller, thinner, and softer, with breasts tipped in raspberry and a wet, delicious center.

Althea.

He replayed the soirée over and over. His white-hot fury at her question, her assumptions. His spate of angry words and ridicule. Her attempt to explain.

Could Ford be right? Could it be a simple misunderstanding? Did Althea meet with Charlotte the next day? Did she follow up with any of the other investors or had he inadvertently interfered with her expansion endeavors?

Even if she had been after his money, Evan rarely lost his temper. Every time he remembered his diatribe, he cringed. He wanted Althea to be successful. Hell, he still wanted her in his bed. He owed her an apology at the very least, but he was unable to put aside his doubts.

Ignoring Franklin's unsubtle overtures, Evan vacated the house to ride the estate whenever the weather allowed, ending each outing with a visit to the dower house. In addition to wanting time with his mother while he could, he needed the reminder of his future.

On the occasions his mother napped or was not present mentally when he visited, he made small talk with the nurse. Often, he brought the subject around to how she knew Beth and Althea and talked about his own relationship with them, which quickly narrowed to discussing Althea.

On his last day there, she handed him a letter sealed with his own mark in the wax. The Cheltenham seal. Frowning, he looked at her.

"Lucy told me that shortly after she'd arrived, she suggested your mother write you a letter. She'd found in past experience it helped the patient's family once communication had tapered off. I love the idea. I shall use it in the future."

Evan's lips twisted at the reminder that his mother would not be her patient forever. But the realist in him accepted that.

"Lucy said that your mother had asked we give it to you when you needed it the most. While I am sure there will be more difficult times ahead with your mother, need can be sparked by struggles beyond that. I think now is as good a time as any. But open it when you are ready."

****

Althea remained despondent despite having won funding. On Tuesday, Beth surprised her by announcing that she had traded days with another instructor, and they were due at Mansfield House, where Penelope and Michael lived, in two hours. Only the promise of testing some new pastries Penelope was considering for her bakery drew Althea out. She was not in the mood to be social, and she'd only met Beth's school friend twice.

Penelope ushered them into the drawing room as the housekeeper bustled in with tea and pastries.

Althea sipped tea, distracted with missing Evan and her continuing anger at him.

Penelope and Beth talked about Penelope's preparations for the bakery and the staff she'd need.

After a few minutes, Penelope turned to bring Althea into the conversation. "Althea, what is happening with your shop?"

Althea explained Evan's idea, and Charlotte's willingness to invest.

"Oh!" Penelope bounced in her seat, and Althea had the random thought that Beth was wearing off on her friend. "Lady Peterborough is also funding my bakery. I am so glad she agreed to help you as well. 'Tis almost as though we are keeping it in the family."

Charlotte's husband had died two winters ago, leaving his younger brother as the earl. Pen's closest childhood friend, Sophia, had married the new Earl of Peterborough last year and in the process had reunited with Penelope.

"But…why is Evan not funding it for you?" Pen frowned in confusion.

Althea nearly growled.

"Er…sore subject, I'm afraid, Pen." Beth interjected, patting Althea's clenched hands. "There was a bit of a misunderstanding. 'Tis what I referenced in my note about needing a day out."

"I beg your pardon." Penelope grimaced at her inadvertent faux pas.

"No, 'tis quite all right." Althea assured her. "You had no way of knowing. He said he'd help, and I assumed that meant he'd fund it himself. He took offense with that, as he meant he'd introduce me to investors."

"Evan? Offense?" Penelope tilted her head. "I've never seen him upset to even the smallest degree."

"Yes, well apparently, he thought I was sleeping with him for his money." Althea gritted her teeth.

"Oh." Penelope bobbed her head once, the details of Althea's relationship with Evan, her upset, and the misunderstanding obviously becoming clear. "Poor Evan. I'm sure he was frustrated at what seemed like yet another request for funding. They do seem to never end."

Althea's eyes narrowed. From the corner of her eye, she saw Beth's expression mirror her own.

"Gor, I beg your pardon again." Penelope hastened to adjust in the face of their glares. "Althea, I know Evan through Michael, so I have heard his complaints. But he had no right to be rude or abandon you there. As I said, 'tis very unlike him."

"I wouldn't know," Althea said stiffly, her spine

rigid.

"Oh dear, I've really put my foot in it. I do apologize. No matter how strange his behavior was, it was not warranted or acceptable. I am very glad you've found Lady Peter—Charlotte, as she insists."

Althea gave a slight nod, still uncertain of Penelope's allegiance to Evan.

Penelope turned to Beth and changed the subject with an overly bright tone. "Beth, what have you been doing?"

"At least 'tis no longer a question of who," Althea interjected, only half under her breath, relieved at the subject change.

Beth shot her an annoyed frown.

Pen's brows shot up. "Really? Do tell." She leaned forward, folding her hands in her lap in an eager pose.

"'Tis nothing serious. I've been helping Robert."

"Ford? With his cock?" Pen asked. Then as the other two hooted, she blushed and apologized. "I swear, Beth, you bring out the worst in me. Or rather, the naughty. My apologies. Please continue."

Althea drifted away from the conversation to wonder why Evan had not funded Penelope's bakery. Did he have some strict rule about women he knew? Or certain types of businesses? Both hers and Penelope's would be storefronts, and he'd mentioned he'd invested in more service-based businesses owned by women. She returned to the conversation abruptly when Beth explained Ford's work.

"He creates leather cuffs, often attached, sometimes in shapes which make for very interesting sexual positions. Some are incredibly adaptable to whatever piece of furniture he wants to put to use. And corsets and cock and bollocks corset thingies and…"

Penelope sat back, gusting out a breath. "I shall say it again. Still waters run deep. Oh my. I am not certain I can ever look at him the same way again."

Althea was furious. Again, Penelope was putting a friend of her husband's on some sort of pedestal, while only pseudo-accepting Beth's wilder nature. Everything she'd learned about the School of Enlightenment, albeit secondhand, countered that.

Before Beth could respond, Althea interjected, "Come now, Pen. That is not very fair, is it? None of Michael's friends look questioningly at you, despite how your relationship began."

Pen blushed and looked down at her hands. "You are right, Althea. You have my apologies. As does Ford. I did not mean it as critical, more that I shall feel awkward thinking of his creations. But that is no excuse."

After an awkward silence, Penelope turned back to Beth. "Mayhap the three of us should have a viewing party of Ford's work one day soon."

"We can have a private party at some point," Beth said. "He also takes them to the demi-monde parties at Sarah's for custom orders, albeit anonymously. All orders go through Sarah."

"Excellent. I shall be on the lookout for one of those." Penelope nodded.

When Beth began asking Penelope about her stepfather's connections in the world of blacksmithing, Althea smiled at her cousin. Ever resourceful, she always seemed to know who in her network could help another. It was an amazing skillset, and Althea wasn't sure Beth recognized her own worth sometimes.

She'd hoped the school would help with that. It had to some extent, but she still worried about her cousin's happiness in the strict London society. Perhaps they'd have been better served retiring to the country. Surely, they would not need as much saved to live simply there. But Althea knew she'd go mad. It would feel too similar to being kept isolated and quiet by her husband.

Unlike Thomas, Evan always asked her about her business. He seemed interested in learning how she managed it, rather than wanting to offer advice simply because he was a man and therefore knew better.

Wondering what he would think of the school, she felt almost sure he'd support it as much or more than she did. She wondered about Penelope's experience there, and how it differed from Beth's. Her cousin had mentioned at least one class they had attended together. She supposed it was an advanced class, as their introductory courses would have been separate from what she'd understood when she'd sponsored Beth.

Not that Althea would have stopped her cousin. The whole point of sending her was to support her open-minded attitude. That was why she'd been shocked at Penelope's responses. But the girl had apologized, and her enthusiasm over Ford's creations was certainly mollifying. Given Beth's lack of anger at Pen's comment about Ford, Althea suspected her reaction might have been inflated by her frustration at Evan. She took a breath to calm herself, vowing to be more tolerant of simple reactions.

Damn Evan for interfering in every aspect of my life, even when he's not part of it. She would ignore him until he apologized for his assumptions and overreaction.

Chapter Fifteen

The sennights after Charlotte's offer of funding were busy. Althea and Beth made one pilgrimage to Bath, a covered delivery wagon full of goods plodding behind them. Althea was that confident the partnership would be finalized. Correspondence until that trip had been by special messenger, hastening the process with letters discussing plans so the formal documentation would hold no surprises for any party. Emily had been in business long enough and shop rents were low enough in Bath that she had not needed an independent investor to increase her inventory for London sales.

After unloading then reloading the wagon with some of the fabulous products from Emily's suppliers, they returned. More would come directly to London in the coming months.

Althea rushed to rearrange the store while it was still the slow season as September became October, crops were harvested, and the days grew shorter.

Having so much to do kept her from missing Evan. Or so she told herself throughout the days. At night, she tossed and turned. She told herself she did not need him or want him if he was going to so easily doubt her. But her heart disobeyed, hurting even as her mind remained focused on independence.

Was she so easily dismissed? Of course she was. He had the world at his feet, more offers for intimacy—

fun as he called it—than he had hours in a day. She had been a challenge, the uptight shopkeeper who thought she didn't like sex. But did the others keep his interest intellectually? Were they as eager for his guidance in and out of the bedroom? It seemed they wanted his money more than his thoughts, and that saddened her. Even more so because she had misunderstood and appeared like them and possibly hurt him.

His silence screamed that he wanted nothing to do with her. Then Beth's words from before Bath echoed in her head. *Cheltie never chases. He doesn't need to. You will likely need to go to him... 'Tis clear he wants you and will flex on the terms. Use the negotiating tactics he would.*

But how?

Finally, she stayed home one full day, having forsaken her Tuesdays and Sundays at home for a fortnight. As it was Friday, Beth was home, and Althea searched her out to see if they could plan another fun day together like they had with Penelope. She needed something engaging to prevent her from obsessing about Evan or the store.

At the door of the front parlor, she halted abruptly and stared.

Her younger cousin was seated by the fire, muttering to herself as she jabbed a needle back and forth through fabric.

Althea could not remember the last time she'd seen Beth attempt needlework. Nor could she tell what Beth was attempting to sew. She knew it had been many months, because this frustrated jabbing was impossible to forget. Why would Beth resort to a pastime she hated? "Beth? What is amiss?"

Her cousin did not even look up. She jabbed again, then yelped and brought her hand out from beneath whatever it was she'd been attacking and sucked it into her mouth.

Althea perched on the edge of a chair facing the younger woman. "Talk to me."

"I like to have fun. With other people. Naked fun. And now. That man." She shook her head and looked back down at the needlework in her lap. Althea rushed to rescue whatever it was, tucking it beside her hip on the chair.

"What man?" She waited a beat, but no answer was forthcoming. "Ford?"

Beth made a wordless growling sound, which Althea interpreted as confirmation.

"So does this mean you and Ford did not...ahem, were not intimate?"

"Ha!" Her cousin's laugh was short and bitter.

"You were?"

A nod.

"And now...are not?"

Another nod, and Beth folded her arms below her rather bountiful bosom.

"Ah..." Althea found herself commiserating, something she could not have envisioned before Evan. "And you are frustrated?"

"Yes, darn him! Always, before now, I'd have simply replaced him with my next bedmate. But not a single footman, maid, or stable boy appeals."

"That is a relief, in any event." Althea sighed, only to earn a glare from her cousin. "My apologies, do go on."

"I can't stand it." Beth dropped her hands and

gazed up woefully at Althea. "Cuz, I tried to help him with sales. My ability to pair people and opportunities is the most valuable aspect of my admittedly shallow life. But he didn't appreciate it. He rejected it."

A tear slid down her cheek, and Althea leaned forward to hold one of Beth's hands, her thumb running soothing circles on the back of it.

"He dismissed me then ran. He and Cheltie disappeared to Cheltenham with only a one-sentence note to inform me. Mayhap I should not have interfered, but I really thought I was helping." She snorted a bitter laugh. "'Tis the story of my life, is it not?"

Althea allowed herself a moment of relief that Evan had not been gallivanting around London with other women, then shook her head. "Absolutely not. You help so many people. Look at your conversation with Penelope before our trip south. You were assisting Ford through your incredible network. You found Evan a new nurse for his mother when he needed one. You connect so many people, and they trust you."

Beth stared at her, lips parted and wet eyes wide. "Thank you, cuz. I needed that."

"So…'tis not only sexual frustration by the sound of it?"

"Ahh. Don't get me started on that part again. 'Tis not like he forbade me from relations with anyone else. We did not speak of it. And he knows my past. I do not think that is why he ran away. Although I shan't learn the reason if he will not talk to me." She shook her head, as though to rid herself of a thought. "I just do not want to risk disappointing him, so I cannot bring myself to…play. Besides which, he may have ruined me for anyone else." She sighed.

Althea was at a loss. Part of her wanted to giggle at Beth's sudden struggles with the idea of faithfulness, previously anathema to her. But mostly, she wanted to cheer the girl up. "I am not sure why you thought making"—she peered at the pile of fabric and thread next to her—"use of a needle and thread would help. I think a girl's day out is much more the thing, don't you? Come on, we shall wander some shops and then get pastries."

"'Tis raining. Again."

"Then we'll take the carriage. 'Twill be fun, you'll see. Go on, fetch a wrap."

Beth grumbled but went.

****

After a rare day of frivolous spending on books, ribbons, and other fripperies, they searched for a tea shop. Driving by Penelope's bakery-in-process and spying movement inside, they alighted and knocked.

Lady Peterborough trailed Penelope to the door across unfinished dusty flooring.

"Lady P—er, Charlotte," Althea said, smiling.

Pre-empting any curtsies, Charlotte grasped her hands and leaned in to kiss her cheek, then did the same for Beth.

"We are on the hunt for pastries and tea but saw activity in here and thought to view the progress," Althea said.

Penelope swept a hand to half-built display cases. "Allow me to give you the grand tour."

After they stepped carefully through the construction, eyeing the large-scale oven and long countertop in the back room that were already in, the four ladies adjourned to a tea shop across the back alley from Penelope's location for sustenance.

"How was the trip to Bath?" Charlotte asked.

Althea beamed. "Excellent. I have begun rearranging the shop for the goods I brought back, and more are due to arrive within a sennight."

"I sent the final contracts back to my solicitor yesterday. Copies for you and Miss Anders should go by messenger within a few days as well," Charlotte replied with a nod. "'Tis all coming together nicely. Evan will be quite jealous."

Althea's brows shot up, but she pressed her lips together to avoid commenting.

Penelope's head bobbed in agreement. "Yes, 'twill be quite fun, after not allowing him or Michael to invest in my bakery either."

"Oh? He *wanted* to invest in your business?" Althea felt her lips twist in bitterness despite her efforts to remain calm.

Penelope wrung her hands. "I've put my foot in it again, haven't I? Michael and Evan and Ford consider themselves family. Once Michael and I were betrothed, I was part of that family, and universal support comes with that. I am sorry, Althea."

"I never mix business and pleasure." Charlotte chimed in. "Nor does Evan. He could not tell me enough wonderful things about you and your business, though, Althea. I was ready to invest before I even met you or saw your projections, based on his recommendation."

"Oh. I got the impression that he didn't trust people asking for money."

Charlotte laughed. "Apologies, my dear. But that is

not universally true in my experience, and I've known him longer than any of you, I believe." At Althea's continued dubious stare, she continued. "He needn't invest in any small ventures, which are riskier than shipments and real estate. But he does—for women only. His network rivals that of Miss Jenkins here"— she tilted her head at Beth—"and he finds those who are struggling and gives them what they need to thrive. 'Tis only the lazy, avaricious lords and ladies of the Ton he despises."

"Hmph." Althea's response was non-committal.

Penelope had watched the exchange silently and now changed the subject. "Beth and Althea, what are you doing tomorrow evening? Michael has theatre tickets that we cannot use, and Charlotte has a prior commitment."

Beth lifted an apathetic shoulder, and Althea suspected she'd been reminded of her lack of evening plans.

"Come now," Althea coaxed her. "It will do you good to see people for something other than charity work. I'm accepting, and you're accompanying me."

The next night, they dressed for the theatre, both choosing gowns that were almost ballroom-worthy in their favorite colors of garnet and peach. But overdressing for the theatre provided a boost to their spirits. Every woman wanted to look pretty in public and never more so when recently spurned by her gentleman.

****

After almost a month at the estate, longer than his usual trip, Evan desperately needed to return to London to meet with his solicitor regarding several investments.

Expecting to have to drag Ford back, given his grumblings about a disagreement with Beth, Evan had been shocked when Ford was packed within hours and ready to return.

Settled at his desk in his London home, Evan struggled to focus on correspondence needed for current investments and the unending appeals for new funding. Charlotte had sent a note thanking him for directing Althea to her and informing him she had funded the expansion. He alternated wondering where Althea was and replaying her explanation of the miscommunication. He refused to whine about it to Ford like a silly girl stewing.

Althea would kill me for that remark. Come to think of it, any of the women I know would.

He sighed. He could not even talk to himself without censure.

He pulled out the letter Nancy had given him, seal still unbroken. Why had she given it to him? Uncertain why she thought it would help, he remained frustrated and angry. At Althea. At his mother, as unfair as that might be. At his cousin's lack of soul, and therefore, at his own need to marry. At life.

Standing, he wandered away from the desk, then back, still stewing. He sorted through the mail left on the small table by the door, his movements desultory as he wondered what Althea's silence meant. Guilt? Righteous anger because he'd snapped at her? Mayhap interest in expanding her sexual knowledge with someone else?

Stationery crinkled in his tightened fist, and he looked down. The usual cluster of invitations included a note from Michael. Scraping it open, he read the offer to use the owner's box the following evening at Michael's theatre. Deciding a distraction was just what he needed, Evan dispatched a servant to Ford's to tell him they were accepting—he knew better than to ask—and then to Michael's and Penelope's homes to ensure the couple received their reply.

His carriage pulled up in front of Ford's house early the following evening, just in case he'd ignored Evan's message or become engrossed in leather. Sure enough, he had to pull the work from his friend's hands and push him to get dressed. He popped into the pub next door for a meat pie wrapped in linen for Ford to eat on the way to the theatre.

They walked in just as the house lamps were being lowered, but they knew their way to Michael's seats, and with him absent, they needn't worry about disturbing him with a late entrance.

Entering the box as the stage curtain opened, Evan saw two forms already seated, one taller than the other. As his eyes adjusted to the dim light from the stage and the hall behind him, the ladies turned.

He might yet murder Michael, friend or no. 'Twas Althea and Beth, and they appeared as surprised as he and Ford. He scowled at the women even as he sketched the shortest, shallowest bow in history. He owed Althea an apology, but he had been procrastinating. He hadn't yet determined the right words to use when he saw her again.

Althea, remarkably, did not return his scowl. Why was that?

After making a quick bow, Ford continued toward Beth, leaning down to whisper in her ear.

Althea stood, offering Ford her seat and retreating

two rows to give the couple a modicum of privacy to talk.

Evan remained standing at the end of the row Althea entered. When she sat in the second seat of the row, he was forced to either sit next to her or choose another row in a blatant snub. A snub would be magnified by the busybodies in the neighboring boxes, which could affect Althea's sales. He would not do that to her, nor did he want to. Apparently, he would need to find words of apology quickly.

He sighed and sat, then reconsidered and stood to pull the curtains on either side of the box, isolating their foursome while still affording a view of the stage.

Settling again in his chair, he inhaled the mixed scent of flowers and citrus that was unique to Althea. Out of the corner of his eye, he caught the subtle movements of her hands on her lap, her sidelong glances.

He had not seen this particular production before yet was unable to follow the story line. Nor could he put together words of regret for his actions at the soirée. His lack of concentration was not helped by his cock, which refused to ignore Althea's presence and interfered with his thought process.

Finally, the intermission arrived. His time was up. Turning to Althea, he murmured, "Our last conversation...my reaction...'twas not well done of me."

Damn me, could I be less coherent?

Her right eyebrow arched.

"Mayhap I could call on you tomorrow? Day or night, your choice," he said, hoping he'd do better with planning.

Finally, she answered, "Tomorrow, I am at the shop. Mayhap the day after?"

Evan breathed out a sigh of relief and nodded. He rose and sped out of the box, mumbling about seeing to refreshments. He sent a waiter in with champagne, returning only as the bell rang to signal the end of the recess.

Beth's and Ford's heads were together, whispering at a furious pace, almost over one another. He shook his head.

"They've been like that the whole time." Althea's voice was soft, tentative, next to him. She held out a champagne flute as though it was a peace offering.

He arched a brow and nodded his thanks, taking it to sip.

"Evan, I—"

"Oh, look, the curtain." Nervous, not ready to dive into their last conversation in whispers in a dark theatre, he turned and focused on the stage.

The play reopened, but the couple in front of them did not notice.

Instead, Ford hauled Beth onto his lap, her back to his front, so they could both still watch the performance. Beth's skirts rustled, and she gasped.

Evan squirmed in his seat.

Ugh. If he is intimate with her right in front of me, when he knows Althea and I had a falling out, I may kill him immediately after dispatching Michael.

His cock ignored his frustration, remaining focused on the woman beside him and the couple in front of them. Her enjoyment of watching others in intimate acts at the demi-monde party flooded his thoughts, inflaming his lust further. He squirmed again as his dress breeches grew uncomfortably tight. He slid a sidelong glance at her.

She too focused on the couple in front of them rather than the stage. Her breath gusted through parted lips, her tongue darting out to lick them. Her hands fisted in her skirt as her gaze darted to his lap where his shaft lay thick and obvious along his thigh.

It twitched under her regard, and it was all he could do to hold still and pretend oblivion.

Her back arched a few degrees, and he wanted to feel the pert tips of her breasts against his palms or flattened between his finger and thumb.

He groaned low, but she heard and turned to him, eyes wide.

And said the most shocking thing he'd heard from her. "I dare you."

****

Althea's dare fell between them as she continued to stare at Evan. Her temerity shocked her as much as his expression reflected.

She had not been prepared for him to walk into the box in his signature colors of bronze and gold. She wanted to be mad at Penelope, but lud, he looked and smelled delectable.

She sat next to him for the first act, looking blindly at the stage while fully aware of every play of muscle in his arm, the tensile strength of his thigh, the long nimble fingers that brought her so much pleasure so facilely. The scents of sandalwood and ginger from his preference in shampoo, combined with an underlying hint of starch and…Evan.

When Ford dragged her cousin onto his lap, she was lost. Her secret delight combined with the sexiest man alive next to her—who knew her predilection to watch—heated her body from head to toe. Glimpsing the iron rod of his cock fanned the flames. At his moan, her question of how to use Beth's advice became clear. He'd just given her the perfect opening. She waited for his response.

He narrowed his eyes at her for a long moment before leaning forward and grasping the hem of her skirt and petticoat.

"Eyes on them." His voice guttural, he dragged the fabric upward to expose her legs. "Imagine what they're doing in that chair. Imagine what they could be doing without clothes in the way." He tilted his head to Ford and Beth.

As she watched their heads next to each other, Ford's tilted to put his lips to Beth's—ear? neck?—she decided on the spot just under the ear. Evan lifted her leg and tucked it over his, spreading her open.

She dared to reach over and palm his erection. His free hand covered hers to squeeze it against his length and hold it still. She knew from past experience that meant he liked it so much he needed a moment for control, and she reveled.

Once he freed her hand, she gripped him, stroking intermittently, as his other hand dipped under her skirts and stroked her damp folds. Slow passes of fingers were too gentle and unspecific to take her up the cliff of ecstasy.

Finally, he pressed the lips apart, dipping a finger to gather dampness before rising to circle her most sensitive spot.

She squeezed the head of his cock through his breeches in retaliation, and it twitched. His free hand rearranged his cock to ease her access. His legs slid open wider, and his length thrust an inch into her fist.

He grunted and turned in his seat to face her, forcing her to lose purchase.

He withdrew his fingers and brought them to his mouth to suck them clean. The change in position brought his other hand within reach, and it slid under her skirt to dip and rub.

He leaned in. "What are they doing now?"

She struggled to breathe and speak through the circling on the exact spot he knew would take her to the cusp. "Likely something quite similar to what we are doing, I should imagine."

"Then picture it and tell me. Use your words."

She smiled and groped for the phrasing. "His hand is beneath her skirt, teasing her as you are torturing me, my lord." Her breath hitched as he made a faster tiny circle with his finger, and it was her turn to thrust her hips.

His finger stilled. "More."

"As he strokes her, she presses her bottom back against him, trying to align her center with his hard length. But alas, he needs her off-center to keep her on his lap and reach everything. So his—he digs into her hip instead." Gasp, breathe, gasp. "His other hand is gripping her breast, weighing its heft in his hand before slipping into her neckline and fondling her."

"*Yes*." His voice was almost a grunt.

The curtain came down on Act Two. Two male voices said, "Hellfire," in unison. Her thoughts were so scattered by pleasure she could not even voice a curse.

"A server or usher will check on us during this break. Can you climax before they arrive?" He sped up his strokes.

Althea tried to bring her concerns of discovery of their relationship to the front of her mind. But she could not focus on anything other than the back of Ford's and Beth's heads and the feel of Evan's hands.

Please don't let them turn around. Please don't check on us, even in the owner's box. I am so close.

She panted.

Beth made as though to rise, and Ford whispered to her. Althea watched his shoulders bulge as he held the girl in place, and she reverted to her mental picture of where Ford's hands might be.

Evan's finger rubbed faster, then he slid two down and into her, curling them as his thumb pressed where he'd circled.

Althea thrust repeatedly, unable to do more than clutch his shoulder and the arm of her chair. She begged under her breath, "Oh, oh, oh. Please, Evan. Yes. Please."

Then she was over the cliff, her head thrown back, her lower back fully off the chair even as her shoulders pressed into it. His fingers pinched her nipple, and she flew higher, her whole body shuddering in pleasure, her muscles spasming under and around his fingers, over and over and over. Breath whistled between her teeth, clenched in an effort not to cry out. His muscled arm, taut with tension, was her anchor as she tried not to sob with sensation.

This man. Only he can summon this response from me.

After a long moment, she sagged, and he withdrew his fingers to cup her gently. After a moment, he produced a handkerchief to wipe his fingers before drawing her skirts down as her awareness of her surroundings returned. She dared not look at Beth and Ford for fear of smug grins at her release. Enervated and energized at the same time, she wished for more time with his cock, despite her satiation.

Activity sounded outside the curtain. They all waited through the usher check-in, neither couple acknowledging the other, as though each pair existed in a bubble where the other was merely there for their entertainment. Althea's eyes kept straying to Evan's cock, still rock hard.

At long last the bells were rung, the hall curtains drawn, and the stage curtain pulled back on Act Three.

And Beth's head, silhouetted in the stage lights, disappeared. Althea sat up, alarmed, before remembering what Evan had mentioned seeing in the demi-monde party, then taught her during one of their clandestine meetings.

Not waiting for direction or to be stopped, she turned to him and shoved his knees apart. She slid to her knees between his legs. Looking up at him, she repeated, "I dare you."

"Godsakes, Althea. You know I cannot resist a dare." He was already fumbling at the fall of his breeches.

His cock sprang out, longer and thicker than she remembered, almost hitting her in the eye.

Grasping it with one hand, she licked her lips with hunger and slid them over it. Sucking hard, she withdrew. "Can you see them? Or hear them? What are they doing?"

"I cannot see anyone but you." His focus was on her, his hand gentle under her hair so he would not muss it, his other cupping his breeches out of the way of his bollocks. "Please, Althea. 'Tis my turn to beg."

"There is no need to beg, my lord. I am happy to please you." She sucked him down, their gazes locked in the darkness as she teased him with her pace for long minutes before she drove him up, bobbing faster. His cock pulsed and grew harder in her mouth. He stifled a groan with his fist to his lips, his other hand tugging her hair a warning. Her tongue curled around the sensitive underside of his cock, and he exploded in her mouth. She swallowed the hot spurts down before licking him clean.

The final act continued to play as he helped her back into her seat. They each stared blindly at the stage, sipped champagne, and watched Beth, giggling quietly, resume her position on Ford's lap. As the theatre emptied and they followed the herd to the stairs down to the lobby, Evan was silent again. His reserve had returned, a veil over his emotions.

Uncertain how to reach him, she knew 'twould be impossible in a crowded theatre. Her hand was on his arm, and she squeezed it to garner his attention. "Evan, I look forward to your call two days hence."

He nodded once before handing her into her carriage after Ford had done the same for Beth.

She'd see what he had to say, then hopefully find the right words to ask him to continue their secret affair.

Chapter Sixteen

Evan arrived at White's for a long overdue visit with Michael. They, along with Ford, tried to meet once a fortnight when they were in Town.

Seeing he was the first to arrive, he ordered a round for all of them and settled into his preferred chair. They always chose this particular seating area and always sat in the same chair within that grouping. Much as Evan embraced new experiences, this one habit was comforting, as was the prospect of catching up with his friends.

Michael's voice sounded behind him. "Good chap, ordering me a drink."

Evan stood. Ignoring formality, the men clasped each other on the shoulder before sitting.

"Tell me about marital bliss. And Pen's bakery. Did you bring me any treats?" Evan always asked, even though White's was not a place Michael would bring food.

Michael laughed at him and shook his head. "Marital bliss is delicious, and that is all the detail you'll get. And the bakery is still under construction, but you'll be the first to know when she needs someone to test recipes on again."

Evan glanced around to ensure no one was sitting nearby before leaning in. "While 'tis just us, I wanted to mention something. Given your ownership of the

236

theatre where Pen was auctioned and your betrothal, I have no doubt you're aware of the School of Enlightenment."

Michael's eyes darted left and right. "I was sworn to silence."

"Bah, always the drab fellow, even now. I make my own rules, and you know I don't do anything by half measure. Why d'you think my servants have always been comfortable with the house party activities? Heck, they sometimes join in when they want."

Michael nodded in remembered agreement. "I should have wondered about that. Before Pen, I was too busy having fun with any and all interested." He pondered that for a moment, then directed his gaze at Evan. "What was it you wanted to discuss?"

"I wanted to hear more of the scholarship you are sponsoring."

"'Tis for other girls like Pen to have a path out of poverty."

Ford plopped into his usual seat, and they sat back, reaching for their drinks.

"Gentlemen." Ford's greeting was terse, said through tight lips. He waved a hand in a circle. "Pray, do continue."

Evan knew him too well for that. "What's the matter, old chap?"

Ford leaned in and hissed, "Does everyone in White's know about the school? Or just you two, and apparently your ladies, and their friends, and God knows who else?"

Evan's brows had risen at his first question, and he and Michael both leaned forward again.

"I suppose Beth told you about it?" Evan said as Michael's eyes widened at the discovery of yet another student.

Ford growled.

"I'll take that as a yes." Evan remained calm. "It is a very closely held secret, I assure you. No one who isn't directly connected hears about it, or you know I would have said something. As for talking about it here, consider the background noise. No one can hear us. 'Tis the perfect foil."

"So how did he learn about it?" Ford flung a hand toward Michael.

"The auction that Penelope participated in was hosted by a group connected to the school and the girls came from there." Michael attempted to diffuse the situation by answering Ford's question. "If you had bid for a contract with someone, you would have been brought into the fold."

When Ford started to speak, Evan held up a hand. "Really, Ford. I am sorry. Even students who know one another are told to be careful when they discuss it. And those they meet after attending are not to know."

"If you'll remember," Michael added, "Sophia and Penelope reunited well after I won her. They only discovered their mutual education because one of the auction leaders specifically approved it."

"The new Lady Peterborough?" Ford's voice went high in surprise.

"You'll remember Peterborough dropped his membership to Sarah's around the time of his marriage." Evan arched a brow. "Either way, why is it shocking for a countess to attend the school and not for an earl to visit a spanking club?"

"Good point. Well said," Michael added, nodding.

Ford threw up his hands, still glaring at them.

"Now that you know, what questions do you have for me—us?" Evan asked, glancing at Michael.

Michael nodded, elbows on his wideset knees. His hands hung between cradling his drink.

"Hmph," Ford grunted, his brow furrowed in thought. "Who else knows of this school?"

Michael ticked them off on his fingers. "Sophia's husband, Peterborough. And her cousin and his wife, Suffolk and Lady Roslynn. Sarah Potter. My theatre manager and the other ladies who ran the auction."

"Oh, and a good number of the servants at Greenborough Park are graduates," Evan added, grinning at Ford, who knew of his policy regarding the staff there and had joined him in partaking in more than one naked and sweaty evening.

Robert nodded slowly.

"Wait. Sophia was gentry, even before Peterborough married her. Penelope was…not." He slid a careful glance to Michael, who nodded. "And…servants?"

"Yes. Three separate courses, but with similar teachings. Young ladies destined for Ton marriages are of course in separate classrooms and dormitories but have lots of leeway in choosing the subjects. And every student has a sponsor to help direct them. I am presently working on adding a fourth program."

The other two men frowned in confusion. Then Michael snickered. "An enterprise path, mayhap?"

Evan grinned. "Don't knock it. Your countess can benefit from it. Wouldn't she love to staff her store with young women who she is confident have the basics of inventory management and customer service?"

Michael's smile turned thoughtful. "Indeed she would. Do I have permission to share this with her? When do you expect to invite the first class?"

"Who was Beth's sponsor?" Ford interrupted, still focused on the parts most relevant to his circumstances.

"Althea." Evan shot a glance at Michael, promising him an answer later.

"And Althea's?"

Evan shook his head. "She did not attend, but she fully supported Beth attending."

"So there are people *directly connected* to the school who have never attended, floating about the country as well?"

Evan arched a brow at his strange phrasing. "Yes. You're looking at two of them. Why?"

"Never mind that for now. How did you first hear about it?"

Evan grinned. "How d'you think?"

Ford rolled his eyes. "Of course, you probably help fund it."

Evan wiggled his brows. "I helped *found* it." He raised his glass. "And you're welcome. Cheers."

The other two gave reluctant chuckles as they raised their drinks to toast him. Evan wondered if Althea knew the extent to which he was involved in the school, then cursed himself for wondering. He'd deal with her tomorrow. For tonight, he'd enjoy the residual glow from her excellent oral skills and savor these hours with his closest friends. With Michael married and he and Ford dabbling in relationships, opportunities like this were becoming more rare.

And Althea has become one of my closest friends. If

only I knew what more I want from her.
****

The next evening, dusk turned to twilight as Evan rode to Althea's home. To avoid risking her reputation, he turned the horse to the alley leading to the stables behind the house. Leaving his horse, he was faced with a dilemma. It felt odd to knock there like a servant, but he could not very well use his key when servants were about, making dinner.

He knocked, dredging up every ounce of panache he could to nod as though it were normal for an earl to call at the kitchen door.

As they stepped aside for him to enter, he nodded and used his most imperious tone to announce himself. "The Earl of Cheltenham to see Lady Althea at her invitation."

The servant scurried away. Moments later, the butler hustled into the kitchen, gesturing. "Right this way, my lord. My apologies to keep you waiting in the kitchen."

"'Tis no bother. It was my choice. I took the liberty of ordering tea to be delivered to Lady Althea's office, assuming that is where you're taking me."

The man nodded, holding the door for him, then stepping out and pulling it almost shut.

Althea rounded her desk and walked toward him. She held her hands out. "Evan. Thank you for coming."

Taking them in his, he pulled her in and kissed her cheek. "Althea. You look lovely, as always." He stifled a grimace at their stilted exchange.

"Come, sit with me." She led him to the plum-and-gold-toned seating area.

"Thank you for seeing me." *Ugh, I sound like a*

right prig. I need to unbend to properly apologize.

"Beth and Penelope helped me understand your reaction to my misunderstanding," she inserted before he could start.

Evan's brows rose at her mention of Penelope. Women's gossip never ceased to amaze him.

"I hope you realize I was not trying to take advantage," Althea continued, oblivious to his reaction. "It truly was a misunderstanding. In fact, I am happier to have Charlotte—Lady Peterborough—as an investor. With no man shadowing me, vendors and the like are forced to deal with me as the owner."

"I do. I was happy to hear from Charlotte that you'd made progress with the shared space model."

"Yes. We already have some of our goods in Emily's store and her ink and pens in mine. We are waiting on a further delivery, but things are going extremely well. Thank you for suggesting this approach." Althea plucked at her skirt. She glanced down and away, then drew a breath.

He twined his fingers together in his lap and sighed. She had not only beaten him to the apology, she was attempting to repair their relationship. Did he dare hope they could move forward? But first, he needed to respond in kind. "I am glad. But I must beg your pardon for my harsh words, Althea. I overreacted."

Her face cleared. "Yes. You did a bit." She arched a brow. "But I suppose if you can forgive me for my misunderstanding, I can forgive you. Especially as the girls gave me perspective on why you might react that way."

"It does get tiresome to always be seen for my deep pockets." He nodded once, still anxious to see how she wanted to progress.

Althea gulped again. "I care naught for your deep pockets. Your big cock is another story."

Evan's gaze shot to hers in surprise. Had she really said that? Her steady stare said yes. He laughed so hard he thought he might pop a waistcoat button.

She grinned.

"I am certain we can fix that, my lady." Evan began to stand, but his breeches had only barely cleared the seat cushion when the housekeeper strode in with the tea tray.

"Sustenance first, mayhap?" Althea asked with a half-smile.

Evan growled. With a quick check of the housekeeper's progress out the door, he said, "If I did not know how much you hate cold tea, I'd lock the door and show you my priorities."

Althea busied herself pouring and doctoring tea. After she'd passed him his cup and saucer, then a plate of small bites, she set down her tea.

Evan cocked his head at her in question.

"I have missed you, Evan. Not just your, er—" She gestured at his lap, having apparently lost her bravery after the one reference. "I've missed you, but my concerns about my reputation still stand. After the soirée, rumors of our relationship could undermine my sales if people think you are driving the expansion effort, and I have even more at risk financially now. I should like to continue to spend time with you. It simply must remain private."

His heart sank. *What did I expect? This is short-term for her, and I know her reputation is more susceptible to gossip than mine. Why do I care? 'Tis temporary for me as well. Is it not?*

Unable to identify why it felt like one step forward and two steps back, he nodded, attempting a smile. "Of course."

"Evan…" Althea's conciliatory tone made it clear his expression had not masked his disappointment.

"I do not have to like it, but I do understand." Without overthinking it, he added, "I missed you. I find myself willing to spend time with you any way you'll have me." He stood. "If you'll excuse me, I shall return later tonight, under cover of darkness then?"

As he ate a light supper alone and waited for traffic to slow on the streets to venture back for his assignation, Evan pondered their relationship. Having toyed with the idea of marriage, he could not set it aside. Despite their argument, he'd missed her for the month they'd been apart, missed more than her body.

But even if he overcame his fears and asked for her hand, she did not want more than a secret affair.

****

A week later, Althea was more tired than ever. Before their reconciliation, she had slept poorly without Evan's late-night visits. Once those resumed, she had hoped their renewed routine would resolve her insomnia. However, Evan seemed to be following a script. He'd arrive, ask perfunctory questions about her day and her business, then seduce her.

The sex was amazing, as always. She was still learning new things, techniques, positions, pacing just when she thought he had run out of new approaches. They'd discovered she liked the flogger more than spanking but only occasionally, he liked being in control, and that orgasms were more intense when she was on her hands and knees with him behind her, but they both preferred face to face. Neither admitted it, but she thought it was more intimate.

However, Evan's attitude now lacked the easy affection they'd had. He was playing a part, and she was frustrated. She wanted the warm, supportive, caring Evan back, not only the expert lover.

How does one complain that a partner's expertise, as profound as it might be, is not enough?

Beth was struggling as well. It seemed that Ford found her background intimidating, to say nothing of her current network. He'd been quick to accept her assistance in finding another blacksmith but rejected her suggestions on how to sell his pieces.

Althea understood his concerns. Like her, he did not want to be the center of gossip, albeit for different reasons. When she'd attempted to explain that to Beth, her cousin had insisted she could be discreet, and Althea did not have the heart to point out her history that said otherwise.

Gaining the front hall after another grueling day on her feet at the store, Althea handed off her cloak to the butler. She noted the pile of correspondence in the salver on the front hall table and sifted through the combination of posted missives and hand-delivered invitations. Among the correspondence, she found a fancy invitation. "Here, Beth, 'tis to both of us. Open it. I want to see what my solicitor sent."

A moment later, Beth bounded into the library behind her, not letting her get to her desk. "'Tis perfect. Please, Althea? We must go! 'Tis the best way to get over that man."

Dread stole over Althea. What could possibly have

taken her cousin from the doldrums to bouncing except something naughty? Bracing herself, she reached for the invitation.

Beth held it tight. "Please say yes, Althea. We've already been to the one during the Season. And then Cheltie's house party and the off-season fête here. This will be much tamer than that, and you enjoyed Greenborough Park. Please?"

Ah. We've been invited to a demi-monde party again. Beth and her connections. Althea's blood ran cold when she realized her name was on it as well. Concerned anew about her reputation, she held her hand out. "Allow me to see the invitation, please."

Scanning it, she found the hostesses names scrolled at the bottom. Sarah Potter's name she knew from the ball during the Season. "Who is Mrs. Lockhart?"

"Do you remember Penelope attended the school with me," Beth answered, "and participated in the virgin auction at the theatre?"

"Yes."

"Both ladies were involved with the auction. They have school connections, and Prudence Lockhart manages the theatre. They are very careful, and invitees are thoroughly vetted."

"I see. Will Evan or Ford be there?"

Beth shrugged, then admitted, "I think the upstairs is for demonstrations of his wares."

"Is this something you really want to do? And what if they're not there?" Personally, she thought it would be torture to know the heights of pleasure she could achieve with the right person and be surrounded by others interested in that same pleasure, but not have the person she wanted available. She supposed she could broach the subject with Evan later that evening if he was willing to talk for more than a minute. And her body still hummed when she remembered the last two balls like this and the scenes she'd watched.

"I darned well do. I am tired of pining for him, and self-pleasure is not at all the same."

Althea blushed at her cousin's bold words, even though she could commiserate. "Right, then. If you are certain of these ladies' discretion, I am willing."

"Oh, thank you, cuz, thank you!" Beth bounded out of the room.

****

Evan was exhausted. He still had not decided what he wanted from Althea. He only knew he was not happy about her request for continued secrecy, despite his claim that he'd accept her terms.

Where will all this lead? How do I decide that without daylight hours with Althea to the extent her work allows. Damn me, I'll take a supper, a breakfast, anything that allows us to further our relationship beyond the bedroom.

He snorted. His silly girlish side was dramatizing again. A few months ago, he would have been more than happy not to have to speak to a sexual partner at all, with no thought to the future. There were a hundred men and women behind Althea who would leap into his bed given the chance, with no questions asked. Why worry about the future?

Because I care. He'd snapped at her when she thought he would fund her business because he was hurt that she was yet another person after his money. She wasn't, but she didn't want all of him, either. She had the power to hurt him, because he cared for her more than he ever had for a bed partner.

He sighed. Something had to change. He could not keep playing this clandestine role.

You say you want more, but how is she to know this? Last time they discussed it, he'd had his own limitations for the relationship. He'd told her he had no interest in marriage, and warned her about his public profile. He desired the freedom of a public fling with none of the responsibilities of marriage or the repercussions that society imposes on women.

The idea of marrying Althea was sitting more comfortably in his thoughts. But the risks of marriage felt far more serious than the risks to her reputation. Weren't they? Or was that a selfish point of view? He had no idea. But one thing he was certain of was that he was done with sneaking around. He needed her to choose him. Then he might be able to trust in the future.

Rifling through his usual pile of invitations, he let them drop one by one into the wastebasket. A familiar logo—a scourge and mask—caught Evan's eye, and he pulled it free, dropping the rest of the stack back to his desk.

Sarah and Pru were hosting a demi-monde masquerade in two nights. He grinned. 'Twas the perfect opportunity to get past Althea's walls and end this sneaking around. The temptation of viewing debauchery might distract her and lower her guard. Mayhap she'd be more willing, more open to suggestion. His desire to take advantage of the situation might be underhanded, but he wasn't sure he cared. He was at his wits end. He wanted Althea but could no longer live with her terms. It was time to up the stakes.

He scribbled two notes out and called for a

footman. Ford needed warning that his presence was required. The other, he sent to Althea, making his excuses for the evening and telling her he'd be at the party the following night. Let the next time she saw him be at the gala. After another quick thought, he sent a note to Sarah to ensure Althea and Beth had been invited.

*****

Trying to take a page from her cousin's book, she'd allowed Beth to dress her for the masquerade. While she had no interest in marriage or a high-profile affair, she could not resist the allure of these parties now that she had discovered the pleasure to be had in physical intimacy.

If I'm being honest, that pleasure may well be dependent on being with the right person, and my prurient interest in watching others performing intimate acts.

She kept an eye out for Evan, having received his note the day before.

Beth had chosen a garnet dress for Althea, her favorite because it suited her light skin and dark hair so well. While the one she'd worn at Greenborough Park had been somewhat daring, this dress's neckline skimmed her nipples. She'd need to breathe carefully tonight and not bend over. Beth only allowed her one petticoat and no drawers, so she felt naked from her ribcage down, where the dress draped away from her short form corset. The dress was a leaner cut than her other dresses and skimmed along her body, highlighting her willowy height.

In contrast, Beth had donned a buttery yellow dress that matched her hair and had a wide square neckline that displayed her impressive cleavage without being as low cut as Althea's. Instead, Beth had rouged her nipples and foregone a corset. She had declared earlier that her goal for the evening was carnal acts right at the party. Althea hoped she meant in an upstairs room, not the theatre-ballroom.

Slipping on their masks, they stepped down from the coach and knocked on the unassuming door. Althea tried to ignore her misgivings about entering the private men's spanking club again. She reminded herself of her mantra the first time she brought Beth to one of these as an outlet for her cousin's overactive libido.

In the main room, she accepted a glass of gold bubbly liquid from a servant's tray and sipped. *Champagne rather than lemonade. Ah yes, this could be a very good night.*

They strolled the perimeter of the room. There was another dark-haired woman in a ruby gown who Althea remembered seeing at the last party and that she was within a few years of Althea's age.

Althea wondered if Evan had been with the slightly older lady. Then, looking around she grimaced. *Gads, he may have been with all of them.* If only she could claim him publicly, so they'd know he was not available.

Giving herself a mental shake, she realized how silly that thought was. She was the one who wanted it secret. She did not want to marry any more than he did.

Trading her empty glass for a second one, she frowned into the gold liquid.

A gentleman's voice said teasingly, "Now what did that poor drink ever do to you to cause you to frown at it so?"

She looked up. One of the prospective investors Evan had introduced her to stood before her, with a small mask that did nothing to hide his features.

"Lady E, I believe?" He kindly forewent her full surname given their surroundings.

She nodded.

"And what brings you to this establishment?" His smile was wicked.

"Ah…" Lud, she was out of practice at flirting. "My cousin…" She gestured vaguely, but Beth had seen someone interesting and was halfway across the room. As Althea's gaze followed Beth's progress, it stopped on two men talking just inside the entrance. One was taller and slimmer than the other but with nicely muscled shoulders and a mane of dark gold— *Evan!*

He turned in her direction, perusing the dancers.

She gasped.

He hadn't even bothered with a mask.

He wonders why I worry about being with him in public.

Her lips twisted at the bitter thought. Not ready to see him yet, particularly in the large crowd, she murmured a garbled excuse to the investor and turned to flee up the stairs, seeking refuge.

Chapter Seventeen

As Ford greeted their hostesses and stepped away to speak to Sarah privately about adding two new items to the demonstrations, Evan gazed around the room. When he spied Beth, his blood surged.

Where one goes, so does the other. Althea is here. His body hummed at the thought. The mere idea of her did what Franklin's fine arse could not. His cock sat up and begged.

A sycophant approached, but Evan listened to his fawning with one ear. Hopefully, Ford's samples would create a viewing opportunity Evan could use to his advantage, to help convince Althea to change her mind. He trusted that she wasn't after his money. Why could she not find faith that he would protect her reputation?

Because neither your reputation nor hers is wholly within your control.

Damned internal voice nagging at him. He no longer cared. If he was not worth the risk, he'd rather know now. Otherwise, how would she react when the stakes were higher and his mental faculties were fading, preventing him from fighting back?

Anger and frustration reclaimed him. He'd show her what she would miss without him, here in this place that held her favorite vice. Then he'd walk away and await her decision.

He climbed the stairs, peering in the first room—a

man getting his cock sucked. Eh. Second room—two women kissing with their tits pulled over their dress and rubbing. Pretty, but eh. Third room—he sucked in a breath. Not because of what he saw in the room, but because he smelled her. Althea.

Turning his head slowly, he saw her a half step in front of him, clutching the doorframe. In shock? Lust? No matter. He was sure he could make it lust in moments.

He slowly slid back a step, edging right to stand behind her. As he did, she sucked a breath in and hummed under her breath. Another couple to the left of the doorway gasped as well. Evan looked. Ah, just as he'd expected. The couple was using one of Ford's leather harnesses. Come to think of it, he'd never thought to try one of those with Althea. Mayhap he would…if she chose him.

Refocusing on his goal, he inched closer to Althea, his gaze flickering between her and the occupants of the room. As the activities unfolded, he judged her body's responses.

The man, an earl Evan had a passing acquaintance with, had three leather straps of varying length joined in the middle of their length, so they could lay flat side by side. He was buckling the first length around one of the woman's calves.

The woman was on her back on the bed, and her dress was up around her hips. She faced away from the door so her face was not visible, but she was not the man's wife. The hair was dark blonde, and Evan knew the countess's locks were closer to Althea's brunette.

His lips twisted at the reminder of how easy it was for men to withstand gossip than women. He did not want to consider that now.

The man pushed her dress out of the way, and Althea drew in a breath, shifting her weight. He bent his partner's knee to bring her calf parallel to her upper leg. The other two leather straps hung free from the one on her calf. He buckled the middle strap around the thigh. She could no longer straighten her leg.

Althea squirmed again, and Evan inched even closer.

The third strap was much shorter. The man held his hand out to the prone woman, and she placed her hand in his. Before she could blink, he had buckled that shorter strap around her wrist along her thigh, and her left side was immobilized. He ran a thick finger under each of the leather circles, to ensure they were not too tight, then quickly performed the same steps with her other side.

Althea's skirts rustled as she shuddered, and Evan's blood surged. The woman's most private folds lay spread open for the man to do what he wished, with no way for her to close her legs or stop him. It was a powerful vision, mayhap not something Althea would want to try but titillating to watch and imagine.

Evan's breeches, led by his cock, brushed the folds of Althea's dress. He watched the man lean over and scoop his partner's breasts out of her wide-necked bodice. Leaning in, Evan took a moment to watch Althea's chest heave against her dangerously low décolletage, to spy her nipples poking through the thin layers of fabric, and to inhale her scent once more.

His lips almost touched her ear as he whispered, "Do you like that, Althea? Shall I pull you back to lean against me and plump your breasts that last inch so that

I can pinch their hard little points?"

She gulped but did not jump. He suspected she'd sensed him as he had her.

He gripped one hip to tug her against him. His cock sighed in relief to feel her bottom cheeks shove backwards. It pulsed eagerly and attempted to get to her through the fabric. Holding her against him to satisfy his ambitious cock, he trailed the finger of his other hand along that ever-so-deep vee of skin above her neckline.

They both watched the bed as the earl's hand disappeared between the woman's legs. Evan snuck his hand from her hip between them, forcing his cock back to make room so that he could press a finger between her thighs to mimic what they watched. As her hips twitched, he tugged her dress down in front and covered her freed globe with his waiting hand.

She squirmed, but was still quiet, surprising him. Mayhap she was loathe to talk or even face him. That was fine. He did not want her to think about the others in the hallway. But neither did he want to risk her reputation too much.

"Shh, follow me." He pulled her dress back up and ran his hand down to hers, dragging her with him. He paced to the end of the hall and found an empty room. Ducking in, tugging her after him, he locked the door.

He wanted her physically. But if she started talking, he swore he'd gag her. Well, after he received her agreement, of course. His golden rule. He wanted to show her what the physical was like without the face-to-face intimacy and caring they'd had previously. What an orgasm without a relationship felt like. He wanted to be a little mean.

"Now, then, Althea." Fueled by lust and frustration at the need to interrupt their rising passion to get to privacy, his words sounded gravelly. "I seem to remember you wanted orgasms." He waived a hand at the lock. "*Private* orgasms from me, despite wanting to watch others. Let's make this one good, as it will be your last. I find I cannot be with someone who is ashamed of me."

****

Half-dazed with excitement, Althea took a moment to register Evan's harsh words. *My last? He thinks I am ashamed? Am I?*

He spun her halfway around behind a large leather-bound settee and stepped behind her. Spying movement, she flinched, only to realize he'd turned them to face a mirror. Watching their reflections, she could see as well as feel her surprise.

They were both tousled and flushed, but while her gaze was slightly unfocused, his was sharp, intent. He grabbed her hips and shoved against her. His eyes flickered closed for a moment, his mouth slackening with pleasure, before he shook himself and stared hard at her in the mirror.

"You enjoy watching. And you told me that every time we were intimate, it was more erotic than anything you'd heard or read. Shall we see if we can reach a new height? How will you react to watching *us*."

A bolt of lust shot through Althea, and she moaned, unable to find words. Unease slithered through the back of her mind. He'd said something she should worry about...

He thrust against her bottom again, then reached around and yanked her dress below her breasts with both hands this time. Cupping her breasts as though offering them to her in the mirror, he asked again, "Althea? I'll need your answer."

His finger and thumb pinched each nipple, bringing her on her toes. All coherent thought fled.

"Yes. Please, Evan," she whispered, pushing her bottom back and her breasts forward.

"Right, then. Imagine I had a set of those cuffs, and I wanted you to watch me use them on you."

And watch she did.

Evan skimmed his hands along her sides, his lips feathering over her skin where her neck met her shoulder. He bit there, lightly.

She saw it as much as she felt it. 'Twas as though they were animals, and he was holding his mate still.

She writhed, her eyes closing as sensation shot through her from where his teeth held her skin. Her breasts tingled, feeling every waft of air from his actions. She shifted her feet to widen her stance.

"Keep your eyes open, and there would be no moving if you were bound." He bent her at the hips, folding her over the settee back and drew her hands together behind her. "Lace your fingers together or I shall use my cravat."

She shuddered at the thought, the image of the woman's wrists strapped to her thighs fresh in her mind.

"Can you see in the mirror still?"

She nodded.

"Good. Watch us."

He leaned forward to plump her breasts where they dangled, pinching the tips. She could smell her shampoo in his hair. That and the twinge of erotic pain in her nipples made her squirm against his hips.

Grabbing her skirts, he tossed them up, flipping them over her back.

She watched his reaction to her bare bottom, a smile creeping across her lips when his brows quirked.

"One petticoat? No knickers? Not even a long chemise?" He tsked.

"Oh please. As though you don't like the convenience," she mumbled, twitching her rump.

He spanked one cheek hard, then the other.

She gasped, arching her back, bottom pushing up toward him. "Evan…"

She needed his cock or his fingers or something. Her core clenched with desire, her pulse pounding. Her nipples throbbed from his pinch, increasing her pleasure.

He grabbed her hands from where they'd fallen to the seat cushion and put them to her thighs. "Hold your legs, as though your hands were cuffed to them."

She tentatively reached, grabbing her upper thighs, still watching in the mirror. His eyes flared with lust as he stared downward at her bottom and hands. She realized she had unwittingly opened herself farther to him. If only he would touch her, not just look.

"Are you still watching?" Evan's voice was thick. He had not spared a glance for the mirror, his focus was on her, from her hair where he fisted one hand to her bottom where his hand slid across her buttocks into the crevice between then forward to check her readiness.

The quick swipe of his fingers tingled, a terrible tease more than a caress. Then they were gone, and he was fumbling with the fall of his breeches, then one of his cock socks.

Pulling her hair, he forced her head up to ensure she was watching, only then meeting her wide-eyed gaze through her mask in the mirror. He shoved into her.

He'd never been this rough with her. His harsh countenance combined with his near-violent thrust had her bracing for pain. Instead, in the mirror, her breasts bouncing from the force of his invasion juxtaposed against his waistcoat and cravat, which remained unrumpled, and his face tight with focus while hers slackened with sensation sent her over the edge. Her channel convulsed in ecstasy around him, squeezing him rhythmically.

He reached around her, and her gaze locked on his hand as it slid under her hips, the mere sight escalating the fire in her to inferno levels. His touch on her hard, quivering pleasure button was almost painful, but he was slower there than his plunges into her had been. Her orgasm soared higher rather than ebbing. She wailed with the intensity, unsure where it would end. All through it, she stared at him, held in thrall by his mastery of her perversity and her body.

His jaw clenched as he thrust out then back in once, then held still as her shudders slowed.

Her walls continued to pulse around his cock, albeit lessening until he began to thrust again.

"My turn," he gritted out through clenched teeth. He grabbed her hips, wrenching back then jerking forward again, hard enough to shift the sofa an inch.

She sobbed, looking for his hands against her flesh in the mirror. The sight was blocked by her skirts. Seeing their reflection but unable to view the act itself created more intimacy. Her breasts swung with every jolt of his thrust as his cock hit a fraction deeper with his grip. Her hair slipped from its pins on one side.

The couples she'd seen in the other rooms wound through her thoughts. A man holding a woman's hair as he fucked her mouth, another man literally tying a woman open to do what he wanted with her. She and Evan were another couple in another room, available for her viewing, one more man directing a woman for his pleasure and hers. His intent furrow between his brows, his focus on where their bodies touched, and her mask still in place despite her dishabille lent them anonymity. They could be anyone. For this moment, they were. And it inflamed her further.

She dropped her hands to the settee cushion and drove back against him, watching his face.

"Holy hell," ripped out of his throat, and he raised his gaze to lock on the reflection of hers.

He sped up, pounding into her with his thumbs digging into her bottom. They'd leave bruises, marks that would remind her of this new pinnacle. She tilted her hips another inch, leaning forward, and he hit a spot inside her that had her keening.

One of his hands covered her mouth to keep her quiet, and his hips pistoned even faster, the skin around his eyes crinkling as it did when he neared climax. That sight more so than all the internal sensations took her over, and her eyes finally fluttered close as heat poured through her. Her breasts rubbed the settee back, her knees and back softened while her internal muscles tightened, feeling every convulsion and leap of his cock as he came with her, groaning quietly in her ear.

Afterward, he helped her up, offering his handkerchief for her use. Taking it back, he swiped at himself, then pocketed that and the cock sleeve.

Awkwardly, she tucked her bosom away and shook out her skirts, hoping for a kiss or a hug. This was beyond the emotional distance she'd worried about those late nights at her home. A coldness emanated from him.

Tugging his waistcoat flat, Evan checked a mirror on the wall. He turned to her and tipped an imaginary hat and shot his cuffs. His tone was indeed frigid when he dismissed her with the words, "My gratitude for the secret orgasm, my lady. Enjoy your evening."

He walked out.

****

Shocked, Althea stood frozen for long minutes after Evan left the room. He had closed the door behind him, so there were no hallway gawkers.

I cannot believe he would simply leave after that. Did he not feel what I felt? If he was angry with me, why did he fu—she couldn't even think the word—*want me?*

With her brain cleared of the fog of passion, she remembered his words after locking the door. Damn him, 'twas a deliberate act of vengeance. He'd planned for it to be their last encounter. Yet he'd told her repeatedly he understood her concerns about a public relationship.

She sighed. This was his world, far more so than hers. Men such as he made the rules, and he'd made his more than clear.

She bit her lip, took a deep breath, and made her way downstairs, where she was relieved to find Beth in the main room and fully dressed.

Her cousin knew her well enough to call the

carriage as soon as she saw Althea's face.

Althea made it into the vehicle with the door shut before she broke down.

Between sobs, she related the events of the past hour. As she came to Evan's parting words, her sobs abated, replaced by anger. Straightening her back, her heart hardened. "I am done with him. This is twice he's been heartless and dictatorial rather than having a rational conversation. I thought I loved him, thought I had seen beneath the façade, but 'tis clear he does not care for me—"

Beth opened her mouth.

Althea sliced her hand through the air. "—or at least does not trust me. I am done."

Beth patted her hand. "I understand. I still think he might have been protecting himself, but that was unnecessarily cruel. Or if 'twas meant to spur you to a change of heart, 'twas poorly thought out."

"I'll show him. This Bath expansion will explode. Mayhap I shall go beyond it to Brighton. Hell, I might even put one in Cheltenham to spite him."

Beth watched her dubiously.

"What?"

"If you are truly done with him, why are you worried about showing him? The thing to do is show yourself. You have nothing to prove to anyone…besides maybe Lady Peterborough."

"Fine." Althea gave a firm nod. "That is what I shall do."

****

For the next several weeks, as more and more of the Ton returned to London after Michaelmas and the London shop became busier than ever, she and

Charlotte applied themselves to unadulterated success.

When Althea wondered what Evan would think about something, she asked Charlotte instead. When she lay in bed at night, her body craving his, she reminded herself of their last encounter. As erotic as it had been, intimacy had been absent. That was not what she wanted in a lover.

Oh, who am I kidding?

Without Evan, she would never have known what she desired in a bed partner. What she truly craved was the old Evan back. While she could not risk a public affair, he had every right to want more. He had his choice of women. Indeed, he had likely already chosen one. Or more than one. Then her guilt turned to anger at how he handled the conflict, and her thoughts circled endlessly.

Despite her inner turmoil, she remained outwardly focused, and business flourished. Despite being only two months into the formal partnership, profits had been encouraging enough that Charlotte wanted to fund her expansion to Brighton in the spring, as soon as the roads grew more passable.

"What do you think of a second London location instead?" Althea asked.

Charlotte shook her head. "Your shop is in the best location. If you open a second store, it might eat into that store's sales by being too close, or you'd have to change pricing or product offerings."

"I was thinking of offering different products, more accessible to the merchant class. Still nice, but mayhap not as nice as the first store."

"What happens if a Ton snob walks into that location and buys a product based on your first store's reputation? Then finds it inferior?"

"Hmm."

"Here is a suggestion. Mayhap we open it under a different name, so no one associates it with the Mayfair location. If it will carry different products and cater to different clients, then you cannot capitalize on your store's reputation. But you will be able to leverage your knowledge of the business and your connections. The question is what your profitability will be with lesser products. We really should look at that first, especially shampoo."

"Right. Mayhap after Brighton then. Thank you. I would not have considered that."

"I might not have thought of Evan's shared space idea. It simply goes to show that two brains are better than one for most things."

Still incredulous at his actions and subsequent silence, Althea inwardly flinched at the other woman's mention of Evan.

"What is it, dear?"

"Nothing." Althea straightened in her chair, resolving to forget him. "I appreciate your help and guidance, Charlotte."

"'Twas not nothing." Charlotte leveled a stern look at her.

Althea found herself responding before she realized she had. "Lord Cheltenham and I do not see eye to eye on things other than the expansion of my shop."

"Mmm. Like what?"

"Like the fact that I did not want an equity investor—particularly a male equity investor. And that I worried about—" She could not very well share her concerns about an affair with Evan.

"Come now, you cannot stop there." Charlotte grinned. "Mayhap I can allay your concerns?"

Althea tried to tiptoe around the subject. "He has a...reputation. And I do not know how it would reflect on my shop given the gossip among the Ton if they thought there was a personal connection between us..."

It sounded terrible when she said it out loud, exactly as Evan had taken it. 'Twas as though he had to remain a dirty little secret.

Charlotte was snickering. "Ah. I think I understand. Frankly, my dear, I think you'd get as many new customers as you might lose. Evan's net is cast wide and far. But I can commiserate. Women's reputations are ever more fragile than men's. Just as men's egos are ever more fragile than women's. I bet he hated that."

Now it was Althea's turn to laugh. She had never heard anything truer in her life. Then she sobered. "He did, rather. Which is understandable. But he did not handle it well. He was rather vile to me, actually."

"Really? Cool, calm, collected Evan—vile?"

"Quite."

Charlotte looked thoughtful. "Then you are well rid of him. 'Tis a good thing you had a superior option for an investor, is it not?"

****

Evan wove the letter through his fingers, contemplating it. Althea was supposed to respond to his ultimatum by choosing him, dammit. Instead, she'd taken his words at face value and moved on, unwilling to fight for their relationship.

Then he'd received this note from Charlotte, who

was too perceptive by half. He supposed he was lucky she was only just starting to socialize after mourning her late husband, or else the widow would likely be lording it over him in person. She was full of praise for Althea, both personally and professionally, and noted some highlights of their first few months in partnership with the Bath store. It had done every bit as well as Evan had anticipated, and then some.

He riffled the foolscap once again. *If 'twere anyone else, I'd be happy for the investor and the shop owner. The investment did not meet my criteria, but I matched another successful partnership.* Why, then, was he so disgruntled at the update? And Charlotte said they were already contemplating further expansion. He was excited for Althea's success. Really, he was.

He scanned the letter again.

The last lines niggled at him. He'd had a few conversations with Charlotte these past months, both in person when he called on her to offer his condolences and by letter. She'd never been one to wallow in her widowhood, despite it being obvious that she missed Charles desperately.

I look forward to having these conversations and friendly competitions in person again soon. As you know, women must be that much more careful than men about observing society's rules.

His eyes narrowed. 'Twas as though she knew Althea's concern about being seen with him. Just how close had the two women become? He shook his head.

Why had he thought it was a good idea to introduce them? Oh, right—because he assumed he'd be in a relationship of some sort with Althea and 'twould be nice to have the two women he spent the most time with be on friendly terms. Instead, he was odd man out. Which was…unsettling. He could not recall the last time he'd not been in the inner circle of any social gathering, group, or otherwise.

He'd spent enough time with Charlotte to read between the lines. Not one to waste words, she'd effectively let him know that not only were rules different for women, but women's concerns were different than men's, and behavior might follow that. In short, she, too, believed that a public relationship with him could affect Althea's sales.

His conscience twinged, as it had countless times since the demi-monde party, at the words he had thrown at Althea when their bodies were still damp from lovemaking.

And making love it was. He knew with the ironic clarity of a broken heart that he'd loved her and still did. He'd behaved badly to hide his vulnerability. But with every visit home now a futile search for his mother in the body living in the dower house, his fear lingered. He dreaded being hurt, but also hated the thought of causing someone the same pain he felt watching his mother leave him even as she stood before him.

He looked beyond the letter in his hands to the one sitting on his desk. He had not felt brave enough to open it when the nurse first gave it to him, then there had been the party and Althea, and here he was, still staring at it more than a month later. Yet another thing he dreaded. Wouldn't all those panderers from the Ton who vied for his attention like he was a minor deity laugh if they knew? Just as they'd have been appalled at his lack of interest in copulation.

It seemed Althea had cured him of the latter, but

only he could solve the former.

Reaching forward, he cracked the wax seal and sucked in a sharp breath at his mother's handwriting.

Chapter Eighteen

My darling Evan,

I don't know where I'll be when you read this. Given my memories of my father, I could be long gone, even as my shell of a body sits with you hand in hand. For that, I am sorry. If I could spare you this experience, I would. Sometimes I contemplate hoarding laudanum, but I confess I am selfish. I want these last months with you. Even if I may not end up aware of them, I value the idea of them in my heart now.

I am so grateful Lucy suggested this letter. 'Twould have been lovely to have such a letter from my father. My hope is that it helps you.

In that vein, let me share my wishes with you and suggestions from my own experience.

Please do not feel guilty if you get frustrated. Even in my father's final months, I'd continue to search for lucidity in every visit. 'Tis difficult, mayhap impossible, to reconcile this person who acts like a stranger with the parent you remember. 'Tis natural to feel anger, despair, shame, and all sorts of other emotions. Absolve yourself. In case you need the words, I understand, and I forgive you.

Evan sniffed back tears and looked away, only to be inexorably drawn back.

Please live your life. Oh, of course I adore your visits whilst I know you and the current world, but when I cannot, go and enjoy yourself. Find someone to love and have fun. When I no longer have the words, I trust this letter will remind you. Your devotion is apparent in many ways even when you are not present, not the least of which is the care with which you select the lovely ladies to help me. But if I do not recognize you, do not torture yourself with visits. I promise I shall know in my heart that you love me.

Last and most important, do not waste time worrying about this illness and your future. If you stew, you shan't fully embrace all the hard work you've done to make this life so wonderful for our family. Find your happiness and enjoy it for however long it lasts.

Look to your father's circumstance. He died far too young in a racing accident, not from any mind-wasting illness. Remember, this condition does not happen to every family member. I hope that you of all people— who loves to gamble with money, weighing risks and rewards of investments—will see that the rewards of love far outweigh the risks. I have worried these past years that you were unwilling to take a chance on marriage because of this disease.

Aside from the need for heirs, I wish love and a family for you. The greatest happiness of my life was my time with your father and you. Can you imagine if I did not have that to look back on as a legacy? Raising such an incredible young man, smart as a whip, who took the reins of the family far too young, yet so deftly. More than that, loving your father, having a partner through thick and thin, holding you in my arms, watching you grow. Those are things I want for everyone in this world—except maybe that nasty cousin in the south...ah, see, you can still smile—and *especially you. You deserve all that and more.*

You don't deserve to be held back by me or fear of this disease. Ignore it, and me as needed, and go find your happiness.

My love always,

Mama

Evan gave up trying to remain stoic. He lowered his head across his arms on the desk and sobbed.

****

Althea had pretended to ignore Beth's nocturnal comings and goings. She supposed she should ask if 'twas Robert her cousin was sneaking off to see, but she could not bring herself to care. Nor did she want to expose herself any further to the younger woman's happiness. As it was, she could barely look at Beth's exuberant countenance some days.

Quite the guardian I am.

Finally, Sunday arrived, and they lingered over tea in the study.

"How have you been?" Althea ventured.

"Fabulous. I have a lead on placing two more students from the charity school, and I think one of them is an excellent candidate for the School of Enlightenment."

"How exactly do you determine that?"

Beth gave a small shrug. "It really depends on the girl and the situation."

"Fair enough. What caused you to consider this particular student?"

Beth slid a sidelong glance toward Althea and smirked. "I decided when she stayed after class and attempted to kiss me."

Althea's brows rose. "Attempted? You are usually

271

quite open to that sort of thing."

"Yes, well." Beth glanced away, mumbling, "Robert made me promise not to anymore."

"Hmm. We'll get to that in a minute. I have a different question first. Why would a girl who likes girls qualify for the school? I'd think 'twould take a bit more than that."

"The school is one of the safest paths to placement in a like-minded household, but you are right. The girl also has to want to learn independence and/or be open to a multitude of households. The fact that she is one of the brightest students in her class, and I'd seen her kissing a messenger—a cute boy a couple years younger than her—also contributed. But I could not resist getting a reaction from you, so I oversimplified a little." She chuckled.

"Thank you for explaining. So back to your other statement. Robert has extracted a promise from you, eh? What did you get from him in return? I know you too well to believe you made any unilateral promises."

"He may have had to promise to entertain me enough I wouldn't get distracted."

"Ah, that explains the late-night comings and goings I've heard." Althea smiled as Beth blushed.

"My apologies for disturbing you, cuz. I shall try to be quieter."

Althea laughed. Trust her cousin to offer to tiptoe rather than to stop. Incorrigible, but loveable. "Do you know what you want from him?"

Beth narrowed her eyes and shrugged. "Maybe? But what of you? What do you want from Cheltie?"

"Nothing. Damnable man." She pressed her lips together in annoyance.

"Even with a baker's dozen shops, the future sounds rather dim without someone with whom to share it."

Althea fell back on her litany of old. "Sharing is overrated. Men share by taking control. I want none of that after working so hard to succeed."

"Are you sure all men are like that? More specifically, that Evan is?"

Althea started to retort but snapped her lips shut. Was she? Was he? He'd wanted an equity share, yes. But he'd offered to be a silent partner then offered free advice with nothing in return. She snorted. *Nothing other than sexual pleasure, that is.*

Her cousin was watching her.

"'Tis too risky to test it."

"Have you and Cheltie ever discussed the School of Enlightenment?" Beth asked, cocking her head.

"No, of course not. 'Tis not allowed." Althea recalled she had thought he'd be supportive. She probably should have considered that more with his respect for her independence. Instead, she'd obsessed about society's perceptions of a male investor.

"His servants at Greenborough Park include a number of students from the school. And he knows you sponsored me. I thought he might have raised it with you."

"Why?"

Beth shrugged. "To prove his support of you remaining in control of the shop. He did help found the school, after all."

Althea's jaw dropped. "He *what*?"

"I should have known. He never brags about his charitable work." Beth shook her head. "I only found out recently. I recognized some of the servants, so I knew he was aware of it, but I did not know the extent of his involvement. Cuz, I told you because that should give you some reassurance that he supports women's independence. Lud, even in other ventures he backs, he prefers to remain behind the scenes. He only invests in ventures where he believes there is strong leadership."

Althea's lips twisted. "What if that was the reason he did not choose to invest in mine?"

Beth sighed. "Don't be obtuse. He did not invest in yours because it would muddy the waters with your personal relationship. And frankly, because you would not allow him an equity stake. You did not trust him. That has been the issue all along."

Althea stared at her cousin, eyes suddenly brimming. "Are you saying 'twas all my fault?"

"No, of course not." Beth rushed to sit by Althea and gave her an awkward hug where she sat. "Rarely is an issue in a relationship one person's fault. Except maybe when it comes to Robert." She winked.

Althea smiled wanly.

"I should have said that has been *one* of your issues," Beth corrected her earlier statement. "Others include his wariness of allowing people close and his propensity to walk away when he feels defensive."

"So, what do I do now?"

"I do not know, cuz. I am sorry. If I knew, I'd have shared my wisdom with you sooner. My guess is you both have to decide whether to trust and risk further pain or whether 'tis smarter to walk away."

His hurt reaction to her wanting secrecy was his ego being bruised, just as Charlotte said. Wasn't it?

Both Charlotte and Beth acknowledged the risks in

a public relationship, even though they both believed there was an equal possibility of gains. Was there an alternative path to being with him? She did not see one, but she was miserable without him. She knew her request had been less than fair to him, but she desperately wanted her cake and to eat him, too.

Now I can taste his mouth, his skin, his essence. I miss that flavor, that soft lush hair to curl my fingers into. Beyond the physical, I wish he could see my success. And he could, if he wasn't so stubborn. Damnable man. Damnable beautiful man, so supportive and encouraging, until he isn't.

She contemplated consenting to a public relationship, but she did not feel she could afford that. Conservative by nature, she was loathe to risk business losses, particularly now she was leveraged with debt to Charlotte.

She considered marriage. But even if she was open to the idea, he was not.

Was she willing to marry Evan? He invested in women's enterprises. He helped found the School of Enlightenment, to offer independence to many more women. There was still society's perception of a woman-owned shop needing a man behind it. On the other hand, she had come so far already. *She* knew she could do it, no matter what society believed. Wedding Evan would give her the best of both worlds.

Her lips twisted. Even if her concerns were fading, he had no interest in marriage, not only because she hadn't trusted him, but also his mother's illness.

Then there was his horrible habit of lashing out when he felt vulnerable. He had some bowing and scraping to do before she was ready to forgive and forget.

Nonetheless, Althea suddenly could not help wondering how she'd respond if he asked for her hand.

****

Evan straightened his cravat, checked the drape of his jacket, and shot his cuffs. He could not remember the last time he'd been nervous to call on a lady. But here he was, not even having knocked yet. He raised his hand, finally rapped on the door, and heard footsteps across the front hall in response.

The butler opened the door, stepped back to allow him to enter, and took his hat and gloves before going to announce him.

As the servant returned to direct him, Evan found his hands fidgeting again, wanting to recheck his cravat once more. He fisted them and entered the library.

Althea and Beth were both seated, one behind and one in front of the desk as usual. Neither rose to greet him.

He ignored the obvious slight, understanding from whence it came, and bowed. "My ladies. Thank you for seeing me without an appointment."

He received silence accompanied by raised eyebrows. *Right. I suppose groveling should not be made easy, after all.*

"Lady Althea, might I have a private word?"

"Anything you have to say to me can be said in my cousin's presence, Lord Cheltenham. Do sit down, I don't like you hovering over me."

As though he'd been invited to sit. He gave a mental shrug. He'd been in worse situations and managed to smooth them over. *This, too, shall pass if I can finesse it.* Mayhap she preferred to have her cousin present to protect her from being hurt again. Hopefully, that would not be an issue.

He sat. "Althea, I must beg your forgiveness. I was exceedingly rude the last time we spoke." He shot a glance at Beth, who smirked at him, waiting for the rest just as Althea was. "I should not have said what I did."

Althea's eyebrows twitched up again.

"I cannot apologize for my actions before that. I will never regret sharing pleasure with you."

Beth stifled a snicker with a cough, earning a glare from her cousin.

"I have come to understand your concerns for your reputation a little better—"

"Oh?" she interrupted. "How?"

"Does it matter?" He did not want to cause a rift between business partners and was not certain what Althea's reaction to Charlotte's letter would be. *Damn me, why did I not consider this and think more about how to word my apology?*

"It matters to me."

"If you must know, Charlotte wrote to me—"

"What?" Her tone was outraged.

"She reminded me that by necessity, women must work harder at protecting their reputations than men. It occurred to me—"

Beth shifted and muttered, "Belatedly," under her breath.

"—that there is a double standard, and I had not fully taken it into account when I—"

"Sulked?" shot from Althea.

Heaven save him from these ladies' assistance with his apology. He stifled a sigh. "Right, then. *Sulked* at being kept a secret." He paused, looking for a reaction.

"Yes? And? You've shared your new, belated, understanding with us."

"Not true. I led with begging your forgiveness. Please, Althea?"

"Fine. You are forgiven, my lord. Does this mean—" she slid a sidelong glance at her cousin "—you would like to resume our interactions?"

He managed not to grin at her discomfort labeling their relationship in front of the audience she'd insisted upon, but he could not resist quirking an eyebrow at her choice of words.

She flattened her lips.

"About that. I have also rethought my concerns about marriage and have decided that, for the right person, it could be worth the risk."

"And what, may I ask, caused that change?"

He barely refrained from rolling his eyes, resisting the desire to ask again what it mattered. "A letter from my mother that her last nurse, Lucy, helped her write a year ago. She explained a few thoughts she was having as the disease…progressed." His throat had clogged, his voice going thick by the end of the explanation.

Althea nodded, her voice softer. "Thank you for explaining. I hope the letter helped you handle her current circumstances as well."

He shrugged and swallowed, looking away for a moment.

Beth nudged him and hiss-whispered, "How does that pertain to my cousin?"

He slanted her a look, grumbling, "Don't you have anything better to do?"

Turning to Althea, he straightened in the chair, throwing his shoulders back and cleared his throat.

"Althea, Lady Egerton, I find myself bereft without you and would prefer to spend more time with you in the light rather than sneaking through the darkness. Would you do me the honor of marrying me?"

Althea gaped at him. Undone by the silence, he glanced sideways. Beth was lounging back in her chair with a happy smile on her face.

"No."

His gaze whipped back to Althea. "Pardon me?"

"You heard me. Oh, was your ego expecting me to fall all over you in thanks?"

"But-but—"

"Yes, I know. You're a catch." She gave a negligent wave of one hand. "Richer than Croesus, handsomer than Zeus, blah blah blah."

It was Beth's turn to gape at her cousin.

Evan stared at her, his eyes narrowing with each phrase, each "blah." This is what she thought of marrying him? Of his apology and declaration of how much he missed her and wanted to be with her? How did he misjudge this whole thing so badly?

Wait, handsomer than Zeus? Damn me, I shall have to bask in that later.

"I confess, you have me at a loss." The trite words, hammered into every aristocrat from the cradle, rolled off his tongue while he fumbled for what to do next.

"Thank you for the kind offer, Lord Cheltenham, but I am afraid I must refuse. I am sure my cousin can walk you out." Althea did not sound grateful in the least. And she was staring daggers at Beth.

****

Beth was back through the library door in no time, slamming the door behind her before stomping back to her chair in front of Althea's desk. She folded her arms over her chest. "What in heaven's name are you thinking?"

"He offered marriage because—what? Two women told him to? He was 'bereft'?" Althea heard the sneer in her voice. "Where was the declaration of love? Where was the feeling that he cannot envision life without me? The need to be together? For that matter, what about doing better the next time and not walking away when he gets angry in the future? 'Twas as though he was admitting a minor mistake and correcting his error and doing me a favor by it. No. I shall be no man's charity. I know you say he supports women's independence, but how can I trust that he will do so in a marriage given his actions to date? I need an affirmation that we will be equal partners."

"It mayhap was not the best." Beth nodded her head side to side in acknowledgment. "But my word, those dismissive things you said to him, cuz. They are actually true. He's considered the catch of the Ton, as good as a duke and probably better in bed."

That was certainly true. Althea shook her head and refocused. "There was no mention of love, much less allowing me to keep my shops. He likely saw some of our profits in that letter from Charlotte and feels as though he's missing out."

Beth gave her a withering look. "Althea. The man's worth probably increases more in a month than what you make in a year. You cannot truly believe that."

Now Althea folded her arms to match Beth's belligerent expression. "He told me himself he and Charlotte are quite competitive."

"Not to the extent he'd *wed* someone to win! You are in love with him. You wanted respectability in order to spend time with him. He offered you the most respectable choice we women get. Yet you declined." She threw up her hands.

"'Tis only respectable with respect. And I never said I loved him."

"Oh, please. At least admit it to yourself if not to me or him. And how can you doubt his respect? He has never offered a woman marriage before."

Althea preened internally, just a little.

Beth continued. "I will accede that his offer was not the most romantic, but you could have discussed all that." The younger woman took a deep breath, her already-impressive bosom heaving upward. "Cuz. I love you. I will always love you. I am not sure I understand your reasoning, but I support your decision. I hope you won't regret it."

"I am perfectly happy."

"I think not. You said so yourself when you wanted to succeed to spite Evan and you have proven it every day these past weeks overworking yourself and then skulking around the house with a dour face. Now, you not only know what you're missing, but you cannot avoid the man who showed you how wonderful it can be between two people. Cheltie's circle is broad."

Althea frowned in disgruntlement. She'd managed well enough before his house party. Their paths had rarely crossed. But is that what she wanted? And their circles had certainly overlapped more and more recently.

How will I face Evan at parties? Charlotte's house? Even the streets of Mayfair? What if he has another lady on his arm?

Pain stabbed through her chest, stealing her breath. Gasping, she stood and circled the desk to pace the length of the room.

Gads, Beth is right. Not only am I not happy, but I am irrevocably in love with Evan.

Evan of all people should have understood what she needed—more even than an admission of love, a confirmation that she'd be able to maintain her independence. And yet, there had been no mention of that.

She was stuck. Unable to return to her blithely ignorant state pre-Evan but unwilling to trust that her business would remain her own in a traditional marriage. Yet miserable without him. She yearned to marry him. The rest could have been negotiated. Two business-minded people should have seen that.

"Lud, what have I done?"

Chapter Nineteen

Evan left Althea's house in a fog, taking his hat and gloves from the butler and forgetting to put them on, despite the drizzle. He walked halfway to his London residence before he remembered and was soaked by the time he walked in his front door. He supposed he should be grateful he hadn't ridden there, as he might have forgotten his horse.

Completely nonplussed, he sat in the rapidly darkening study, with only a fire for light, and contemplated where he'd gone wrong.

He had not taken into account the possibility of his suit being rejected. It had never entered his purview.

"Ha!" His bark of laughter startled him in the silent room. *Of course it didn't. I am not accustomed to having to work for a woman's affections. No wonder I made a muddle of it.*

But how? He'd told her he cared for her, he'd missed her. Godsakes, he'd even used the word bereft. He had thought through all the risks of his future, and they could determine how to handle that for her sake. But she hadn't even let him get to that.

"Bah. I need a whisky and a friend. Mayhap Ford will have some ideas."

Grabbing a different hat and an umbrella, he did not bother changing his damp clothes, given the continued wet weather, but he did take a cloak. A few minutes later, he pounded on the door of Ford's home.

"Ford. 'Tis me, Bags. Come on, man. 'Tis dog's soup out here."

Ford opened the door in shirtsleeves, and Evan pushed past him.

"Right. Please, do come in. Allow me to take your outer garments, sir."

Evan looked around, distractedly handing his cloak and hat to his friend. He'd had a sudden idea of an even better source for help.

"Is Beth here?"

"Why would you think Beth would be here?"

"For godsakes, Ford. I am not the morality constable. I would very much like to talk to both of you if she's here."

Ford gestured to the parlor. "Pour yourself a whisky, and I shall fetch her. And pour me one as well if you please."

"Thanks, old chap. Will Beth want one?"

"Mayhap, but pour her a sherry. She's better behaved with that."

Evan managed a laugh at that, despite his preoccupation.

Once everyone was ensconced in chairs by the fire with drinks, Evan gave Ford the highlights of his marriage proposal and then sat back. "What now?"

His friend was looking at Beth who was attempting to stifle her giggles behind her sherry glass.

"May I ask what is funny?" Evan frowned at the petite woman.

"Really, Cheltie? You still do not see it?" She smirked.

"Obviously not, or I wouldn't be here." He drew

himself up, affronted at her laughter but still needing her help. "Mayhap you could elaborate?"

"You solved *your* problems. All right, and *one* of hers."

"But-but—" His brain caught up with his mouth, and he groaned.

"Ah, I see you are beginning to understand what your offer lacked. But just to be certain any subsequent proposals are more comprehensive, why don't you tell me what you view as Althea's fears?"

"She does not want rumors about an affair between us among the Ton."

"Yes, yes. We know you did not like that."

We? Evan let it go in the interest of knowledge. "She wants sole proprietorship over her business."

"And did you address that concern?"

"I would have."

"Not good enough, Cheltie. You addressed the issue that had hurt your ego. Then you addressed your other interests. I bet when you are coaxing someone to invest with you, you lead with how it will help *them*, not you. Seems like that approach might be even more important in asking someone to spend the rest of their life with you."

Evan grimaced.

"What about love? 'Tis obvious you love her, simply from observation. But women like to hear the words." At that, Beth cast a sidelong glance at Ford. "And she's already been widowed once. Mayhap she worries that she'll be a widow again or worse, given your mother's health. She may not want that."

"Is that it? Is that why she declined?" Evan hung his head in despair. "There is naught I can do about that."

"Oh, please." Beth rolled her eyes.

Evan gaped at her.

"Of course there is. You can give her the best years of her life until death—or mental illness—end them. But to do that, you must love her. Not just miss her from your bed. And show her, not just tell her. You are so single-minded in your investment ventures. I am shocked at what a muddle you've made of this."

"I say—" Evan stopped there.

She's right.

He glanced at Ford. Placed his still-half-full glass of whisky on the table and stood, then bowed to each of them. "I beg your pardon for interrupting your evening. And words cannot express my gratitude for your help, Miss Jenkins. You have given me much to think about. I have one small request?"

Beth and Ford looked at each other, then turned to nod at him.

"If I have any further questions, might I intrude one more time? If, say, I send a note round first?" He gave them his famous grin, hoping like usual it would get him what he wanted.

"Yes." Ford waved a hand. "No note needed, you know that. Now go think. And please have a better plan for your next sojourn."

"Oh, and let me know when you're trying again," Beth said with a snicker, "so I can be there to enjoy—er, coach."

****

Having had help from friends, Evan saw no reason to stop there. He knew that an earl's countess had many responsibilities, and he had no idea how a woman would balance those with a full-time job as a proprietor.

But he did know someone who had thought about it already and was putting it to the test—Michael and Penelope.

They'd spent time in the country because Michael's father was unwell, and their time with him was limited. But after his death they'd returned to London for Penelope to oversee the construction of her lifelong dream, a bakery using recipes from her East Indian grandmother.

Michael was planful enough, and Penelope wary of making the leap from commoner to countess, that Evan knew they'd given the balance of duties some thought.

He sent a note around to Mansfield House and received a quick response.

As he knocked, gift bag of shampoo in hand, he wondered if he even knew what questions to ask. Knowing he'd get some ribbing from Michael for his quandary, he braced himself as the door swung open to the butler.

"Gilbert. How have you been faring?" Evan knew Michael's butler almost as well as he knew his own. "And the children?"

"Sir, lovely to see you as always. Oh, the baggage, they're just fine, thank you. The eldest is a chambermaid here now."

"Excellent. Put them to work, keep 'em out of trouble." The men laughed as the butler bade him wait with one finger and went to announce him.

Then Michael was there. "Bags! I cannot wait to hear this tale. I wish we'd thought to invite Ford. Come in, come in, my lovely bride is here as well."

Beaming, he stood aside for Evan to enter and bow

over Penelope's hand before leaning in and pecking her on the cheek.

She laughed at his flirting. "Even in love, you cannot stop yourself, can you?"

"There's time enough for that when I am dead." *Or lose my mind.*

They sat, Michael and Penelope choosing the settee with Evan across from them. As Penelope poured tea and passed delicious pastries she'd made, Evan regaled them with his story, ending with Ford's and Beth's guidance.

"I need to address the shop," he said finally, "or likely shops. Althea has worked so hard to build those, and they are not only her passion but her retirement plan."

Penelope snorted.

Why do my friends' women find this so amusing? Evan gritted his teeth.

"You need to address the fact that you are in love with her."

"Yes, yes." Evan flapped a hand. "That I can handle." He ignored Penelope's doubtful moue. "I thought you might have some specific suggestions about balancing her independence and the duties of an earl's wife."

"Hmm. Yes. We discussed that." Michael clasped Penelope's hand in his between them. "As you suggested, we are hoping to use the new merchantry program you created at the School of Enlightenment to staff the bakery with paths to management and to head baker at the store."

"Excellent. I am glad to hear that," Evan said with a smile.

"Yes, 'twill be very helpful. I was not willing to give up the dream of the bakery, even when I capitulated to Michael's demands of marriage." She snickered at her husband, and he outright laughed back at her.

"Can you two please temper the newlywed silliness long enough to help me?" Evan teased them with a big grin.

"Probably not." Penelope shrugged. "But Michael's point is that you've created the very solution you're looking for, Cheltie."

His head fell forward as the pieces fell into place.

Penelope giggled. "The rest will take discussion. For Michael and I, the solution is a manager who we trust and can run the bakery for a fortnight at a go, and I am training a sous-baker. We also plan to close the bakery during the quietest times of the year, with notices posted well in advance so customers are not upset. August through Michaelmas, Christmas through January, that sort of thing. But to show your support of her independence, one need look no further than that new program."

Evan nodded, feeling dumber than he had since secondary school but grateful for good friends.

****

Ignoring Beth's wishes, Evan decided to visit Althea at her London shop.

He came bearing gifts, knowing her employees would likely take over governance in the face of obvious romance.

It took him a few days to decide on the right gifts, appropriate for her practical nature but still romantic. And then a few days to obtain them. Given her love of the inks and pens from Bath, he considered an inkwell and wax seal set for her desk. Or a new leatherbound journal for her accounting. On the other end of the scale, he knew she adored the few fancy lingerie pieces that Beth had talked her into purchasing. But that was not something she could open in the shop.

Finally, he chose garnet earrings and a pack of hand painted playing cards with—if one looked closely—rather outrageous pictures of lewd acts on them. Both reminded him of the first times he had met her, and the path they'd traveled to date.

He walked in with just over an hour left to closing time, hoping that would make it easier on her staff.

Althea's back was to him as she fiddled with a display on a table. When neither of the other shop girls approached the newly-arrived customer to ask how they could help, she looked a question at them. Their gazes bounced between her and him.

She turned and frowned for a moment before smoothing her brow and pasting on a smile. "Lord Cheltenham, how kind of you to grace our shop with another visit. How can I help you? Mayhap shampoo for another lady friend?"

"No, thank you. The only lady friend I would want shampoo for has a lifetime's worth at her fingertips." He strolled toward her as he spoke. His hand reached out for hers and he bowed low, hat tucked in the crook of his arm. His lips skated across her knuckles, and it jolted in his. He smiled in satisfaction but wiped it from his face before straightening. "My lovely Althea. I come bearing gifts, in the hope that you will give me a few minutes of your time."

He produced a black velvet bag encrusted with

teeny jewels. One of his protégés was a jeweler and made these gift bags with the remnants of jewel cuts to sell, minimizing waste and maximizing profits.

"Hmph. I suppose that is a better start than your last visit."

Ouch. "I promise. If you allow me, I can do better at the whole visit." He did not want to show his hand quite yet.

"Right, then. Shall we adjourn to the back room?" Her cheeks pinkened, and he was sure she was remembering their last interlude there. But he had more important things in mind, a frame of reference he'd never thought he would have toward sex.

He gulped and nodded. *'Tis now or never. I must convince her to accompany me to the school. Besides showing her proof of my support, the journey shall give me the time to convince her to accept my suit.*

Once the door closed behind them, Evan tossed his hat on a pile of boxes and turned to Althea. He daren't reach for her hands, as he did not want to give her the opportunity to reject him in any way. He needed all yays and no nays or he—known for his worldliness—might lose his nerve.

"I find an apology is always better accompanied with gifts." He handed the bag over. "And these made me think of you."

When she shook the bag into her other hand, the playing cards fell out first. She glanced at him, then perused the provocative design on the box.

Evan grinned as the blush rose on her cheeks. "These seem particularly appropriate for future games of strip whist, should you choose to indulge, my lady."

She glanced up at him through her lashes. "Thank

you, Evan." She clutched the cards in one hand and the bag in the other.

He eased the cards from her grip and placed them on the table. Nodding to the bag, he said, "There's more."

She shook the bag again, and the earrings fell into her hand. Her mouth dropped open, and she stared at them, then up at him.

"They come from a store I invested in and are one of a kind. Both gifts reminded me of the night I first met you."

Her brow furrowed. "Garnet? I wore plum that evening at your house party."

"Ah, but you wore garnet at the demi-monde party when we were first introduced, back when Michael asked Penelope for her hand."

Althea's mouth went slack.

Did she doubt that he remembered such a detail? He'd been so struck by her lithe beauty. He would never forget that first glimpse of her.

She shook her head. "Evan, I cannot accept jewelry from you."

"When is your next day away from the store?"

She blinked at his change in subject. "Tomorrow."

"Excellent. Might you hold them until tomorrow and decide after you accompany me on a day trip? Please?"

"Evan—"

"You can bring Beth, of course. Or I can pull up down the block and use an unmarked covered carriage. Please?"

Althea's brows rose at what was essentially begging.

He didn't care. He needed the yes. "Althea, I haven't said the words. I am very sorry for my rather awkward and incomplete proposal. I should have said that the minute the door closed, along with this." He took her hands in his, holding them loosely between them. "I love you. I am in love with you. I can only plead inexperience at my fumbling approach the other day and for not saying those words early and often. And now, I am asking only for a few hours of your time, to correct my mistake."

She narrowed her eyes.

Yes, Althea. I am going to propose again, but this time I shall do it better. I shall do it the way you need.

She nodded slowly.

His knees nearly buckled in relief.

****

Evan loves me! Althea nearly skipped home from the shop.

Evan had left quickly after her nod of acceptance, lingering only to set a time and a place for pickup. He had hinted at another proposal or at least a discussion of an intimate enough nature that she'd chosen to go alone. She had learned her lesson by keeping Beth in the room last time. This might at least preclude another lecture from her cousin if she found his comments lacking.

She doubted she would. Certainly, she needed to not get defensive, hear him out, and ask questions. It would help if she knew what she wanted.

She had asked herself that every hour of every day since his proposal. She wanted him and her business. Did he see that? If he offered that, could she trust him to make good on that promise? Her heart wanted to say that, with love, she could. Her brain was not as sure.

They had set the hour to meet early, so she could sneak out of the house without Beth's knowledge. After choosing a maroon day dress, she pinned her hair back but eschewed earrings. Tucking the gifts from Evan into her reticule, she paced her office until it was time to meet him.

Strolling the block, she attempted a guise of apathy while her insides quivered in eagerness at spending hours with this man she loved. She darted nervous looks back and forth across the street as she walked, in an attempt to identify his carriage.

As she reached the corner, she spied it parked just back from her street on the side lane. 'Twas the nicest carriage in sight. While she examined it, the door swung open.

"Thank you for coming, Althea." Evan sounded as nervous as she felt.

"Will you tell me where we are going now?"

Evan rapped on the roof to start the carriage. Once they were underway, he shook his head and replied, "I want to show you something. 'Tis about a two-hour ride. Will you tell me more about your expansion while we travel?"

This is what I wanted. To share my successes with him. He is asking all the right questions and—thinking of his declaration of love the day before—saying all the right things. Dare I hope? Dare I trust?

Beth's criticism rang in her ears, as did her subsequent wonderings. Was Evan the key to her future happiness? She could not fathom falling in love with anyone else. She'd been in lust with him since her first orgasm and in love with him since his first tip for her shop, if she were honest.

This was not the soothing warm milk of care and respect for her husband, nor was it the baffled affection she felt for Beth. Those were candle flickers compared to the conflagration that was her adoration for Evan. But despite Beth's assurances, she worried that if he did not feel the same, did not put her first, that very inferno would consume her independence and leave her in a similar position to when Thomas died.

Her inner critic argued. *You shan't be in a similar position. You have educated yourself. And Evan has helped you, not taken that away. You will not lose what you have built. And he brought gifts!*

She groaned silently. Her inner critic sounded a lot like her cousin.

He watched her expectantly, mayhap hopefully.

"Sales have already exceeded our projections." Althea was happy to brag. "They did so in the second month, in both stores. We had to reinvest our profits to obtain more inventory quickly, and I worked with the shampoo-makers to build their business. I asked Charlotte whether we should open a second shop in London to garner more customers, but she likes our current location too much. Instead, we shall evaluate Brighton in the spring when the roads are better."

Evan raised his brows, a smile blooming. "Excellent. Using the same model?"

Althea's shoulder rose noncommittally. "Mayhap. If profits continue as they are, we could afford a joint venture in a new space with Emily, rather than trying to forge another relationship with the need to vet quality of goods as well as management. 'Twill also depend on competition there, available spaces, and rents, as you know."

He nodded.

"Then we may consider another store in London, but under a different name, with less expensive products, to reach the next tier of customer."

"Hmm."

She frowned. "What?"

"What did Charlotte think of that?"

"She suggested it in lieu of a second location of my store. But mentioned we'd need to evaluate profit margins." She continued to frown at him, knowing his tells. His tactful hum was his way of remaining neutral until asked. "Why?"

"I do not want to interfere in your business relationship with Charlotte. Nor would I dare to question her approach. But I shall be interested to see— if permitted—the profit analysis."

"And? I know you are considering another dimension. Please, I should like to know your thoughts. I've—I've missed sharing ideas with you these past weeks."

He grinned and relented. "I suppose I wonder if you'll be happy working with inferior goods. If you can bring yourself to be as passionate selling them as you can when you are confident that the product you are offering is the best available."

"Huh." She hadn't thought of that.

"Charlotte is likely looking at it from a numbers perspective. And the profitability may well be there. But I am looking at it from an overall business perspective. Your enthusiasm goes a long way in driving sales. Well, that and your ardent interest in observing people." He winked.

Althea blushed and looked away.

"While we are on the subject of your shop or shops…" He took a breath. "I know I made a poor showing of myself the other day. One thing that I did not have a chance to say is that I had my solicitor draw up papers to ensure your stores remain yours, should we marry."

She opened her mouth to speak, although completely at a loss as to what to say. He hadn't actually proposed again, had he? Had she missed it somehow?

Evan continued before she could form words. "But before we get to that, let me show you the reason I've brought you here." He nodded out the window.

She peered around. The front gate of the School of Enlightenment was swinging open for their carriage.

Chapter Twenty

Althea turned back to him.

Before she could ask anything, Evan said, "Please bear with me for a few minutes. I shall attempt to explain."

She nodded, and he sighed in relief. He hoped for greater coherence than his last attempt.

They both watched out the window as the carriage rolled toward the main building with its grand entrance, then beyond it down a narrow drive.

A clearing with a partially constructed building came into view, and the driver pulled to a stop.

He jumped down, then set the step in place and handed Althea out. As she shook out her skirts, he surveyed the progress. The façade was complete, the double wooden doors with iron hinges arched under a peaked roof. Above the doors, a long narrow wooden sign sat empty.

As she gazed about her in question, he turned and clasped her hand to draw her to face him.

"Lady Althea Egerton, I am completely in love with you and shall be forever." He squeezed her hand as he was reminded of the risks to his future cognition. Refusing to be distracted, he continued, "I need you. I want to marry you and, indeed, plan to state my case more clearly here. I want to help you own more apothecaries in England than all the others combined.

Or"—he quirked a brow—"if you do not want my help, I want to stand back and watch you succeed. You have all the control here, Althea. If you prefer not to marry and to simply live in sin, I will abide by that. I hate sneaking around, but I'll do that, too, if I must. Although I will ask you to meet that evil cousin of mine, so you know what impact a lack of heirs will have on all those employed by my estate."

Althea giggled once, and he smiled.

"I also spoke with Michael and Penelope, as she is a bakery owner as well as a countess, to see how to balance the demands of a proprietorship and an earldom."

Althea's eyes widened with interest.

"I thought about buying a storefront in Bath or your loan from Charlotte and ripping the note up. But I know you value your independence and I do not want to infringe upon it. You need to be confident that you are an equal partner in this relationship. Other than love, as I love you more."

Althea sniggered at his competitive nature coming out in that particular way.

"I was one of the founders of this school, a few years ago. But more recently, after getting to know you at my house party and learning more about Beth as well, I undertook adding this building to the school. This will house a fourth program, one for young ladies interested in merchantry rather than serving in the aristocracy's homes or being at a man's beck and call as a courtesan."

She stared at him, her dark eyes pooling with unshed tears.

"Althea, this program will be named for you,

regardless of your decisions today or in the future. I will do anything to make you happy. But more, I want to empower you and other young women to make yourselves happy. I hope that this helps you trust my words when I promise you independence."

He gulped. *Please let her answer be yes.* He hadn't dared let himself want to marry, but his mother's letter had given him the strength to ask, and now he craved Althea as his wife more than anything.

"I agree to any terms you want if you'll have me. I shall ask again, though. Should the sign read Egerton Hall or Cheltenham Hall? Will you marry me? Please? For love, not to avoid sneaking around in the dark. For forever or as many years as my health and yours allow."

He held his breath.

****

Althea fought tears at Evan's first sentence, declaring his love for her forever. When he explained the purpose of the building and why he wanted to show it to her, she could not hold them any longer. Her eyes welled. She may have only recently admitted to herself that she adored him, but she had been falling in love with him since she'd touched his hair and discovered his playful nature at Greenborough Park. And he had just resolved all of her doubts, one by one.

When he asked for her hand, one tear escaped in a narrow rivulet down her cheek.

His hand trembled as he lifted it to swipe the tear track away with his thumb.

"Evan, 'twould be my honor and pleasure to marry you." Relief filled her, lowering her shoulders a fraction, as though her body had known what she needed and had been waiting for her mind to catch up.

He blew out a gusty sigh.

She smiled gently, adding, "You see, I am very much in love with you as well."

She thought his grin might split his lip, it was so wide, and an answering thrill shot through her. But she only had a moment to ponder it before he swooped in to kiss her. His arms circled her and tightened to lift her off the ground.

"Mmph!" She had not been lifted since she was young. The fleeting thought that her height made her too heavy for such play was diverted by her happiness. Never had she expected to marry again, especially not for love. She was gratified that Evan was mayhap more excited than she, given that no one in the Ton, including him, had expected him to wed.

He set her down, and they stood grinning at each other like loons.

Finally, he released her to offer an arm. "My lady, may I show you a bit more of the building, as incomplete as it is?"

"Certainly, kind sir." She looped her arm through his.

The inside of the building was rough enough to prevent much exploration, though, so Evan promised to bring her back at another time.

He was strangely quiet in the carriage, and Althea grew nervous.

"Is something amiss?" She was relatively sure he did not regret offering for her, but he was distracted.

He looked at her, his golden eyes glowing. "I am afraid to believe this is real. I was contemplating asking you to say it again but daren't in case you change your mind."

She reached for his hand. "One might say you just did, but never mind." She smiled. "I shall happily reiterate my answer as many times as you need. I love you, and I want to marry you."

He sighed, his shoulders relaxing, but his brow creased again.

She arched a brow. "What is it?"

"We have not discussed my mother or my future in light of such a commitment."

"Do we need to?" Althea was surprised.

"Beth pointed out that you've been widowed once—" He stopped when her brows rose higher.

"Do I understand that you discussed this with Michael, Penelope, and Beth?"

"Um. Ford was there, too," he mumbled.

"Anyone else?"

"No. In my defense, 'twas obvious I needed the counsel."

"Hmm. True. Please continue." Althea smirked and rolled her wrist to encourage him to continue his thought.

"As you know, you'll likely be widowed again. Unfortunately, it may feel like twice more. Once when I go mad and then when I die."

Althea clutched his hand in a grip so tight it likely hurt him, horrified on his behalf at the vivid imagery. "Oh, my love, I hate thinking about that."

"'Tis not enjoyable for me, either, dearest, but 'tis my reality. And whilst I trust you to handle things as needed should the earldom require it, I want to ascertain that you are truly prepared to take that on."

"I have observed the extra care you take with your

mother." As his other hand rose to their joined ones, she loosened her grip. "Whether that is a certainty for your future or not, I have always understood 'tis a possibility. That risk does not mar my affection. Indeed, 'tis more important than ever to enjoy the time we have together. My first marriage taught me that tomorrow is never guaranteed. 'Twas less relevant without a grand passion"—she returned his smile at her use of his phrasing in Greenborough Park—"involved. Now, however, I want it all as soon as possible. A special license, a wedding as soon as it can be arranged, and on to marital bliss."

"And heirs."

"Yes." She smiled. Then it was her turn to frown.

"I was not able to give Thomas heirs. What if I cannot do my duty for you?"

"Frankly, I do not care. I could never wed someone else. So we shall muddle through. Besides"—he leered at her—"I am certain we have already practiced more than you did with him."

Her laugh ricocheted around the carriage.

He chuckled, watching her.

"Oh. I brought your gifts, as you said today would be a better day to decide on accepting them." She grabbed her reticule off the seat and dumped it into her lap. Sifting through coins, a scrap of paper and pencil nub, and the pack of cards, she found his earrings. Tucking her hair behind her ears, she offered them to him. "I should love to accept these. I wore this dress in the hope I'd have reason to put them on. Would you care to do the honors?"

Evan accepted them and attached one, then the other to her lobes. Sitting back, he smiled. "Perfect.

With or without the ear bobs."

Althea blushed and looked for a subject change. The playing cards provided the perfect path. "Shall we play?"

"I am not sure I am up for whist against you, but have you looked at the various art on the backs?"

Althea opened the box and fanned the cards out. Then she held them toward the window. Dropping a chunk of the deck, she passed cards from hand to hand, one at a time, peering at them. "Oh, this looks...challenging."

Evan peered at the card upside down. "Overrated. You would not get much pleasure at that angle." Then he gulped.

Althea lowered the cards, watching his reaction. She hid a smile.

He was nervous.

"Evan." A part of her relished his fear. His good looks and charm, never mind his bags of money, had made navigating relationships too easy. But a much bigger part of her loved him for all of that and in spite of it, and she wanted to soothe his unease. "I love you. Your charm, your wit, your unconscious flirting with every girl from eight to eighty. The depth of your love and care for your mother. Your teachings and your willingness to be taught." She thought of his tutelage in sensuality as well as his willingness to ask Penelope, a common-born woman, for guidance. "Your humility. And yes, your skills in the art of intimacy, however they were learned. Besides, 'twould be rather hypocritical of me to condemn a past that has awakened me to so much pleasure these past months."

He closed his eyes, his exhale whooshing out in

relief. "How many people do you want at our wedding? If 'twas small, we might have it within the sennight."

Althea shrugged. "You are the earl. I need only Beth there—and Charlotte if she is available."

Epilogue

In the end, Evan and Althea were married in the chapel at Greenborough Park a fortnight later. Evan was disappointed his mother could not attend. He had hoped she would have one of her few lucid periods that day, but it was not to be. They stopped by the dower house after the ceremony to visit with her.

Only their closest friends were in attendance, Michael and Penelope, Beth, and Ford. Charlotte declined to travel quite yet but sent a long letter of congratulations to both of them. Her gift, only given after approval by Althea, was her loan note, stamped as forgiven, with the stipulation that she would receive a lifetime supply of free shampoo.

He'd needed the extra time to arrange paperwork of his own. Althea had been ecstatic when she'd received the formal documents securing the shops in her name, with a separate account also in her name for all profits from them. They'd worked out a rough schedule of the amount of time each of them needed for their business ventures, to allow together time. She would help him with his responsibilities, and he arranged for his clerk to handle the shop books under her watchful eye.

He supposed they'd renegotiate when and if she became pregnant. In fact, he looked forward to it. He always enjoyed bargains with Althea, as even when he lost, he was happy she won.

He leaned toward her over the wedding breakfast table. "I have a wedding surprise for you after breakfast. 'Tis why I put the guests, even Ford, in the other wing."

"Oh?" Althea's voice was breathless. Then she leaned in. "I have something to show you as well, husband."

He'd never imagined being someone's husband. But already he could not imagine his life otherwise. He wanted to spend every minute with Althea and leave the damnable estate and investment paperwork to his solicitor. Conversely, he was proud of Althea's desire to drive her shops forward and succeed in business in her own right.

He dropped his knife to reach for her hand. Squeezing it, he whispered, "I love that title. You have made me so happy, lady wife."

As soon as breakfast was finished, he stood.

Ford and Michael immediately hooted and hollered. "Leaving so soon, my friend? Shan't we get another toast from the groom? Mayhap a drink in your study?"

He smirked at them. "Jealous, lads? Just like in university, I must lead by example. This"—he gestured—"is the way to happiness. Michael, you drab fellow, you ought to know."

They all laughed, including the ladies.

"And now, if you will excuse my lovely bride and I, we are off to the family wing of the house. We shall see you on the morrow." He offered Althea his hand to help her rise, then bowed at his guests.

She blushed prettily.

"Are you feeling shy, wife?" he teased.

"I cannot imagine why. I've literally seen Beth in the throes of a sexual encounter. But I am."

"I have just the thing. We shall give you something else to focus on." He led her to the room that had been used for whist the first night of his house party. The room was darker, and the furniture was quite different, however.

A settee in a deep sapphire was set in a corner. A low table with a bottle of champagne and two glasses sat in front of it. A soft cream-colored blanket was thrown over one end, matching the decorative pillows on the couch. Strangely, the candelabra on the wall were not lit, nor was the chandelier in the center of the room, and all the window drapes were drawn.

Althea turned her head and gasped.

In the corner opposite the settee sat a chaise longue and a bed. All the candelabra in that corner were lit, as well as candles on a table in the center of the tableau. On that table sat a flogger that Evan had procured from Ford. Given her enjoyment of the flogger, he rather thought watching it being used would titillate.

He steered his still-blushing bride to the darker corner, gesturing to the settee before pouring her champagne.

Observing her gold gown, he hoped for as few petticoats as possible. He removed his bronze jacket, worn over black trousers for the church wedding. Perching beside her, he undid his cravat and slid it from his throat, leaving his white shirt open at the neck and his waistcoat that matched her dress and his eyes.

"Evan? What is this? Why is there a bed in here?"

"You recall that many of my servants are hired

from the school?"

"Yes."

"And I recall that my lovely wife enjoys a show." He arched a brow, allowing her to reach her own conclusion.

She glanced over to the lit corner, then back to their darkened surroundings, realizing the lighting created an impromptu stage with them as the audience.

"Oh." Her eyes were wide. "Whoever you asked to do this is truly all right with it?"

He nodded.

"Will they be able to see us?"

He stood and offered his hand, leading her over. "Sit on the chaise longe, and I shall return to our settee."

She sat, and he returned to lounge. Picking up his drink, he lifted it. "Can you see what I am doing? What clothes I am wearing?"

"Somewhat, but not in great detail."

"The plan is that they shall be otherwise occupied and not looking at us. But if they do, you can judge the extent of their view."

She nodded and returned to his side. Leaning down, her hands disappeared under her skirt, and she unwrapped something from her leg.

What is she doing? He heard a metallic clink. *Is that a buckle?*

"I think this is the perfect time to show you what Beth gave me for our wedding." Althea's voice rose from her lap as she continued to work at her ankle.

She rose slowly back to sitting, twisting to face him.

Unsure where to look, he watched her face.

Her expression combined nerves and eagerness. He hoped it included anticipation for the show.

He felt a jumble of straps fall into his hands and lap as he smelled the leather. Glancing down, he shouted a laugh. Beth had given Althea one of Ford's simpler X-shaped contraptions, and she must have secured it around her leg to save for when they were alone. He licked his lips, visions of these on Althea or on either of the servants who had agreed to perform. He'd let her choose.

Running his hands over the leather toward a buckle, he looked questioningly at his bride.

Her lower lip was caught in her teeth as she watched his reaction. Releasing it, she said simply, "I dare you."

A word about the author…

Maggie Sims began her love affair with romance before her teen years, drawn to the Regency by her mum's British influence. She did her best to live the Carrie Bradshaw life in New York City, albeit with less expensive shoes.

Despite reading hundreds of romance novels in her life, she was still blown away when she met the love of her life, an ex-Marine cinnamon roll with creative culinary skills.

Having retired from corporate life, they live in Central Texas and are parents to a varying number of dogs and cats. When not writing, Maggie is a wine enthusiast, a travel junkie, and a romance reading fiend. She also sporadically crochets for KnotsofLove.org and does just enough exercise for that second glass of wine at night.

~*~

Want a bonus scene between Althea and Evan?
Sign up for Maggie's newsletter here:
https://tinyurl.com/4kt22erb

~*~

Visit Maggie at
www.maggiesims.com

Beth and Ford's story due out Fall 2023

Thank you for purchasing
this publication of The Wild Rose Press, Inc.

For questions or more information
contact us at
info@thewildrosepress.com.

www.ingramcontent.com/pod-product-compliance
Lightning Source LLC
Chambersburg PA
CBHW051138030726
47504CB00004B/938